LONG ROAD TURNING

LONG ROAD TURNING

Irene Bennett Brown

Five Star
Unity, Maine

Copyright © 2000 by Irene Bennett Brown.

The Women of Paragon Springs, Book One.

This novel is a work of fiction. Names, characters, places and incidents are either the product of the author's imagination or, if real, used fictitiously.

Five Star First Edition Romance Series.
Published in 2000 in conjunction with Multimedia Product Development, Inc.

First Edition, Second Printing

Cover design by Shana Chandler.

The text of this edition is unabridged.

Set in 11 pt. Plantin by Anne Bradeen.

Printed in the United States on permanent paper.

Library of Congress Cataloging-in-Publication Data

Brown, Irene Bennett.
    Long road turning / Irene Bennett Brown.
        p. cm. — (Woman of the Paragon Springs ; bk 1)
      ISBN 0-7862-2813-X (hc : alk. paper)
    1. Women pioneers — Fiction. 2. Kansas — Fiction. I. Title.
  PS3552.R68559 L6 2000
    813´.54—dc21   00-057309

Dedicated in memory
of a very special Kansas woman,
my aunt,
MARY ELLEN WAMSER

Chapter One

She needed a cash sale of her millinery goods nearly as much as she needed the next breath. Meg Brennon wiped her perspiring brow at an additional thought: Even with cash in hand, her life was not going to have the worth of a candle to the sun if Frank Finch caught up.

She nervously divided her attention between the hat shop owner, Mrs. Isaacs—an aged sparrow of a woman at the hat display counter in the musty-smelling shop—and the goings-on outside the dingy front window.

"The feather quills with rounded tops come in black, brown, cardinal, and navy." Meg shoved a fan of samples into the milliner's hands, wanting to urge, *hurry.* But Mrs. Isaacs, one of her best customers in eastern Kansas particularly, could not be rushed. Again Meg's glance sped to the scene outside the blurry window. An odd-looking trio in the dusty, sun-baked Emporia street were showing high interest in her little green drummer's rig tied at the hitch rail.

A raggedy, travel-worn old woman in black peeked into the back of her fringe-topped wagon. A girl—maybe fourteen in washed-out brown and beaten-down looking for one so young—crept around the wagonette twice. The third party, a scarred, wispy-haired, grubby boy, followed close on the girl's heels. The three of them seemed to be checking if anyone watched as they came together to stroke her old buckskin driving horse, Butterfield.

Meg's anxiety rose. "Five cents each for the straight-topped quills." She wagged a handful of white, pink, purple, and black feathers under Mrs. Isaacs's eager, parrot-like nose. "I recommend a good supply of all colors, so you don't run out." Aware of the value of patience, and Mrs. Isaacs's penchant for taking her time, her palm still fairly itched for the money. Her head spun with the wish to be outside, to shoo the suspicious trio away from her wagon, her *world*.

"Mother of God, they are going to do it!" Her sharp shriek caused poor old Mrs. Isaacs to start, eyes widening as the bouquet of feathers in her hand went flying like birds given sudden life.

In a flash of motion at the hitch rail, the hag in rusty black skirts was boosted onto the driver's seat by the brown-pigeon girl who then ran around and vaulted up beside her. The crone caught the lines as the boy undid them from the rail and tossed them to her. He made the back in a flying, tumbling leap. In shocked disbelief, Meg watched her olive-green wagonette career away, beyond the window's frame.

"I have to go, those hooligans stole my rig!" She frantically gathered her scrambled goods, stuffed them into her supply case, and snapped it shut.

"Eh? Huh? What?" Mrs. Isaacs's mouth pruned. Her watery brown eyes were puzzled and a shade frightened. She stared toward the window. "Thieves, where—?"

"Outside! Gone with my things. I'm sorry, Mrs. Isaacs, I have no time—" Meg raced out to the street as fast as her lame hip would allow. She watched as her flat-topped wagon shook from side to side and almost tipped over as it reached the end of the street and headed toward open

8

prairie. Dust settled over her.

Mrs. Isaacs followed from her shop, looking doubtful and confused, but shrilling just in case, "Thieves! Robbery! Somebody help!"

In a sweat of panic, Meg started to run along the dusty boardwalk, her sample case banging painfully against her leg. "Come back here! For the grace of God," she shouted, "return me my horse and wagon!"

She looked around for help, took note of a lean, plain-garbed cowboy riding a tall roan slowly up the street toward her. When she yelled at him, "You!" his sun-strained eyes looked at her in reserved question from the shadow of his hat. When she motioned, he looked over his shoulder at the fleeing wagon marked by a coil of dust. His dark, sharp-chiseled features behind a shadow of whiskers were deadpan. A drifter from the looks of him, likely headed for the saloon up in the next block. And the saloon more important to him than any trouble of hers.

"For God's sake, help me. Go after them, stop them!" Meg ran into the street, waving frantically, her sample case abandoned on the dirty plank walk. "That is my horse and wagon they're stealing. There's no time to lose!" Her anger at the stranger for being so slow wasn't fair but she couldn't help it.

Fortunately, he snugged his dusty hat down tight and growled, "Don't get het, Miss. Stay here and I'll get 'em back for you."

Ignoring his order to stay and not get "het," she grabbed her case and followed at a jig-jagging run down the street as the drifter reversed his direction and, elbows high, flew ahead on his horse. Shading her eyes as she ran, she saw him catch up to her wagon, sweep out in front in a dust cloud, and flag the thieves to a halt. He appeared to be having words with them.

Determined to add her own say, Meg kept going, panting from exertion and the afternoon heat. Relief flooded her when she saw her rig turning, the rider leading it back at a fair clip. The trio was still aboard and appeared to be at least temporarily cowed.

She met her wagon in the middle of the street, and for a moment she was unable to speak. Her face was like fire; her small bosom heaved. Her straw-colored shirtwaist was damp with perspiration. Dust coated her lilac skirt. Her self-designed bonnet would have flown away if not held to her choking throat by its ribbons. She fought for breath, yanked the bonnet off, slammed her bag at her feet. Her dark hair tumbled loose from its combs and blew in the wind, revealing the thin scar at her left temple. She glared from eyes so big and light they looked silver.

The reedy cowboy sat his roan, knee hooked around the saddle horn, Butterfield's lines in his big brown hand. Butterfield snorted and blew, looked around for some grass to graze on as long as they were stopped, then tried to draw away to the side of the road but was held fast by the cowboy. The three thieves, faces unreadable, stared down at Meg from her wagon. "They claim," the man grunted with little interest either way, "that the horse and wagon is theirs."

"A pure lie!" Amazed at their audacity, she pointed toward the sample cases stowed behind the boy squatting in her wagon. "Tell me what is in those cases if you can? Of course you can't. Well, I can. There's identification in the bags. They belong to me—" she hesitated, "Meg Brennon. I can identify every item in every case, parcel, and box because those are *all* my possessions. And," she panted, "you're not taking them from me." She took a moment to gather her breath and then addressed the cowboy, "Thank you for stopping them. I don't know what I would have done." She smiled, her dove gray eyes softening with apology for being angry at him earlier.

He nodded, looking embarrassed, his chiseled face showing reluctance to be involved at all in this fuss between women and children. She turned her attention from him and examined the others, who had yet to make a move to get down from her wagon.

The freckled-faced boy cowered with knees drawn up, his back against her food box. His blue eyes had a blank, fixed stare at nothing. His nondescript clothes were dirty and tattered, and a breeze pulled at the few, wheat-colored hairs he possessed. Besides being filthy, his bare feet were scraped, bloody and bruised.

The old woman mumbled a belligerent oath under her breath and reached out to place a dirty, gnarled hand on the girl, who had a haunted, desperate look in her light, pearly blue eyes. "Stay settled now, lass. You don't want to do nothin' foolish."

The girl's shadowed face, the defeated set of her shoulders, the final-straw-need Meg felt emanating from the trio, snagged suddenly at her feelings. Her anger at what they'd tried to do to her lessened slightly.

She stepped closer, her back to the rider, and asked, "What on earth possessed you to try to steal my wagon? You had no right."

There was no response from them, no change to their stony, static silence. She wondered if they weren't afraid of *her*, now the tables were turned. Afraid of what she could do to them, like turn them over to the law. She could hear the cowboy shifting restlessly in his creaky saddle. "You can go," she said, turning to face him. "I can manage from here." The lines lay lax in his hands. Under the shadow of his hat brim, he looked relieved to hand them back to her.

He then hesitated and scratched his stubbled jaw as if re-thinking the situation. "Do you want me to send the marshal back, Miss?"

She considered for a moment, then smiled. "I don't be-lieve that will be necessary." They were a couple of waifs, after all, and an old woman. They had failed at their thieving attempt. For all intents and purposes she had her wagon and possessions back. She waved him off. "I thank you kindly for your assistance."

He touched his hat, rode off at a lope toward the saloon.

For several minutes of silence she calculated what she might do, or say, by way of punishment. "Get down from there, all three of you," she ordered. "Count yourselves lucky I'm going to let you try and explain your way out of this."

She caught her breath at the sudden glimmer of a blue-nosed pistol pointed at her from the girl's voluminous skirts. The grubby hand holding the pistol shook, the grip tightened.

Meg sent a darting glance over her shoulder for aid from the drifter. A block up the street he was tying his roan at the saloon's hitch rail; in a few seconds more he would disappear inside. Mrs. Isaacs had vanished too, but wouldn't have been much help anyway. She took a deep breath. She was alone with the thieves, who were a lot more dangerous than she had thought. She looked at the gun still clutched in the girl's shaking hands. She ought to have agreed to let the drifter get the marshal. Her heart thumped. "What do you think you're doing? You don't frighten me."

She turned a hopeful glance up the empty street. Would the girl shoot her if she yelled, and then take her wagon anyway?

The old woman, whose hickory-brown face was mostly nose and chin, studied Meg from squinty, coffee-brown eyes. With a sudden, crazy-crooked grin from the depths of her ratty sunbonnet, she hooted, "You can come with us, Missy, if you want." A strange gingery scent mixed with sweat and dirt wafted from her as she leaned forward.

Before Meg could recover from shock at the offer and protest, the girl waved the pistol for Meg to get aboard the wagon. Her voice came lifeless, low: "Get up here with Sally." She nodded at the old woman. "For now, me and my brother will walk since your wagon ain't big enough for all of us to ride. Just keep in mind I got this .44 trained on you ever' minute." She added, as though it made her offer fair, "We'll give your horse and wagon back to you when we don't need 'em anymore."

Meg, her scalp crawling with fear and worry, didn't move. "When might that be?" She wondered with a fragment of hope if the drifter might send the marshal after all. Was the marshal's office where Mrs. Isaacs had disappeared to? A glance toward town revealed nothing moving in the lazy afternoon sunshine except a dog angling at a trot down the main street. Hope evaporated.

The pigeon-shaped girl in faded brown answered in a voice so quiet Meg had to strain to hear her, "After we get to Dodge City and to my Uncle Ross's homestead north of there, you get your rig back. You got any food or money we're goin' to need that, too."

Good grief! She fought her creeping panic. "Go with you as far as Dodge? I should say not! That's two hundred and more miles from here. There is nothing in that country but rattlesnakes and buffalo, desperadoes and their—their fallen frails. Your blessed uncle is an outlaw for all I know." She shook her head, sputtered, "I-I can't go off with you like that, allow you the use of my wagon for two weeks. My work is here in eastern Kansas."

The dismaying thought struck her that if she went with these people, she could vanish and no one would be the wiser. There were two sides to that. Finch, the man following her for the past year, might lose her trail for good—and that she'd welcome.

But how safe was she with these thieves, in spite of their promise to give her back her things once they were through with them, and her? What about her work that so far kept her body and soul together, though sometimes barely? Following as irregular a route as possible, these last months she had sold millinery goods to several shops in Kansas City and in Lawrence, to a few in Topeka, to Mrs. Isaacs in Emporia.

She came and went, almost a stranger to everybody. She had no family, no permanent home, she never gave her real name, Cassiday Rose Curran. She slept in boardinghouses and cheap hotels, signing the register *M. R. Brennon, Sales* with a flourish that looked like *Mr. Brennon Sales,* which might later fool someone asking about a woman. She felt some safety because most traveling vendors were men. She slept in her wagon when it seemed safe to do so and she needed to save money.

If she never showed up again at any previous stop—millinery shops, hotels—folks would likely guess she'd taken other work. In conversation she'd commented on the penny-poor, and not always safe, life of a traveling vendor. They would conclude she had quit for something more secure. Except perhaps to Frank Finch, her disappearance would cause little stir. A terrible feeling of aloneness engulfed her.

She eyed the gun, considering for one brief moment trying to run for it. Say the girl didn't gun her down, let her run off. As slow as she was with the bad hip, it would take her a while to get back to town, find the marshal, and discuss her problem with him. If she couldn't find him, these crazy-desperate folk would have time to be long gone with all she owned. And where would she be then?

She couldn't risk staying in this town one more day. Finch could catch up, take her back to St. Louis to face torturous hell, or worse. He could be a month behind, or a week, or a day. She had changed her name, changed her location with each new job, but she couldn't change the fact that she was lame, slender, and had silver-dark eyes. Maybe her only choice was to risk life and limb going with these folks, though it wasn't much of a choice.

Her reluctant conclusion must have shown on her face.

"Laddie, boy," the crow-like old woman ordered over her shoulder, "git on down and walk." The boy scuttled wordlessly out of the back of the wagon.

The girl clambered down to stand beside him, the deadly gun in her fist waving at Meg. "Give Sally the lines and get in the wagon."

"If you insist," she said as though they had invited her to a parlor tea. Head high, insides quaking, she stowed her case with the others and climbed up into her wagon, settling her skirts around her. Her mind scurried for a scheme out of this predicament. Soon as she could, she would find a way to be rid of them, be on her rounds again. They stank to high heaven, all three of them. Manners, tinged slightly with pity for their state, was all that kept her from holding her nose.

Oddly, she didn't hate them altogether. She, too, was as homeless as they appeared to be. She would near give her soul for a place to call her own, for an opportunity to stop running from the man bent on taking her back to Kerry Patch—the old Irish neighborhood in St. Louis—and the husband she feared and hated.

Could she use these folks as a means of getting away from Finch? Forcing her along at the point of a gun, though, was hardly friendly, and they sure didn't add up to much as companions.

Chapter Two

Meg, when she was still Cassiday, had been told by her father, Red Pat, that Kerry Patch, the shabby St. Louis neighborhood where she was born, bore little resemblance to its namesake, Ireland's pretty County Kerry where the Lakes of Killarney were located.

Most early immigrants to St. Louis were very poor, he said, and had few contacts on arrival. They had a choice of living in filthy boardinghouses or squatting on open land. Arrivals from Ireland in 1842 chose the latter, and set up their tents and shacks in an open commons in the northwest section of the city. They called the place Kerry Patch. Luckily for them, the commons was owned by the heirs of a self-made Irish millionaire, John Mullanphy, who chose to let them be.

From that time on, Patch residents were predominantly Irish immigrants and their American-born children, as in her case. A few Germans, English, and French were sprinkled in.

The area, which reeked of poverty, grew to consist of overcrowded, flat-roofed box tenements with flimsy galleries marking each story. Here and there a small clapboard shack, or more than one, was squeezed into the shadows of the tenements. Like wounded features on a homely face, shutters were broken and patched. Straggly plants in window boxes struggled to grow in the industrial soot-filled air. Except in the coldest days of winter, flies swarmed over piles of rubbish.

Narrow, rutted dirt streets dissected the neighborhood in haphazard fashion. Children in raggedy dress played everywhere with a noise like swarming bees. Housewives stood in gossipy clusters, their clucking going silent only when a stranger passed and they stopped to stare.

Few outsiders, though, ventured into the strange land of Kerry Patch. Few insiders wanted them there.

There was a constant turnover of Patch residents, as people struggled to leave or died; fires and disease were common.

She, and her parents, Red Pat and Maria, had lived in a crude little whitewashed shanty. Goats and chickens grazed a nearby vacant lot. Patch life had been bare-bones simple, made brighter periodically by noisy, joy-filled festivals and parades.

There was singing of an evening as people sat on front stoops, singing that told of shamrocks and shillelaghs. Dancing was accompanied by the playing of fiddles, flutes, pipes, and goatskin tambourines. There were boisterous election day battles with fists and stones between the Ulster Irish and the Catholic Irish to see whose man would be voted ward boss. Papa's Presbyterian faction usually lost, she remembered fondly.

Though rich in love, hope, and dreams, her family was as financially poor as the rest. Her proud father would have none of his wife's family's money. It was cross enough to bear that his lovely Maria was educated and well-spoken. Kerry Patch was seen by her father as only temporary, a way station on the road to owning a fine stone house in the country, with snowy sheep dotting the fields. He practiced his philosophy of hard work, "putting the shoulder to the wheel," more than anyone she had ever known. Had he lived, her father would have achieved his dreams. He was that kind of vigorous, forward-looking Irishman. But death came early.

The day they got word that her father had been killed in a construction accident, was the same day her mother planned to tell him she was pregnant with a long-hoped-for second child. Six months later, her mother died in childbirth, the new infant surviving but a few hours. Cassiday was suddenly alone at sixteen.

If only she had had the courage to strike off for the West and new opportunity right then. But she was a meek, frightened little mouse. She had gone no further than two doors down, moving in with her mother's spinster friend, Meara Dolan, to help her with the sewing she took in.

It was during that period, out and about making deliveries for Meara, that Teddy Malloy, in his early twenties, first began to pay her attention.

His friendly overtures to her on the heels of her parents' deaths had been like a breath of spring in days of clouded loneliness. He was witty and lively, and his sweet attentions thrilled her. He brought her small nosegays of hothouse violets. He made up songs to sing to her. Funny songs—gallant songs—with himself as the hero and she as his maiden fair falling everlastingly in love. From his small pocket flask—all the young men carried them—he drank to her health, toasted her "beautiful gray eyes" her "beguiling smile."

He smelled nice and dressed well. He was educated and came from a respectable family. The Malloys in her time at Kerry had risen from shanty-Irish status to far beyond even lace-curtain labeling. His father was important not only in Kerry Patch where he was affectionately known as "King," but his name counted for something in all of St. Louis.

Meara Dolan was delighted that the former ward boss's handsome son had singled out her young companion. The Malloys by now had moved, building a fine new mansion well beyond O'Fallon and Cass avenues, core of Kerry Patch. It wasn't long before the older woman was oohing and aahing over various wedding gown patterns, causing Cassiday to flush in protest because Teddy hadn't mentioned marriage.

But she thought he might and she was convinced she was in love with him. His reputation for being wild didn't matter, was excusable. Most Kerry Patch young men had run in mischief-making gangs when they were boys.

When she was a very young child she didn't know quite what to make of their actions. Their mischief wasn't nice, certainly. The boys would dash an unknowing passerby with a bucket of cold water, just to hear him rage and curse. Or they would knock his hat off, for the opportunity to laugh hugely at his displeasure. Some of their pranks were more serious. They untied merchants' horses from their hitches, and ran the horses off. They derailed streetcars with ropes. There was a great deal of petty thievery. It was the sort of thing Patch boys did to amuse themselves. Teddy was no different, just more charming, more handsome. He didn't mean to be bad. And he was attracted to her, and she, a lonely sponge for his affection.

In the most embarrassing moment of her life late that year, Mr. Malloy caught her and Teddy under the honeysuckle arbor on the Malloy grounds. Their clothing was barely back in place before wedding plans were set in motion. It was time his son settled down, Mr. Malloy ranted. He would not allow Teddy to besmirch yet another poor girl's reputation and continue his path of lazy, reckless living. And there was a bonus: Cassiday was of finer cloth than the others. She was a beauty. Her father, Red Pat, had been a man of good character, and her mother, Maria, so it was said, had come from fine bloodlines and wealth back in Ireland.

It was the first time Cassiday heard that there were other girls; she had foolishly believed herself the only one, the special one.

Teddy, to avoid being disinherited, agreed to the marriage, although neither he nor Cassiday had any real say about the matter. His father was too powerful, too intimidating, for either of the young people to stand up against him.

The newlyweds were given a rustic cottage in the old neighborhood to live in. Mr. Malloy expected his son to bring himself up the same way he had, by initiative and hard work.

Teddy's resentment that Cassiday had no money of her own, and having to labor hard for pennies, began to show almost from the moment they married. She began to see a side of him she wouldn't have guessed. Money he lost gambling he blamed her for stealing. When he was too drunk to make love he insisted it was her fault: she was too "cold" to arouse him. The first time she hadn't cleaned his shoes on time was also the first time he struck her. She had been helping Meara with an extra heavy order of sewing, and hadn't yet gotten to his shoes.

When she stood up to him, saying he was to never lay a hand on her again, he said a good thump to the skull would make her remember better and it was his responsibility "to keep her in line, and teach her a thing or two." In that regard, he believed as most men did. He owned her; he could do what he wanted with her. She had no rights.

She knew she must leave him, leave before she got with child. A child would need his father. She and the child would need security. She would be chained to Teddy forever. She had to escape while she could, she knew, but hesitated. If Teddy's father wanted her to stay with his son, he could force her to do it, somehow. And there was the chance that Teddy would change. It seemed he might; he could be very sweet sometimes. Their love might yet turn out to be what she had believed it was in the beginning. Then he would find an excuse to hit her again for an imagined slight, some trifle.

She could not tell anyone of the abuse. Few would blame charming Teddy, but would believe she had failed her marriage. The beatings became her shameful secret.

They had been married less than a year when she was late one day returning from Meara's to fix supper. While the stew came to a simmer at the stove, she raced to slice bread, put out a pat of butter, set the table. She was nervous and shaking from Ted's ranting at her to "hurry it up!" He was already late for an evening at the tavern with friends.

As soon as she placed the steaming tureen of stew on the table, Teddy served himself, gulping at the food while it was still too hot. The stew must have been like fire in his mouth, the pain intense. She was rushing to him with a cup of cold water when he grabbed the tureen and threw it at her head. She ducked in time, then tried to give him the water.

Shrieking in rage, words unintelligible, he attacked her, slapping her face, grabbing her head to slam it against the table. She fought her way free, nose bleeding, and tried to explain. Her heavy sigh, her attempt at explanation to him was "backtalk," disrespect. She had to learn better.

He kicked her and beat her with his fists. In a painful daze, she watched her blood splatter the walls in a macabre design as he threw her around, too hurt, too weak, to get away or stop him. She thought it would never end, or at the very least would end mercifully in her death.

She was bleeding heavily from a cut over her eye, bleeding from her mouth and nose, was hardly able to move from a cracked hip, when he finally said maybe now she knew who was boss, and stalked out.

After he'd gone, she crawled from the house, humiliated, as angry as she would ever be in her life. No man would ever lay a hand on her in such a way again. Not even his father could make her stay with him.

Meara, shocked, riven with regret and sympathy, hid her and brought a doctor to tend her. Within days, Teddy discovered her whereabouts but was willing to let Meara care for his bloody, broken wife for the next few weeks. He was confident that when Cassiday was healed, she'd come crawling back to him, all the wiser. But by the time he expected her to come home, she was on a train to Kansas City, gone from Kerry Patch for good. Neither of the women believed she could really get away, but they had to try. And she had succeeded.

The first months in Kansas City were a blur of pain and desperation while she completed her recovery in secret at the home of Meara's great-aunt. They heard from Meara that Teddy had tried to force her to tell him where Cassiday had gone. Meara, armed with a poker, insisted she did not know, that Cassiday had slipped off one day without a word. Meara was afraid, though, that Teddy would hire someone to find Cassiday and she should take guard.

She left the home of Meara's great-aunt and found ways to support herself with menial work, changing her location and appearance as much as possible with each job. Eventually, she worked into a business of her own as a lady vendor delivering hat goods.

She accepted that she would have a limp all of her life, but with God's good grace would somehow make a decent life on her own. She would never return to St. Louis. No one could make her. As proud as she was of her own name, she would never use it again: she was now Meg Brennon.

She could guess Teddy's reasons for sending Finch to find

her and force her to return. No man took lightly the fact of his wife running away. To him she was his property. Leaving him was a crime against him, damaging his ego, leaving an ugly mark against his power. Once she was back he could do what he pleased with her.

Without knowing yet what might happen, she doubted any circumstance in which she found herself, including traveling west with her strange kidnappers, could be much worse than that she'd already known. Or would experience, going back. The greater the distance between her and Kerry Patch, the better. And if she were truly fortunate, she might yet find a permanent, safe haven.

Chapter Three

Emporia was several miles behind them by the time the sinking sun spread the rolling hills with crimson fire, filled the draws with purple shadow. Meg and her kidnappers, by common weary decision, drew off to the side of the dusty road to spend the night.

They soon had an aromatic campfire of twisted dried grass and sage, and coffee percolating in a pot. The fire helped some against the tiny sandflies. They were preparing supper when the lawman, a rotund, mustachioed gent on a dappled gray, rode in.

Meg's thoughts wavered. In the beginning she had hoped for a chance such as this to turn her captors over to the law. Some hours ago, though, she had decided against it.

"What can we do for you, Marshal?" she asked tentatively, giving the frying potatoes and bacon a turn. He dismounted, tied his horse to a shrub, and approached the campfire. His eyes were as bright and friendly as the reflection of the fire on his badge. She liked his looks, but the girl, Lucy Ann, had gone pale and was fingering her pocket. Laddie crouched close to the ground, terrorized.

The granny woman, Sally Coalter, eyed the lawman, eyelids at half-mast like a drowsing frog's, but her body tense.

She slowly chewed a piece of spicy-smelling weed that she had picked along the way. The weed helped her digestion, she claimed.

Meg prayed her captors wouldn't do anything foolish, nervous like they were, and make things worse for everybody. She mustered calm. "Sir?" she asked again, "can we do something for you? Would you like to join us for supper?" She poured him a cup of coffee.

"A couple of folks in Emporia asked me to investigate you all." He added in apology, "I'd have caught up with you sooner, but I was out of town most of the day on business." He accepted the coffee, but turned down supper. He looked at the homey scene the four of them made around the fire. The fragrance of their cooking filled the evening air.

The drifter and Mrs. Isaacs had asked him to track them, make sure she was all right, Meg surmised, pleased even though she had changed her mind about wanting aid.

Eyes squinting over the rim of the cup, he asked, "Miss, are you with these folks by your own free will? You got a problem here I can help you with?" He looked a trifle embarrassed asking the question, given how comfortable they looked together. The whine of mosquitos filled the silence.

Convincing him that she was fine was going to be too easy. She hesitated, wanting to do the wisest thing. Lucy Ann had taken up a huge butcher knife and sliced more bacon onto a tin plate. Lad squatted on one knee shoving sagebrush into the fire. The old woman set the coffee, starting to boil over, off the blaze. If she were at real risk from them, this was her chance.

She crossed her fingers in a tuck of her skirts, smiling thinly. "No, sir, there is no problem here. We had a bit of discussion back in town, but now I've agreed to help them reach family in western Kansas."

"You're sure, miss?"

She nodded.

The old woman relaxed. She cautioned with a toothy smile from where she squatted, "Don't let the 'taters burn, daughter."

"I won't, I'm as hungry as you are. Lucy Ann—" she addressed the girl whose name she had learned only in the last hour as they worked together— "will you bring more bacon?" They had learned her name, too, at least the only name she could give them.

The marshal took time to drain his cup, saying, "If you're all right then." He gave the cup back to Meg, took a puff on his stogie, prepared to leave. "Hot this evenin', ain't it? Damn skeeters!" He slapped his neck, took a bandanna from his pocket, and wiped his round friendly face. He lifted a hand in a wave. "Now you folks have a good trip." He stomped off on short legs to his tethered horse.

"Be there Indians about to watch out for?" Lucy Ann, tin plate in hand, called after him suddenly in a stricken voice that took Meg by surprise. The look on Lucy Ann's face shocked her, though fear of Indians was common to all women on the frontier.

He came back a few steps, waving his stogie. "Redskins? Nah. They're mostly south of here, on reservations. A few Cheyenne might of hid out, got missed by the soldiers, but I ain't laid eyes on an Injun in a blue moon." Lucy Ann appeared relieved.

"I was a woman," he went on, "I'd fret more about white-skinned outlaws like the James gang, and their crazy imitators rampagin' the country. Some of 'em be gentlemen with women, but you never know." He shook his head. "Women alone with no man to look out for 'em is easy targets." He didn't say for what, but he didn't have to.

Lucy Ann looked about to collapse, her eyes glazed.

No need to scare her so. "We'll be all right," Meg declared stoutly and waved him off. She had looked out for herself for well over a year, in fact. One just had to be on guard, wherever they were, whomever they were with. It would be only a little more difficult to mind the others' safety along with her own, if it came to that. Possibly it would be easier, if they stood together against trouble.

She watched the marshal ride off into the dark. What did she really know about her companions or what they might try? They could still take everything she owned, abandon her, if they took the notion. It was possible she was making the stupidest, most dangerous decision of her life to stick with them. Time and caution would tell.

The following day, they made a brief stop in Strong City, a small trading center in the high-grass Flint Hills. Meg used a tot of hoarded cash and a pile of items from her goods cases to buy food supplies. Potatoes, onions, beans, and flour were stowed in her food box, which also contained her skillet, kettle, coffeepot, and now additional eating utensils.

Several evenings later, they camped by a little creek in the humid, mosquito-infested shade of a hackberry grove, and dined on a meatless meal of beans and skillet biscuits.

Meg was frustrated and a little angry. "Rabbit would have been tasty with our supper," she said pointedly. They saw hundreds of rabbits daily, but Lucy Ann refused to fire her blessed pistol at a single one. She had seemed to turn deaf the times Meg pointed and whispered, "Shoot!" All of them seemed deaf to her last remark.

They had seen antelope, too, and once a herd of buffalo, but the larger game had been at too great a distance to concern themselves with. The rabbits had been close.

"Don't keep fussin' at the girl to use her gun on them rabbits," Sally cautioned Meg with a deep frown a few minutes later when they took the pots and dishes to the creek to wash. "She ain't agonna heed you."

"Why not?" Meg demanded from where she knelt by the creek. "Lord knows, we could use a little meat with our meals and she's got the only weapon!"

"Shore she does," Sally nodded, "but she's got but one bullet."

"Oh?" One bullet, *for me?* Her throat dried.

"She's savin' that bullet for her ownself." She poked her temple with a wet forefinger.

Meg stared at Sally, then dropped back on her heels feeling like she'd been struck. Her skin popped out in cold perspiration, her mind spun. Sweet heaven! Why would Lucy Ann want to do away with herself? Maybe the old woman was mistaken. "You don't really mean—?"

The lines in Sally's face deepened as she nodded. "Bunch of Injuns got to her up north where she come from. She onliest wants to get the boy to their uncle first, then she means to use that bullet."

Horror crept into every fiber of her. She looked toward where young Lucy Ann sat, a small lump of shadow by the fire. A tide of sympathy swept her, bringing both anger and the threat of tears. No worse outrage could happen to a female in that new country. Some never got over being despoiled. A few lost their minds, like Mrs. Ward on White Rock Creek. Raped by savages, she ran from her rescuers and finally vanished. A few took their lives as Lucy intended to do. Some of the stronger ones did recover, went on with their lives, and endured. Lucy Ann just had to be one of the latter. She said in a choked voice, "I must talk to her, if what you say is true." She jumped to her feet, letting the kettles go.

28

Sally got up and clutched at her. "You can't do no such a-thing! Talkin' about it will only bring the girl shame, don't you see? I swore to Lucy I'd not tell a livin' soul. She likes you. Only if she thinks you don't know, can she hold her head up atall."

"But what happened was not her fault. She's still a—good human being. We have to do something for her!"

Sally's hands gripped and shook her. "Now, listen to me, daughter. We bide our time, give the child a chance to get over the idee of takin' her life. Soon's we get to that uncle, we'll let him know her thinkin'. With family she might feel different, want to live. It'll be his job to see that she does, 'til she's an old lady like me."

Meg looked at Sally in disbelief. Say nothing? *Do* nothing? Regardless of what the savages had done to her, Lucy Ann couldn't be allowed to kill herself! She was young, healthy, she had her brother. But if she tried—?

Lord God, what a pretty pass she'd gotten into. She'd have to keep an eye on Lucy Ann every second of the way. She squatted back down and mechanically rewashed a kettle in the creek.

In the beginning, joining up with this strange lot had seemed simple enough, if scary. Traveling with them had appeared the only way to hang onto her outfit. She'd had thoughts about maybe taking up some of that free land in western Kansas for herself, once she was shed of her captors. She hadn't guessed, though, how complicated things would be as she got to know them better.

They pushed on, day after day, taking turns riding, then walking. Endless rolling hills covered with tall waving grass stretched ahead of them, touching an azure sky.

She kept a near-constant watch on Lucy Ann. In turn, Lucy Ann spent most of the time looking for Indians, or some other terror, to come on them.

Contrasting to the tension, hundreds of wildflowers bloomed in rainbow sweeps over the hills: aromatic pink yarrow, white prickly poppy, purple poppymallow, goldenrod. Tall stately sunflowers swayed in lovely quiet peace, belying any trouble anywhere.

On they went, at times seeming to be buried in a sea of grass along the road snaking ever west. Food for them might be short, but graze for Butterfield was more than plentiful.

One afternoon Sally pounded the shells from three land terrapins with a stone. That night they had turtle soup. "Meat," she told Meg with a toothless grin. Meg grudgingly admitted it was edible, though her mouth watered still for rabbit, for buffalo or antelope steaks, with no way to come by them if Lucy Ann stubbornly resisted using her pistol for game.

With miles behind her, Meg was feeling more free all the time from her own past, as well as expectant of good fortune that *could* lie ahead. She had to remind herself from time to time that she was still a prisoner in a touchy, disordered situation.

She made effort, chiefly through observation—she wouldn't pry—to know her companions. Lucy Ann had little to say. But each time they nooned by the side of the road, fixing a meal in the shade of the wagon, Lucy Ann hopped to, doing more than her share. She helped likewise to cook supper, to clean up, and afterward to shake out their blankets. She seemed not to care one way or another when Meg offered her one of her clean dresses to wear. The pink ruffled gingham was snug on her boxy frame and the hem dragged in the dust, but after she began to wear the pretty dress and matching sunbonnet, there was more life in her round solemn face.

Surely there was nothing to the gun business, Meg told herself; it was a false alarm, the old woman's imaginings. Or Lucy Ann's notion to take her life had faded, was all over with.

Lucy Ann's little brother, Laddie, spoke not at all. But he could hear well, and through those small scruffy ears of his, Meg was beginning to charm him.

In the past she had taught herself to imitate a number of birdsongs. There was little else to listen to, or do, traveling long lonely roads from town to town with her sales goods.

The beautiful song of the meadowlark was her specialty. As she trilled the clear tuneful whistle, in answer to a meadowlark swaying from the stem of a tall sunflower, Laddie's face altered, brightening slightly. She could imitate the song of the wren, sparrow, oriole, blackbird, towhee, and wood warbler. After the first time, witnessing the boy's face, she missed few opportunities to entertain him. She wanted his trust, his friendship, but he would shrink away if she looked to be getting too close. Only his sister, Lucy Ann, was allowed to tousle his hair, help him wash his face, remove the stickers from his abused feet.

Meg said one afternoon, when they had stopped so Lucy Ann could check Laddie's stubbed, infected toe and apply a yarrow-leaf poultice Sally prepared, "Laddie should ride the rest of the way. I'll walk." For an instant, his face held a soft thankful smile, then his vacant expression returned.

"But your—bad leg?" Making a point of Meg's affliction brought a flush to Lucy Ann's face.

"Needs the exercise," Meg answered simply. "I'll be all right."

Sometimes they were met or passed on the road by a single rider. Another time they were buried in the dust of a long freight wagon driven by a six-horse team. There was no attempt made to abuse or rob them. There were several occasions when Meg could have called out for help in retrieving her own conveyance and turning back to the life she'd left. But she couldn't abandon her companions now that they had struck a sympathetic chord in her heart, a liking for them, even. Nor could she set aside her wish to go to western Kansas.

"I'm not very accomplished at this," she explained the night she got out her father's fiddle to play after supper. While they listened, she played a rustic rendition of "Sweet Genevieve," then "Oh Promise Me," and finally, her father Red Pat's favorite, "The Flower of Kildare."

" 'Minds me of the old days in southern Missouri," Sally cried happily from where she squatted by their fire. She clapped, and in a moment, Lucy Ann and Laddie clapped, too. Tears were close when Meg played "Home Sweet Home."

" 'Twas a happy time for me," Sally said solemnly, "afore the War Between the States. Afore everything was tore apart and changed an' the child—" She fell silent when Lucy Ann reached out to touch her arm, gently consoling.

Meg played on, inexpertly, selecting happier tunes. It was the first time she'd heard where the old woman, or any of them, was from. Not wanting to share details of her own past, of what took place in Kerry Patch in St. Louis—which would always shame her—she never probed for information about her companions. Let them tell her if they wanted to, but she would accept them as they were and would hope they would accept Meg Rose Brennon as she was. Legally, she was Cassiday Curran Malloy, but she would *never* use that name. She had no husband.

One night, after Lucy Ann and Laddie had gone to bed in the wagon, and Sally and Meg sat by the fire, Sally whispered,

"I never finished tellin' you 'bout them younguns. You need to know, 'fore Dodge, case they need your help there." She spat over her shoulder, and in the heat from the fire closed her moist eyes, and swayed and talked.

Meg was frozen to the spot the while, listening.

The children's parents were German immigrants named Voss who had settled years before in Nebraska. June just past, four renegade Sioux struck the Voss farm located south of Grand Island. Used to dealing with Indians, the mother hid her fear, offered food, did her best to be sociable. But the renegades, crazed from stolen whiskey, tore up the house in devilment. When the mother struggled with one of them over a treasured china pitcher, she was hacked to death with a hatchet.

Her husband, brought on the run from the field by his family's screams, managed to fire on the Indians, killing one of them. The rest of the band circled on Voss and killed him. Two baby sisters and an older brother of Lucy Ann and Laddie also lost their lives at the savages' hands. Lucy Ann was ravaged by two of the Indians. Laddie was alive but partially scalped when neighbors showed up, firing on the savages and killing them.

Laddie's scalp was cared for and, in time, it healed, but he hadn't uttered a word since. There wasn't much to do for Lucy Ann except scalding baths, which couldn't heal what had been done to her. The dead members of the family were buried. The land, farm implements, and household goods were parceled out to neighbors in exchange for funds to help the two youngsters leave the scene of the tragedy behind them.

Meg sat with her hand over her mouth. She felt sick and furious.

"Them chil'ern," Sally said, "was sent south from

Nebrasky to family livin' near Manhattan, Kansas. They weren't good and kindly folk, not them relatives. They didn't want the burden of a scarified boy who couldn't speak. Weren't about to keep a girl 'dirtied by Indians.' "

"What happened?" Meg asked through a tight throat.

"The girl was turned out on the street to do for herself. Boy was took to the Topeka asylum. Boy and me got to be friends there, even if he couldn't say nothin'. Girl come and broke us out one hot night in July when everybody in the place was sleepin' or was some'eres else tryin' to get cool." In answer to the question Meg didn't ask, Sally explained, "I was in that place 'cause I get a little mixed-up at times, is all. Ain't real crazy, like some they had behind them walls."

Meg nodded; Sally continued her story.

On foot, the trio had set out for Dodge City where Lucy Ann and Laddie had an uncle from their mother's side who would hopefully accept them more kindly. Walking was taking too long, and their blistered feet had gotten infected. Food was difficult to steal; hard grassy beds were getting tiresome. Worn out, on the verge of starvation, afraid they would be caught and sent back to the asylum before they could reach their destination, they tried to steal Meg's wagon and few belongings in Emporia.

"So that's it. I'm glad I know." Meg rose stiffly from beside the fire. For now, she wanted to clean up in the creek they had camped beside, go to bed, and try to sleep under this sorrowful burden of knowledge. But first she had to get her soap.

The moon shed a pale light into the back of her wagon. She climbed in without a sound and crouched there. Lucy Ann lay rolled in her blanket behind the wagon seat. Laddie slept scrunched against her sample cases packed to the side of the wagon. It could hardly be comfortable. She reached out and gently smoothed what hair the boy had over the healing scars at the front of his head. His hair was stiff with dirt and grime. Poor little soul. Like Sally said, the boy was "the most scarified li'l' critter" she'd ever seen.

Stealthily, she got her soap from her satchel of personal things, thumping into the wooden food box in the process. The boy stirred, but didn't wake. When she looked, she saw that Lucy Ann's eyes were open, round and shiny in the dark. Did Lucy Ann ever really sleep, after what had happened to her? The gun was probably under her pillow. She didn't look of a mind to take her life at the moment. If she did want to for certain, it would be her way to wait until the boy was safely delivered to their uncle.

Meg had the blessing of time until then, and when they got there, she would find a way to prevent it.

With a finger to her lips, an uncertain smile, she backed out of the wagon. The remembered look in Lucy Ann's eyes by day, the emptiness of hope, the pain there, cut to her soul even more now that she knew the reason.

Her heart weighed heavily as she moved toward the creek in the dark. This past year had been a hardship to keep herself alive and well. Yet, now that she was tied to these lost souls, she wanted, no, *had* to do what she could for them, too.

Her means were little, but she would get the youngsters and the old woman to the uncle's place north of Dodge. She prayed God that the uncle was a good man, would know what to do to stop Lucy Ann if she still meant to kill herself, would know how to help Laddie speak again. With love, she was sure both could be done. The children needed kindness and understanding as much as food and shelter, or how were they to survive?

If they remembered him as a good man, then he surely was.

The creek water smelled of fish but at least felt cool as she washed. Her own problems pushed to the front of her mind but she shoved them back. She didn't want to think about the bounty hunter, Finch, or her brutal husband, or the fact that she had just left the only means she'd had to survive, her millinery supply business. Nor did she want to recognize how this trio of misfits could only complicate her life further. She would manage somehow, moment to moment, day to day.

The fire had burned down to gray ash and a handful of red coals when she headed for camp. She stopped in her tracks at the sound of Sally's voice, carrying through the night as she sang a lullaby. The pained keening sent shivers along Meg's spine, though she had heard the singing before. Every night on the road the past week and a half, Sally had rocked and sang her invisible baby to sleep.

Swallowing the dryness in her throat, her knees quivering, she stepped to the old woman's side and touched her bony shoulder lightly. "Mrs. Coalter? Sally?"

The old woman continued to rock and sing with a forlorn sadness Meg could feel to her bones.

"Sally?"

Slowly, the rocking, the singing, wound down. Sally looked up at Meg and smiled. She cuddled the invisible child to her breast for a moment, then lay it aside in its invisible cradle, tucking an unseen coverlet around it. "Grandma Spicy," she croaked then to Meg.

"I beg your pardon?" Meg left her hand on the old woman's thin shoulder, stroking it gently.

"Back home to Missoura they called me Grandma Spicy. Have had me a bad stomach for a long time, but takin' a spoonful of nutmeg oil, or chewin' a piece o' gingerroot fixes it fine." She cackled, her mouth open wide, her teeth showing few and far between in her nutcracker face. "Way I smell, is why they called me that. For that an' for the sass I been known to show a few times." She laughed again, reached up, and patted Meg's hand on her shoulder. "Call me Grandma Spicy, daughter."

"Grandma Spicy," she said, with a soft uncertain laugh. "It's time we turned in and got some sleep. With a noodle of good luck, we could reach Dodge City in another day or so."

She had heard plenty about the wild town of Dodge, haven to buffalo skinners, gamblers, outlaws on the run, and sporting women. Some claimed Dodge had a few decent businesses, a sprinkling of honest townsfolk. Some said the country around there was fine for raising cattle.

Soon they would see the town, the people there, for themselves. Anyhow, they didn't have to be in Dodge any longer than to learn the uncle's location and be out again. After that, her companions ought to be a whole lot better off. And the fates could answer what was in store for her.

Chapter Four

Under a brassy afternoon sky, Dodge looked to be as raw, horrible, and fascinating as Meg suspected it might. She drove her wagon into town with Grandma Spicy beside her. Lucy Ann and Laddie, his sore foot much improved, walked alongside, kicking up small puffs of dust.

Wide Front Street was lined on one side with crude business houses the same dun color as the prairie they'd covered on the final stretch west. She counted a billiard hall, restaurant, hotel, tonsorial parlor, dry goods store, and several saloons. From the latter's open doors men of every shady sort spilled in and out, yelling and laughing. The cowboys' spurs jingled as they clumped to their individual mounts tied at the hitch rail.

A newer saloon had the odd name Long Branch. Through the wide open door came the tinny sound of a piano. Just inside, a staggering drunk cowboy and a brilliantly plumed sporting woman danced clumsily but enthusiastically. Grandma Spicy spoke, scandalized, in Meg's ear, "Land sakes, whoopin' it up in the daytime when most folks are hard at work as ought to be. Ever' think you'd see such as that?" Her sunbonnet brim flapped as she whipped around for a better view.

She shook her head and continued her own look around. Few of the hodgepodge businesses had plank sidewalks; the deep dust-and-manure mix that went to the doorstep of most made her cough. Grandma Spicy's hand flew to cover her face as a buggy pulled away from the tonsorial parlor, sending up a cloud of the unhealthy powder. Before the dust could settle, three shaggy-looking men in skin-heaped wagons drove in, sending the dust swirling again.

A halted train sat on the Santa Fe railroad tracks that lined the opposite side of the street. There were no trees, the only shade cast by mountainous piles of sun-dried buffalo hides by the tracks, awaiting shipment. Rank odors rode the hot winds from the hides, but also from outhouses behind the business places and sod houses, and from the cattle yard farther along.

Meg sighed, feeling as dirty as the town looked and smelled. After walking days in the open sun, her skin was blistered, her throat felt fried, and she was choked with dust. She pulled Butterfield to a halt beside the town pump located in the middle of the street, in front of the barbershop and the Beatty and Kelley Saloon. She jumped down, her foot narrowly missing a pile of horse dung swarming with noisy bottle-green blowflies.

She led Butterfield to the trough where he plunged his nose in and began to drink. She pumped while Sally and Lucy Ann—with weary but glad little cries—and Laddie took turns filling the chained tin cup for long drinks before splashing their faces and arms.

Male voices in a furious yelling match exploded from inside the saloon a few feet away. The language was such that Meg and Lucy Ann blushed, Grandma Spicy giggled, and Laddie looked frightened. Lucy Ann hugged her brother to her side, holding a hand over his other ear. Meg consoled, "We'll find out where your uncle is located, and be gone from here in nothing flat. I think the local marshal is the best one to ask directions to your uncle's place." *If* Dodge had any law.

"Ross McCoy? Sure I knew him," the marshal, a chunky, well-dressed, and clean-shaven man told the foursome awhile later. They stood in the street where they had stopped him in front of his small office. He gave them a serious, studying look. "You ain't going to find him out at his place, though. He's dead."

Dead? Meg looked quickly at Lucy Ann, catching her arm in sympathy as Lucy Ann sagged, eyes wide and disbelieving, back against the wagon. She reached for Laddie with the other hand, but with a soundless cry he whirled to hop into the vehicle where he curled into a shivering ball behind the seat. Grandma Spicy looked disbelieving and then angry, a reflection of her own feelings.

Grandma asked, tone sharp, "Are you sure, mister?" Her coffee-brown eyes glinted at him, her pointed chin jutted. "These young ones came a powerful long way to see him, ya' know. Near killed themselves gittin' here, and now you go and say their uncle is *dead?*"

He nodded, his expression sincere. "Wouldn't say he was, otherwise. Only facts I know is he got gored by a bull and bled to death. Harlan, his partner, brought McCoy's body in and he's buried up there on Boot Hill." He pointed out a cluster of crude grave-markers on a low butte in the distance, a buzzard circling slowly in the hot sky above.

What in the name of heaven were these youngsters going to do now? Meg's mind tussled with these new facts. Getting the youngsters here was to take care of everything, her part done. "You say Mr. McCoy had a partner in the homestead?" She tossed back a tendril of hair that blew into her face, and rested on her other hip for a moment's ease. Would the partner take the children in? she wondered. If not—

40

"Yup, he had a partner. Harlan Thorne's his name. Let me give you directions for gettin' out to his place. You can talk to him about McCoy and find out anything else you'd like to know about his dyin'."

"Thank you, Marshal." Meg smiled grim gratitude from all of them.

"Obliged to help, anytime. Bassett is the name, Charlie Bassett."

The homestead they sought was a full day and a half north of Dodge City, Bassett told them. All of them were worn to a nubbin from the trip, but mutually agreed that they should keep going until daylight gave out that night, camp, and set off again at first light. God willing, the partner, Thorne, would allow them to stay awhile until they could decide what to do.

A hawk screeched and circled above as they set off on the uphill climb from Dodge. Meg and Sally walked while the youngsters drove the wagonette along a faint, dusty wagon trace, each of them occupied with his or her own thoughts. In time, Dodge City grew small behind them and finally disappeared.

Ahead, the yellowed short-grass prairie undulated endless miles into the hazy horizon. The big, desolate, unconquerable-looking land was dizzying to the eyes, disheartening to the spirit, Meg thought.

With a weary sigh, she toed aside a discarded rattlesnake skin, watching more carefully for the real thing. A scorpion scuttled out of her path, causing her to stumble in the dust from a few seconds' fright before moving on in long uneven strides.

For hours, no one spoke. Lucy Ann's face, always solemn, was lined with fresh grief and despair. There was no uncle to turn her brother over to, now. She would have to stay alive for

41

the boy; she was all he had. She had asked for a few minutes at her uncle's gravesite, and stood there with Laddie, whispering something to him that the others, standing back, couldn't hear. Meg guessed, *prayed,* that Lucy Ann was giving him assurance that she was there for him, that she'd never desert him.

In that regard, Meg felt some relief. At her urging, both youngsters took to the wagon, Lucy Ann handling the lines. Tears the two had shed back in Dodge had dried on their grubby faces, and Meg thought she had never seen a more stoic pair.

On foot, she and Sally trailed a bit. The old woman broke the silence. "Sorry we got you into this, daughter. Didn't none of us know our plan would come to this."

"In for a penny, in for a pound, Grandma Spicy." Meg tried to smile, managing at best a grimace. At the moment she was too tired to care what she had gotten herself into, or how she was going to extricate herself, or when. All she wanted to do was lay her bones on the prairie and sleep for days on end. But she dragged one weary step after another, jaws clenched due to her bothersome hip.

Sunlight spread its last golden rays on the wide plain. A coyote barked. She looked for him with tired eyes, found him outlined on a ridge to the west against a pinkish sky; a second later he dropped his head and trotted away, disappearing into an inky draw.

Maybe a half hour later, unable to take another step, she called ahead that they should stop for the night, make camp, fix something to eat. They pulled down into the shelter of a draw.

"Uncle Ross didn't come visit often, but when he did he brought little presents." Lucy Ann, who rarely talked about anything, was rattling on in near hysteria about her Uncle

Ross as they sat by the fire following a meager supper. "One time he scolded me when I squashed his Stetson flat, sitting on it by accident. But he didn't really mean it. He dried my tears his ownself, on his bandanna." She reached out to touch Laddie's arm. "Remember the magic top he brought you, Laddie?" He nodded. Her voice broke, "Lordy, how that top could spin, like a rainbow in motion."

Listening, Meg experienced the youngsters' pain, their fear groping toward the emptiness of their future, as if that future were her own, and maybe it was, now, in part. Clearly, they had loved their uncle. His loss was near to the end of the world to them.

The air was filled with no-see-ums, tiny sandflies that had them all scratching. Lucy Ann rubbed her neck, her arm, her ankle. Then she continued:

"Uncle Ross used to say any of us got trouble to let him know. He would have been so good for you, Laddie." She put her arm around her brother. He wore his vacant, detached look. She shook him gently. "I'm—I'm so sorry he had to—to die. He would have raised you, he would have, the same as Mama and Papa would have done. Now—" She let go of Laddie, buried her face in her arms, which were crossed over her drawn-up knees. Sobs broke from her, like water from a ruptured dam.

"Now," Meg said softly, scooting over to put an arm around Lucy Ann's shoulder, "you'll do for Laddie what your mama and papa and Uncle Ross would have done. And we will help you, me and Grandma Spicy."

She hadn't meant to make any such promise toward the future. She had planned to part company with the others and go her own way. But she was in so far now, what else could she do? Until they were safely settled one way or another, she couldn't leave them.

Her thoughts turned to Dodge as she lay on her pallet under the stars a short time later. A woman, she was positive, would run a town located even here in the untamed West very differently. But when did a woman ever get such a chance? By law women could hold no political office, were under male rule in too many ways.

That's what she had fled from, leaving Teddy Malloy back in Missouri. She could live under no man's thumb. Would as soon be dead as have her own dreams stifled, as they surely would have been, if she had stayed with Teddy Malloy. And that providing he didn't beat her to death first. She drifted toward sleep at last, soothed by the song of crickets. The scent of sage and yarrow was a drug to her exhausted body and soul.

When she woke next morning, Lucy Ann and Grandma Spicy were gone, their blankets empty. "Where are they?" she frantically questioned Lad, but he cowered away, wouldn't listen to her, or respond. She ran to the top of the draw, looked north, east, west. Finally, she saw them coming from the southwest, two tiny figures in the silvered dawn. She ran to meet them. "What happened? Are you all right?" She grabbed Lucy Ann.

Lucy Ann gave her an odd look. "Of course I'm all right."

"Then why did you leave? Why did you go back toward Dodge?" Meg couldn't control her voice, her fears.

"I was looking for Grandma Spicy." Lucy Ann nodded to where Grandma had charged ahead and was banging pots and pans, fixing breakfast after stirring up the fire. "She wanders sometimes, looking for the baby."

"What baby? What baby is it that she rocks and sings to?" Her voice was thin, a shiver running along her spine.

"The baby she imagines she lost."

Lucy Ann started toward camp but Meg grabbed her arm.

"Lucy Ann, you've got to tell me more than that, please. I feel sorry for her, but I have to know—" *Is she insane?*

"That's all there is to tell. Grandma Spicy's family was near all killed by thieving bushwhackers near the end of the War Between the States. Her granddaughter, Annie, that Grandma was taking care of, ran and hid but she wasn't ever found, after. She vanished and Grandma feels it's her fault. Sometimes her mind slips and she goes looking for Annie. She's been looking a long time, off and on. Years. It's her grandbaby, Annie, she sings to."

Meg had covered her mouth with her hand while she listened and now let her hand drop. She felt sad and blinked as she looked toward the warming sun coming up over the horizon. "Thank you, Lucy Ann, for telling me." She turned to where Grandma bustled, perfectly happy for the moment, preparing their food. "Poor dear old thing." She shook her head. "We'd better help get breakfast, eat, and be on our way."

The rest of the morning they made good time, but it was afternoon before the homestead came in sight. The dugout, a bleak, uneven lump against the far slope of a wide grassy bowl, was marked by a stovepipe and surrounding ant-like activity from a few thin cows and horses. They headed toward the swale and the only signs of civilization they had seen for miles.

Charlie Bassett hadn't mentioned that they might find someone else besides Harlan Thorne at the homestead. But coming closer they could see a woman moving about the dooryard of the dismal dwelling carved into the hill. There was no man in sight. A pale spiral of smoke lifted from the narrow pipe poking up at a slant through the grassy roof of the dugout.

The woman was a slender, out-of-place figure, Meg

thought, when they got close enough to see her better. She was in the process of emptying a dishpan of water around the roots of a spindly cottonwood tree. She wore a blue, elegantly cut dress that had once been very fashionable and expensive. At the sounds of their approach, she stood in the knife-blade shade of the tree and watched them come, hand over her eyes, shoulders thrown back, her demeanor both mystified and defiant. She spoke to three youngsters making play roads and houses in the dust nearby. A baby sat playing in a large clothes basket.

"Hello," Meg called out. She caught Grandma Spicy's arm to stop her as she cried out and hurtled herself toward a small blonde girl. Grandma Spicy eyed the child intently, then dismissed it and settled back.

"Good day." The woman's large green eyes stared at Meg and the others from under thin, winged brows the same dark, gold-brown of her hair. She tucked escaping tendrils behind her ear, then gave her apron a quick brush with red chapped hands. Her dress was faded from the strong sun, grit looked permanently ground into the fancy hem.

Lucy Ann had fallen suddenly shy and silent, her expression begging Meg for help. Meg introduced her companions, then herself. "We understand this was the home of Mr. Ross McCoy? Lucy Ann and Laddie are his niece and nephew. They've come west expecting to live with him, but we recently learned that he—that he's dead."

"I know of Mr. McCoy, but I never met him. Yes, he's dead," the woman said bluntly. "My name is Aurelia Thorne. These are my young ones." She introduced Joshua, a dark, handsome boy of about seven years of age, and David John, similar in looks to his brother and maybe a year younger. "And this is Helen Grace." She patted the cornsilk-gold hair of a girl about three who had come to peek wide-eyed from behind her mother's skirts, thumb in her mouth. She was the same child who had caught Grandma Spicy's interest for a moment. "The baby, yonder in the basket, is my little Zibby. Joshua, get that dirty corncob out of Zibby's mouth! The baby is teething," she explained to the newcomers. "Chewing on a corncob makes her mouth feel better, but when she drops it into the dirt, she reaches right out, picks it up, and pops it into her mouth again." She sighed. "If my children don't die from snakebite or get killed by a wild cow, I swear the dirt will do them in."

Meg nodded sympathetically, but wanted to get down to business. "We understand a man named Harlan Thorne was partner to Ross McCoy in this homestead. Is Mr. Thorne your husband? We must speak with him."

"That rakehell is not my husband. Harlan is my good-for-nothing brother-in-law. My husband, John, who was Harlan's brother, is dead." She turned on a heel, motioning them to follow. "You may wait inside for Harlan. We might see him tonight, and we might not. We had an argument and I haven't seen him for several days." She added, "I don't have anything fancy to offer company, but you're welcome to what is here."

"We don't want to put you to any trouble—" Meg began, but the woman, her back to Meg, waved off her words. It wasn't hard to figure that in another society, this woman would behave very differently; she would be the epitome of propriety, good manners. But here, trying to make a life in a dirt pile in the middle of nowhere, she was an angry pistol of a woman.

No wonder. The place looked hardly fit for animals, let alone a well-bred woman. The blistering southwest wind stirred dust-devils in the hard-packed dirt yard. The front of the hovel was built of grassy dun-colored brick. Under one dusty window was a wash bench with wooden tubs turned up-side-down. There was a barrel to catch rainwater, next to it a wooden bucket and a stone jar. A grubbing tool rested against the wall, harness hung from a peg. None of it was the accouterments of fine living.

Laddie unhitched Butterfield to graze, while the women timorously followed Mrs. Thorne inside the dim, surprisingly cool dugout. A few battered pots and pans hung from pegs over a mud and stone fireplace where a small fire flickered. Next to the fireplace was an Arbuckle coffee box filled with buffalo chips. Their hostess waved them to the table, a large dry-goods box surrounded by an assortment of beat-up boxes and kegs for chairs. Bed ticks were piled in a corner, and stacked on them were neatly folded but thready Indian blankets; shaggy buffalo robes were spread on two cots.

She brought them cups of cool ginger tea, which Grandma Spicy lapped at like a thirsty puppy.

Bustling about, Mrs. Thorne explained, "I haven't been here long, only a little over a month, and if I'd had any other opportunity I wouldn't have come to Harlan at all!"

She slumped into a chair fashioned from old nail kegs, wiping her perspiring brow with her apron. "I'm sorry for my lapse of manners." The resentment in her eyes lessened only slightly. "I can't tell you much about Ross McCoy, because, as I said, he died before I got here. And Harlan and I can't seem to share a civil word, nor do I care."

Harlan, a gangly cowboy in a wide-brimmed hat, sweat-spotted shirt and dust-coated canvas trousers, rode in shortly before suppertime on a tall, rangy roan. He said he'd been out on the range the past several days, checking water holes for his cattle, then going on a wild-horse hunt further west that didn't pan out. His sister-in-law, Aurelia, accused him of being in Dodge's watering holes spending his time gambling and consorting with the indecent women there.

The one-room dwelling had been crowded before, with the women and children gathered to prepare and partake of the evening meal. But with Harlan Thorne and Aurelia together in the same room, the small space had become fairly combustible. A flint and steel couldn't have caused more sparks.

When it appeared their arguing would go on indefinitely, Meg's own dander began to rise. She didn't give a hang if Mr. Thorne had spent his time in Dodge, or was trailing cows to better water holes as he claimed. Mrs. Thorne, she'd begun to suspect, was taking out on his brother her fury against her dead husband for leaving her alone and helpless with four children. But other than feeling sympathy, the woman's predicament was neither here nor there with her. She wanted the matter of the Voss youngsters settled, *now*. She had no wish to listen to Thorne and Aurelia carry on as if they were the only ones in the world with troubles.

"I beg your pardon," she said. "Pardon me!"

Chapter Five

"Ross made out this paper after his bull gored 'im and he knowed he wasn't goin' to live." Harlan Thorne produced the scrap from his saddlebag of personals. He held the dirtied, bloodstained scrap of paper toward Lucy Ann. After a slight hesitation she reached for it.

While she read Harlan talked. "Your Uncle Ross's will gives you and your brother his half of this ranch, half the cattle including that durn bull, his two horses, and" —he looked around him— "one-half of the dugout to live in. Dugout straddles the line between our quarter sections."

The look of disbelief, then relief, on Lucy Ann's face, raised Meg's own spirits. The youngsters would be taken care of, if not by their uncle, by his land. In the corner, Aurelia rocked hard in her chair, from outside they could hear her children's voices as they played tag in the twilight. Laddie sat in the doorway like a little stone, watching the other youngsters. Grandma Spicy, completely worn out from their journey, was spread-eagled on Aurelia's cot in the corner, snoring peacefully, a small, mysterious being no one else could see tucked safely in the crook of her arm.

She had crooned to the unseen infant earlier, rocking it in

her arms with eyes closed. Meg explained to their hosts in an aside that the old woman was harmless. Occasionally her mind slipped away to another time, another place, to a tragedy involving a child. Hadn't they all had troubles that cut deep, left scars?

Watching Grandma Spicy sleep, Meg realized more than ever how much she would miss her and the Voss youngsters if she moved on without them.

"Mr. Thorne, I am interested in taking out a homestead. Would there be a piece of free land available, close by?"

"Plenty of free government land you could file on," he nodded, "but it'd take you five years to prove up. Before you'd get your final certificate, Jack Ambler would argue you plumb off your place, claim the land ain't yours but his. Your hard work would be for nothin'. Better to buy you a piece of land right off, then you own it free and clear by law."

"Who is Jack Ambler?" Meg asked, although her mind was stuck on the word *buy*. She hadn't the money to buy a pound of butter, let alone a piece of land. Was her dream going to slip away, just like that? And with nowhere else to go, and nothing to go with?

"Jack and his riders is about the only other folks out here. Headquarters of his Rocking A Ranch is located about eleven miles northeast, in the Pawnee Valley. Jack took his place right after we all come to western Kansas in 'sixty-five. He started out with about five hundred cows, a few head of horses, a quarter section he homesteaded, and a full section of land he paid for. His cattle business has grown mighty big the eight years he's been here. He runs cows over most of this country, on his own place and miles of government range. He figgers all these parts is his by right of use, and bein' here first. Me and Ross McCoy used to ride for Jack, 'til we decided to build up holdin's of our own."

"Fanciful dreams of lazy men that in a lifetime would never come to anything," Aurelia commented in acidic tones from her corner.

Thorne ignored her. "My heart ain't been in ranchin' since Ross died. He was my best friend. Him and me got wounded side by side in the battle of Wilson Creek, in Missoura." He tapped his upper arm. "My arm near got shot off. Ross was wounded in the thigh. We was bleedin' to death both, tourniqueted one another, and kept one another goin' 'til help come. Never knew another man like him, he was one to ride the river with."

A small, proud smile touched Lucy Ann's lips at the kindly words about her uncle, although she didn't comment. Meg appreciated, for even that brief second, the absence of the girl's usual look of forlorn despair.

Aurelia rose and called her children in to bed. Beds for the women and children were made on every available surface, including the floor. Harlan volunteered to sleep outside. His look at his sister-in-law before he went through the door into the night said he was more than glad to get away from her sharp tongue and condemning glances.

Meg felt herself sinking fast toward sleep soon after she lay on her pallet on the hard dirt floor. Lucy Ann, next to her, whispered, "I would take it as an honor if you'd stay on and live here with Laddie and me, Meg. We want you to."

She patted Lucy Ann's hand, but was simply too tired to answer. Thankful for how things had turned out for the Voss youngsters, she slept like a stone. In the night she dreamed of green valleys and clear streams—*land,* and it was her own. The "Curry Ranch" it was called, and from every direction around her palatial white house, her land went on forever. And on her land no one beat her or forced her to their will.

She had found paradise. She woke after the dream, stared into the inky darkness, intensely aware of the actual puniness of her possessions.

Breakfast next morning was an even bigger ordeal than preparing for bed had been in the crowded dugout the night before. The teething baby cried, the children fought to be first at the flapjacks, there was no room to breathe, no chance for order.

Aurelia's waspish mood continued nonstop as she complained to Harlan how thoughtless men could be, expecting women and children to live in a hole in the ground. "No proper stove to cook on," she complained, using her apron to pick up a cow chip from the fuel box for the fireplace. "No water except what we lug from the spring by the bucketful, and that full of nasty little wiggly things so bad you have to strain them out—"

"Ross and me didn't expect no women to live here, just us," he growled. "We wasn't going to ask no girls to marry us 'til we was better off."

"Pipe dreams," Aurelia hissed, "that never would have happened!" She snatched his dirty plate away to wash so Grandma Spicy could use it next.

"Well, it ain't happenin' now, for shore." Thorne stormed to his feet, his head nearly striking the low, muslin-covered ceiling. Meg caught the empty molasses pitcher his flailing arm knocked off the corner of the table as he passed.

Over his shoulder, he asked Lucy Ann and Meg, "Would you like me to take you around the ranch purty soon? Won't look like much to you," he spoke directly to Lucy Ann, "but your Uncle Ross was proud of it." When they nodded, he said, "I'll be waitin' outside."

"We're about out of fuel," Aurelia snapped, "and it's time that hole in the roof was patched. The other day one of the cows nearly came through on my head and got filth on every-thing."

He turned a hostile glare on her. "That's what I was fixin' to do. I don't need to be told what to do on my own place."

Meg and Lucy Ann insisted on washing dishes and clearing up the kitchen area, then went outside. Meg was as glad to leave Aurelia's sourness as Harlan must have been earlier.

They found him coming back from the open prairie with a gunnysack of buffalo chips slung across his broad shoulders. He dropped them in front of the door and, with a wide grin, motioned Meg and Lucy Ann to follow him. "Watch out for rattlesnakes," he cautioned, "we got a few in these parts. A man, or a woman," he grinned at them, "is better off on horseback. But we'll walk an' just be careful."

Harlan's half of the 320-acre spread lay north of Ross McCoy's. Most of his northeast forty acres rose in thick lime-stone ridges covered with a smattering of scrubby grass dotted here and there with scrawny cattle, and buffalo bones bleaching in the sun. Meg wiped perspiration from her face as they traipsed over the area, keeping a sharp eye out for rattle-snakes.

"Ain't good for nothin'," he told them of the area strewn with white and gray rock that reminded her of dirty clumps of snow. "But by settlin' for the rocks on my piece, I also got the spring." They turned back south, and he showed them the small trickle coming from a sandy ledge northeast of the dugout. He had started to enlarge the pool made by the spring and line it with rock. "I got called away," he explained lamely of the unfinished job.

Lucy Ann knelt by the spring, cupped her hand in the water, and drank. Meg followed suit. "Sweet, good," she said.

Some of the water could be channeled to a garden if a body wanted to make one by the dugout, she thought, swiping her windblown hair from her eyes. So far, not an inch of the virgin soil had seen a plow. They walked on, circling southward, past the dugout. The spring might supply enough water for household use, but what about the cows? she wondered. She asked Harlan.

"We got the sinks, too," he said. "That's mostly where the cattle and horses go to drink." Ten minutes later, they stood looking at two ponds, each taking up a little more than a quarter acre on the western edge of the claims. The water was shallow, muddy brown, and rimmed with cow and horse tracks and dung. "Thought they was buffalo wallows at first, but since they never go clear dry even when it don't rain, we figured there's a couple underground springs here, too."

There were more bleached bones near the drying edges of the sinks. A huge rack of elk antlers lay a few feet north of the furthest pool. Dragonflies hovered close to the water.

Harlan looked sadly at the cow bones. "Me an' McCoy both lost cattle to blizzards last winter. Cattle can forage fine in these parts most of the winter, but it don't hurt none to put a little hay by for insurance."

On the way back he pointed with pride to three aromatic stacks of cut hay he'd finished making a month before. "Except for the rocks, most of my place and all of McCoy's is fair grazin' land. We ranched together, but we each got our own brand." He pointed out his T Cross on the hip of a couple of cows, McCoy's Pocket 7 on some others. They walked wide around the grazing bull, a huge mottled-tan creature. "We started out with thirty head each," he explained, "but after the killin' winter we got maybe fifty left, total. Couldn't afford to lose none, is the truth of it."

Aurelia wasn't far from wrong in her opinion of the place,

Meg decided. Overall the ranch was scrubby, made up of rocky ridges and grass-filled draws. It was small, and frighteningly far from civilization. Improvements except for the dugout and a halfhearted try at the spring were nonexistent. Lucy Ann and Laddie might eke out an existence by raising a garden and keeping cows. It was more likely the two of them would starve to death.

They headed back in the direction of the dugout. Harlan pointed out a small pinto with a Pocket 7 brand, a little later a long-legged sorrel. "Them ponies was Ross's," he told Lucy Ann, "now they're yours." She smiled, nodded, turning back for another look when the horses nickered and began to follow.

Harlan said from the corner of his mouth, his eye on Aurelia trudging from the spring with a bucket of water pulling her to one side and spilling onto her shoes, "I don't aim to stay on here any longer." He gnawed a long piece of grass between strong teeth. "What I mean to say, Miss Brennon, is my half of this place is for sale, for travelin' money. One hundred sixty acres, and twenty-six T Cross cows is yours if you got a fancy to buy."

So that's why he had invited her on the walk. "Mr. Thorne, I might have considered it, but I don't have the money to buy you out." Just thinking about it, though, made the ranch a tad less sorry than it had seemed moments before.

Grievously sorry for herself for wanting to stay, as for him, desperate to leave, she said with finality, "There's no way I can buy your half of the ranch, I'm sorry."

The truth was, her future was even bleaker than anything she saw around her, she had no idea what she was going to do. Perhaps she could make her way back to Dodge and find a job there. It hardly seemed a fit place for a decent woman, though.

"You got anything you might trade for my half the land and the cows?" Harlan asked. " 'Cause I'm leavin' one way or the other."

"Trade?" In that case—Meg's breath caught, then released softly as she considered it. "I don't know what value you put on your land and the cattle. My own possessions are few."

"Name me what you got—"

They walked slowly toward the dugout.

"I have a fiddle of my father's. It's a fine Paganini violin, worth around" —she had to guess the worth, not being sure— "ten or twelve dollars. Maybe more. I've never considered parting with it before, but maybe—"

"That all?"

They reached the dugout. Parked in front was her little green, flat-topped wagon. Butterfield was staked nearby. If she stayed here, she would need both to help with the farm and for transportation to town. She couldn't part with either. The only other things she had little need for, besides Papa's Paganini, were her millinery goods: cases of ribbons, feathers, fake flowers, and beads. At least half or two-thirds of them could go and they would amount to something, in trade. To the right customers, they could bring in as much as fifty dollars.

"Mr. Thorne, I think I have an idea!"

She led him to her wagon, where she opened three cases of colorful gewgaws for him to see. To his dumbfounded expression, she exclaimed, "There are a considerable number of—fancy women in Dodge City, aren't there?" Her face warmed, but she rushed on, "I'm sure you could sell these goods to them, and to women in other towns, for three times the cost." The thought had crossed her mind to try to make sales to these women in Dodge herself, when she was there.

She had no doubt the women would buy her goods; she just hadn't had the nerve to approach them. If Harlan Thorne was as familiar with the women as his sister-in-law claimed, he'd have no trouble at all.

With a bit of reluctance, she handed him her father's fiddle to examine. Memories of Papa and Mama rushed her mind as she waited.

Papa, given the name "Red Pat" by his friends for his fiery red hair, had enormous hopes for their life in America when he crossed the sea with his new wife, Maria. His ambitions stretched far beyond the poor St. Louis neighborhood, Kerry Patch, where he learned the stonemason trade and where Meg was born. His dream was to own land away from the city. In the country he would have sheep and he would build his sweet Maria a bigger stone mansion than the one where she had grown up in privilege in County Leitrim. Mama, desperately in love with rowdy Red Pat, didn't mind how they lived; she wanted the mansion only because Papa did. Both of them would agree, though, with what Meg, as rootless as a dandelion puff, was about to do.

"Are you sure, Miss Brennon?" Harlan asked. " 'Cause if you are, I think we got a deal."

Her mind went back over all he'd shown her the past hour. There was only one truly redeeming feature she could think of: it was, after all, *land,* something God had long since stopped making more of, and it could be *hers.* One hundred sixty acres of near-worthless land, twenty-six head of scrawny cattle, but still—*hers.*

She hesitated. "What about Aurelia? She's your family. Shouldn't you let her have the property?"

He scoffed. "She don't want it! I offered it several times. What she told me I could do with my claim ain't fit for a lady's ears an' not fit for a lady to say, neither!"

She bit back a smile. Aurelia might not want it, but she did. She reached to shake his hand. "Mr. Thorne, if you're sure, we have a deal."

Lucy Ann moved away from them, a quiet smile on her face.

"One thing, Miss Brennon," Harlan Thorne said, ducking his head guiltily, scuffing the ground with his boot toe. "My sister-in-law stays on here as part of the deal 'til she figgers whatever else she wants to do, without me. I'm sellin' cheap on that fact alone."

Meg stared at him. The property was hers, but she had to look after his pepper-minded sister-in-law and her four children? *Good Lord, no!*

Aurelia had come up from nowhere, and demanded, "What deal? What deal are you making me part of, you scalawag, Harlan Thorne?" She stood with her hands on her hips, fire in her eyes, and more than a little worry there, too.

Red-faced but determined, he explained his plans sketchily to Aurelia as he got a parcel of papers from his saddlebag and nodded for Meg to sit beside him on the wash bench in the shade from the dugout. He held tight to the papers against the wind and told Meg, "Picked up my final certificate just four months ago, at the land agent's in Larned. There's the proof that after five up-and-down, durn-hard years I hold clear title to the quarter section described." His finger tapped the land patent. "We can figure out the wordin' of a bill of sale together, an' both sign it in front of these witnesses. Soon as you can, you'll want to go to Larned an' make sure the change of hands on the property is recorded legal."

"I am not staying here!" Aurelia shouted at him, marching back and forth and stirring up a fierce dust in the yard. A few minutes later, Harlan passed the papers to Meg and she scrawled her signature under his. He stood up, stretching, a smile of contentment on his face. Aurelia, shaking her finger, circled Harlan like a hen after a worm. "You have to take me and my children out of here, at least as far as the nearest civilized town, at which time I'll be as glad to be shed of you as you will be of me. But I won't stay on this godforsaken ranch, I won't. As John's brother, you are responsible for me."

"I'm doing what's best for you, Aurelia. You and me spend much more time together, we'd kill one another. You'll be awright here. There's no way I could take you and the children with me. I just sold Miss Brennon everything but my horse, my saddle, bedroll, and personals. That's all I got now, except a fiddle and some feathery truck, an' my packhorse. I got no way to look out for you, so stop your cryin'."

As happy as she was for herself, Meg felt sorry for Aurelia who continued to rant and rave while Harlan prepared to leave. In Aurelia's shoes she would likely act up plenty, too, she decided. But Aurelia's behavior only seemed to worsen the matter, making Harlan more eager to be gone as he stuffed his saddlebags with his personal items and loaded his small sorrel packhorse. As he rode away a short time later on the tall roan, leading the other animal, Aurelia covered her face with her apron and ran weeping into the open prairie in the opposite direction.

With a sigh, Meg started after Aurelia, then decided she might prefer to cry alone than with a near-stranger.

Where had all these obligations come from? Meg wondered, as she turned back. She now shared a ranch with Lucy Ann and Laddie, that was good. But Aurelia and her children would be here, too, and of course, Grandma Spicy, for the rest of her days. So many to take care of, who couldn't take care of themselves. How were they to be provided for? Where would food, decent shelter, fuel—medicine if needed—come from?

For now she wouldn't dwell on the obstacles to this new switch in her life. She wanted this land she stood on more than anything. Already, seconds after becoming hers, a love for it was growing inside her—affection for every ugly rock and sun-burnt grass blade of it. She would work her fingers to the bone to make this place provide.

She had *land!*

All four of Aurelia's children, deciding suddenly that their mother had abandoned them, began to cry. Meg was brought back to reality. "There now, children," she said, "your mother will come back, she just wants to be alone for awhile." She took a sobbing Helen Grace's tiny hand in hers; Lucy Ann had picked up the squalling Zibby from her basket. Joshua and David John looked embarrassed for their tears as Meg gave each of them a pat.

Over the top of the baby girl's fuzzy head, Lucy Ann's wisp of a smile at Meg vanished as she thought of something. She looked around, her light blue eyes wide and worried. "Where's Laddie? Where is my brother?"

He was not with Grandma Spicy. She had cleared the tubs from the bench in front of the hovel and sat there with her head bobbing in sleep.

Chapter Six

It was impossible to calculate how long Laddie had been gone. None of them could remember when they had last seen him.

Meg worried he had shadowed her and Lucy Ann wordlessly around the ranch and they hadn't noticed. He might be in one of the distant rocky draws, unable to find his way back. Aurelia on her walk might see him, or not. He could wander miles in the wrong direction. Unless he found his voice, he would be unable to call to them.

Standing with Aurelia's youngest still in her arms, Lucy Ann's eyes were glossed with fear. Meg caught her arm. "We'll find him, Lucy Ann. He can't be far."

Her young friend swiftly returned Zibby to her basket and gave her a frayed sock dolly to play with. She put the baby's older siblings in charge. She shouted for her brother in a thin, frightened voice. "Laddie!" She flurried toward the open prairie, stopping every few steps to cup her hands around her mouth. "Lad! Leonard Voss," she used his real name for the first time, "you come to me, right now!"

Grandma woke up and declared that the saving grace was, although Lad didn't speak, he could hear fine. All of them began to shout, until they raised such a bedlam cattle grazing nearby began to bellow, raise their tails, and run.

Riding bareback on Butterfield, Meg set out to cover the ranch, beginning at the spring and riding up to the area of limestone rocks. There was no sign of him in the crevices, or in the draws where the wind murmured in the grasses. She thought of the sinks, and her heart squeezed in her chest. A boy and water just naturally went together; sometimes dangerously so. If he had accidentally fallen in one of those saucered pools, got stuck in the mud, or went under, she prayed to God to be in time.

She found him at the second and deeper pool. He sat in the goo at the edge, not far from the old sun-bleached elk-horn rack, splashing water on himself; a breeze tossed his pale skimpy hair. Rather than shout and maybe frighten him, Meg whistled the "sweet-sweet-sweetie-o-sweet" of a yellow warbler. He turned and looked at her seated on Butterfield several yards away.

"We have to go back, Laddie, your sister is worried about you." She smiled, rode forward slowly, nonthreatening. She slipped off Butterfield, then went to sit at the water's edge several paces away from the boy. She hoped she hadn't imagined that over time he had become less frightened of her and seemed to show a trifle of trust.

"This is a nice place, isn't it?" Around them, vast towers of lonely clouds filled the never-ending sky. Over the water a quartet of white butterflies danced the minuet. She trailed her hand in the water slowly.

A dark, crowned bird she didn't recognize but thought was a variety of flycatcher came to rest on a lavender-topped thistle shrub nearby. She tried a call and the bird repeated its own, "Che—beer," the second note slurring downward. Meg wiped perspiration from her eyes, tried the bird's call until the bird trilled with her in unison, "Che-beeer." Laddie got up and came to stand at her shoulder, watching the bird, watching Meg's lips form the music that clearly thrilled him.

They rode home, Laddie in front of Meg on Butterfield and carrying the huge old elk-horn rack. A shout went up when they were spotted. Lucy Ann, Grandma Spicy, and the other children halted in their tracks at the apparition they made, then hurried to meet them.

With a glad cry, Lucy Ann whipped the horns out of Laddie's hands. She caught her brother as he slipped off the horse, holding him tightly.

"Please don't ever do that again, Laddie. Don't ever go away without my knowing. I was so worried." She looked up at Meg. "Thank you."

"All's well that ends well." Meg grinned and slid down from Butterfield's back.

Aurelia had also returned. She came from the dugout, her eyes still red and swollen from crying. She stared at the rack of horns. "What in the name of heaven did you bring that here for?"

Meg shaded her eyes the better to watch Aurelia's face. "Laddie and I decided the rack is quite admirable and useful. Without a proper clothesline to hang our wash on, the elk horns will do. Pretend," she said, leaning toward Aurelia, "it's a tree of many branches. The first," she beamed, "improvement around here."

Distaste curled Aurelia's otherwise pretty mouth. "Why would anyone want to buy misery by the acre, anyway? You're a fool, Miss Brennon, for staying on here a moment longer than necessary. You'd have been wiser not to come in the first place! Seeing how it is here, you could have taken your merchandise and gone back to Dodge, or back east." The longing to do just that was etched deeply in Aurelia's face, a fresh shine of tears coming to her eyes. Clearly she suffered humiliation, too, of being traded off as part of that "misery by the acre."

You're a fool, Mrs. Thorne, for seeing nothing but bad in every blessed thing, and not appreciating what you have, Meg couldn't help thinking, as much as she felt sorry for her.

She turned to Aurelia. "I have no wish to go back east, and I intend to make the best of my chances here." Grandma Spicy and the Voss youngsters had no more to return to than she did. This bit of desolate, hard-baked western Kansas land was, for all its shortcomings, their only means to stay alive. "If you want to leave, I'll take you to Dodge as soon as I can, Mrs. Thorne. In the meantime, there's much to be done."

She didn't wait for Aurelia to answer, but went to take stock of the food supplies on hand and try to analyze future possibilities. That's what she'd been about to do before Lucy Ann noticed Laddie's disappearance. Nine mouths to feed was a tremendous number when provisions were scant.

Harlan Thorne and Ross McCoy's root cellar was a hole in the ground a third of the size of the dugout, and a few paces north of it, on the way to the spring. She shoved aside the cowhide door and crept in, doubled over, under the low ceiling. In the gloom she kept a sharp eye out for snakes and scorpions, careful where she stepped, where she put a hand. Crouching, she examined the few bags and kegs. Grim reality revealed a half-sack of cornmeal, a little salt, a gallon jug of molasses, a can of lard, a nearly empty sack containing beans. There was a pitiful pile of dried corn, a pile of mostly shriveled potatoes, two pumpkins and a squash that were good. Some kind of melon looked like it had rotted a year or two before, leaving dried rind and a spill of seed. Heaven only knew where the cowboys bought the vegetables, they sure hadn't raised them.

Even parceled carefully, their food would last only a short

time, perhaps a month if somehow supplemented with other victuals. Additional foodstuffs had to be acquired somehow.

Maybe they could try raising a garden, impossibly late in the season though it was. She crawled carefully back out and stood up dizzily in the blazing sun. She wanted to keep the cattle, not eat them, raise calves and sell off the increase from time to time for cash. Thorne, before leaving, had given her a rushed lesson on the cattle business: bull calves born in the spring could be turned into steers—Grandma Spicy interjected that she knew how that was done, he needn't spell out what was unfit for ladies' ears—and the steers sold. Her best heifer calves would become cows and increase her herd.

They could trap wild game for meat. Rabbits were everywhere; there were prairie chickens, too. According to Harlan, their land lay between the middle and southern branches of the Pawnee River. They could fish. A search might turn up berries in the thickets along the rivers. Any kind of fruit would do, but they had to have it, to ward off scurvy.

She took her late-garden idea to Grandma Spicy, who was sprinkling water on the dugout floor to settle the dust and keep it hardened. In her long rambling talks, the old woman had seemed to know a lot about farming and other helpful matters.

"Sure, we got to try!" she agreed with Meg, pulling her faded old sunbonnet off the hook, yanking it down over her thinning gray hair, and tying it under her scrawny chin. "We had calamities back home in Missoura that made late plantin' the only plantin' done atall. There's tricks to it. You leave the gardenin' to me!"

On the way back to the root cellar Grandma Spicy chattered. They would work a small patch of soil extra-fine to cater to the seed, and other things they must do.

Together, in the musty gloom of the cellar, they separated

seed supply from what they must have for food. A few shelled ears of dried corn, with care, would make quite a few plants, each plant could give a couple ears, if it grew. Shriveled potatoes could be cut into chunks, an eye or two to each chunk, then planted. Each hill of seed potatoes, which they would water and care for "like babies," Grandma said, would produce several times the potatoes planted, with luck.

Coming on late and needing a ninety-day growing season, the garden would be subject to early frosts but Grandma had plans for that, too. "We'll cover the plants at night when the sun ain't out and the frost is worse, tuck 'em in like under blankets." With dried grasses pulled from the prairie, with any other covering material they could find.

"Like these!" she chortled a while later, dragging forth a stack of moldy burlap bags from the back of the dugout.

"What do you suppose they held?" Meg asked, as they carried their trove out into the sunlight for examination.

"Flour, maybe. Grain for the cowboys' horses. Lemme see—"

Together with Grandma Spicy, Meg noted the flour sacks that would be useful in many ways. The burlap bags had held oats and, chirruping with glee, Grandma dug tiny oat seeds out of the bags' seams. She gathered the golden whispers of seed into the palm of her hand. "Be a miracle if oats grew in these parts, this late in the year," she said to herself, shaking her head.

"I'll get something to put them in." Meg leaped to her feet and took the seed.

"They be gold, daughter, don't go lettin' them blow away in this confounded wind."

Meg wasn't officially put in charge around the homestead, but from the first day, everyone turned to her for leadership as if she had been.

Chores were assigned for everyone. The garden would be Grandma Spicy's responsibility, after Meg broke the ground. The children and the rest would help Grandma as needed. The cooking, baking, redding up of the dugout, and laundry chores, would be divided between Aurelia and Lucy Ann.

After working the garden plot, Meg would take up Harlan's unfinished job enlarging the spring. The pool was eight or ten feet across and she wanted it bigger. She would dam the small stream, line the reservoir with stone, find ways to channel water closer to the dugout. She wanted to build her own sod house on her own property, but until that could be done they had to put up with overly crowded conditions in the dugout.

"Laddie and Aurelia's boys can learn to trap rabbits and other game for food. Grandma Spicy knows how to make both figure-four traps, and box traps with swinging trap doors. She will teach you. Whoops," she said, seeing a flurry of signing motion from Laddie. "It appears that Lad knows how to trap, so he can show Joshua and David John." The Thorne boys looked at Laddie in admiration, mixed with a little resentment that he was ahead of them in that knowledge.

Meg went on, "We'll all take turns guarding the stock from predators: coyotes, rattlesnakes, rustlers. The children will go out on the prairie every morning to gather cow chips for fuel—"

"No!" Aurelia protested. "I didn't bring my children here to turn them into drudges, to pick up—*filth*. For heaven's sake, they are only children. It would be dangerous for them to wander the prairie where there's rattlesnakes, wild cattle, and who knows what else. These young ones could get hurt or killed."

"Aurelia, who picked up the cow chips stacked outside,

the fuel you've been using?" Meg asked.

"Harlan, most of the time. I had to, when he wasn't here."

"Well, Harlan isn't here now. The work is up to us, to share equally as best we can." She sighed. "I don't like putting the children in danger any more than you do." She remembered Laddie wandering away to the sink, how scared she'd been she would find him drowned or not find him again, ever.

She spoke with reserved caution. "We're going to look out for one another, as best we can. But there will be hard work for all, every day, from now on. For without it, there is no life for any of us. It's best we remember that."

Chapter Seven

The tough prairie sod seemed to fight Meg, unwilling to be broken, to be altered in any way. She hacked with her grubbing hoe at the shallow, but thickly tangled roots of buffalo grass, meeting with force the dry, iron-hard ground. It took forever to turn a single square foot of earth.

Hour after hour she worked; blisters formed and popped, stinging, on her palms. Perspiration dripped from her brow. Her bad hip was a constant knife of pain. She cursed Teddy Malloy for that, and kept hacking, pulverizing, raking. Since she had given herself the job, she would be to blame if she failed and they all starved.

While she worked, and ached, and silently swore, she dreamed of proper tools such as Grandma Spicy had described: a sod plow, cultivator, seeder, cradle scythe, hay wagon. Where were those implements to come from and how were they to manage in the meantime without them?

It took three difficult days to till a plot the size of the dugout floor. Grandma Spicy planted it to potatoes, two potato chunks to a hill. Ahead of her, Meg hacked, chopped, gouged, pulled sod free, to make way for more seed. The additional area, when finally ready, was planted to melons and pumpkins. Back and forth she and Grandma Spicy toiled, hauling water from the spring to mud in the seed.

The next digging was planted to oats, which Grandma Spicy now said didn't have a prayer of a chance to come up and grow. Meg silently cursed the time she'd spent working the ground for the oats, if they weren't even going to sprout. Reading her mind, Grandma Spicy said, "But let the bed be, daughter, an' we'll just see."

Sore in every muscle and bone, so tired she could scarcely stand after days of digging, Meg suggested they plant sod corn and Grandma Spicy agreed. The usual cultivation was skipped. Meg took the axe and made holes in the grassy sod. In each hole, Grandma Spicy carefully tucked in two or three kernels of corn and added a prayer.

Every now and then while she worked, Meg looked to see where the children were. Aurelia's boys enjoyed being turned loose from their mother's apron strings. Guarding the stock was a lark to them. They often got sidetracked, though, climbing off their horses to stir up an anthill, to then run shrieking from the stinging red ants and fly away on horseback. They could spend an unbelievable amount of time and giggle themselves almost sick, decorating a fresh cow pie with purple gentian blossoms. They checked the rabbit traps so often no rabbit came near.

Meg hoped Lad's clear consternation over the nuisance caused by the other boys would induce him to speak, to yell, fuss, and argue like boys usually did. But in that regard there was no change in him, he remained mute.

She admired Laddie for taking his work seriously, using a stick to goad the cattle or Butterfield and the other horses back toward home when they started to stray too far afield. It was obvious the wide, empty prairie was frightening to him, that somewhere in the back of his worried mind Indians lurked. Any suspicious indentations in the dust had to be inspected to make sure they were not moccasin and pony tracks. Yet he held to his post, showing great relief to hurry home each night.

"Don't worry, Laddie," she told him one evening. "Remember how that sheriff said the Cheyenne, Pawnee, and the other tribes are mostly now on reservations south of here in the Indian Nations? There's none close about."

It had been four or five years since Kansas's last Indian raids—a series of murders of railroad workers, rapes and killings of women alone on their homesteads, travelers caught on the road far from town and help. Of course, an uprising from reservation Indians was a constant possibility. Also, there was no way of being certain the army had rounded up the renegades; some could be hid out. A little caution didn't hurt, but she just hated to see the boy in constant turmoil.

Laddie's expression had seemed to stick on the word *reservation,* and she tried to explain her interpretation. "The reservation is not a pen, or corral, but more like a huge camping area where the Indians get to have their tepee homes, or build a cabin, raise a garden, have a cow, go hunting for food." It was probably impossible for the boy to think of the Indians as human, but she continued, "Many Indian children go to the white man's school and learn our ways. They in turn will teach those ways to their children. Eventually, the Indians will become more like us, settled down and civilized."

The end of freedom for the Indians seemed a terrible thing. They had been there on the plains first, and it was hard not to feel sorry for their loss of the land and the buffalo— mainstay of their way of life. But she had no sympathy for their savagery. The white man and woman needed room to spread out, too, in order to have farms, make new lives. The time of change had come and the raiding and killing had to stop.

"I won't let anything happen to you, Laddie. That's why we're all here together, to look out for one another."

She thought she eased his concern a trifle, but mere words would never completely erase what happened to him and to his family that day in Nebraska.

Lucy Ann shared her brother's fears, but showed it in less obvious ways. Most days, she made a special effort to finish her work at the house and hurry out to be with Laddie. She used the excuse that the young boys would be thirsty or hungry. She would take a jug of water to them, and sometimes cold flapjacks spread with molasses and rolled up. Lucy Ann would stay with the boys on the prairie until she had to be back to help in the kitchen. Oftentimes, in a sort of worried trance, she would go to the door and scan the far-reaching distances. Seeing nothing of concern, she would return, expression relaxed, to the task at hand. She liked things clean and would scrub diligently.

Gradually, Aurelia seemed to accept the fact that her boys must work the same as everyone else, that only her two small daughters were exempt. Even then three-year-old Helen Grace, a fairy-pretty child, was sometimes pressed into service helping Grandma pull new young weeds from the garden, or helping to care for Baby Zibby.

As unhappy as Aurelia was being there, she did her part. The meals she made from the little they had were becoming legendary in the small group.

After a hard day's digging at the spring one day, Meg headed for the dugout, half-starved. Never plump like Lucy Ann, she was thinner than ever from hard work. She stopped to wash the mud and dirt off her feet, hands and arms, at the bench outside. She sniffed the air, relishing the fragrance of Aurelia's excellent potato and corn chowder seasoned with wild onion, simmering on the fire inside. The chowder would be served with cornbread and molasses. The delicious smell and thoughts of the meal ahead, made her stomach rumble. The hard work she did now increased her appetite threefold, but she held back on portions, concerned that everyone get enough to eat.

A few days later, the children succeeded in snaring their first rabbit, one of the whoppers native to that country. For two days, they ate heavenly rabbit stew. After the initial success, the boys became more adept at trapping five- to seven-pound rabbits, and fat prairie chickens became routine. Healthy meat became a regular feature at mealtime.

There were nights when a dozen or more chickens were caught. Aurelia cooked the smaller pieces. The breasts were dried and suspended on strings in the dugout for use come winter; rabbit meat was also dried in abundance.

They were so alone in the process of daily living, there were days when Meg could believe their little clan were the only humans alive in the world. Since Harlan had ridden away, they had seen no living soul but one another.

Sometimes a few head of cattle branded with the Rocking A wandered in to drift with their own herd, to be chased off by the boys. One day the youngsters found what they were sure was an old Indian trail, some three miles west from the homestead. Looking it over, Meg guessed it was used by wayfarers headed north to Nebraska, or south to Dodge, and she thought that sooner or later they might have visitors.

So it was no surprise when one day twin dust patterns spiraled off the trail toward the homestead. She breathed a sigh of relief when the riders got close enough she could see that both men were taller and leaner than Finch. Until that moment she'd been so busy she'd almost forgotten he was after her.

The riders looked to be ordinary men, their approach nonthreatening, although there was no way to be sure about strangers. If they were as they appeared, she was glad to see them. Maybe they could answer some of her questions about that part of the country.

"Hello!" she called out, shading her eyes. The older rider in brown took off his hat, allowing the wind to riffle his dark hair. There was a strip of white skin between the bronze of his weather-beaten face and his hairline.

"Howdy," he grinned, pounding the dust from his hat against his thigh. His tall black horse danced sideways.

The other man, on a big chestnut, had longish blonde hair and a sweeping moustache. He wore a well-cut, but wrinkled and dusty, suit. He touched his gray hat brim. "Miss." His glance veered away with a shy, polite grin.

"How can I help you gentlemen?"

They were passing through, would like to water their horses, and could use a good meal.

Their horses, fine horseflesh if Meg was any judge, were eager to be at her new trough. The convenience she had carved from soft limestone was now hardened and held fresh water from the spring. She motioned the riders to go ahead and water their animals. "Noon dinner is about ready and you're welcome to join us. You might want to clean up here at the spring, first." She nodded to where she now kept soap and a towel on a large white limestone slab nearby.

After washing her own hands and splashing her sunburned face, Meg went ahead of them to the dugout, while they unsaddled and watered their horses. She worried that Aurelia would make a fuss about the extra work, the additional food it would take to feed the two strangers. But Aurelia's face actually brightened at the mention of guests. She flew into action, made no complaint, saying it would be no trouble at all to add to the pot. They could also make portions small for everyone but the guests.

The table was spread with white cloth, under other circumstances one of Aurelia's fine cambric petticoats. The lace of it fell daintily just above the dirt floor. "The very gossamer of heaven," Meg called such lace in her former trade. The plain crockery dishes took on a special luster from the fat candle that centered the table, lit just before the men stooped to enter the dugout, hats in hand, grinning self-consciously.

The first course was a thin, wild onion soup, followed by fricasseed prairie chicken, molasses baked beans, and cornbread. The wayfarers claimed it the best meal they had eaten all year, and handed a glowing Aurelia two silver dollars after they had saddled their horses.

"Here," Aurelia said, handing the money for Meg to take. They stood in the dooryard together, the ever-present wind blowing their skirts as they watched the men ride off.

Considering how much Aurelia wanted to leave and needed money to do so, Meg said, "The money is yours, Aurelia, for cooking that scrumptious meal. It is a wonderful knack you have with the simplest ingredients. I wish I could cook half as well."

Aurelia's face reflected gratitude for the compliment, but she insisted, "The money belongs to all of us. You keep it, Meg, until we can spend it." Over her shoulder as she headed back into the dugout she tossed, "We're about out of flour and lard. If we had more, and some dried apples or peaches, I could make the children a pie." *Or pie for guests, if any ever come again,* her forlorn expression said, as she turned in the doorway to watch the riders disappear into the horizon.

Meg put the money in her pocket. They could use the cash a thousand ways. In the meantime, they would continue to explore ways to survive on the land.

In the next weeks, they took to making sojourns every few days farther from home into the surrounding sun-browned prairie. As many as could piled into the green wagonette behind old Butterfield, the others riding the two McCoy horses. They found the rivers Harlan had mentioned. The narrow streams were edged in thicket and alive with fish. Meg thought it was possible no one fished the streams before in all of time and the fish had nought to do but multiply. In great excitement, Grandma Spicy unraveled an old shawl to provide fish line, pins were shaped into hooks, and a small pebble tied on each line above the hook provided a sinker.

Three times the little band returned to the dugout with a catch of yellow-brown catfish almost as big as little Zibby; with baskets of hackberries and plums that, past their season, had dried out on the limb, but were revived and freshened by soaking them in water. Some of the fish was fried and eaten right away; a great lot of it was dried for winter. Berries were dried and stored, some sauced into jam.

Aurelia, who at first hadn't wanted to participate in the outings, would spread a blanket on the ground for herself, little Helen Grace, and Baby Zibby. After the fruit picking, the fishing, the wild splashing as they waded and cleaned up, a picnic lunch was spread on the blanket and quickly devoured.

Meg felt doubly thankful—all of them could enjoy a change of scene from their hard work, and their store of foodstuffs was growing. Still, if there was a way to earn cash money, she had to find it. The worry of providing for so many constantly gnawed at her.

Above all, to make the ranch run properly and provide a living, they needed the right tools. She would like to buy a milk cow, so they might have milk, butter, cheese; some hens to provide them with eggs; and a pig, perhaps. And heaven knew, they must buy seed by next spring! Then they could plant fields of wheat and corn.

If only she had the means to fit her dreams.

Although Aurelia had argued against it, Meg decided they would start picking bones from the buffalo carcasses that had been left to rot on the prairie by hiders who had—and still were, by the stacks of hides in Dodge—decimating what were once huge herds.

One bright morning, she and Lucy Ann, along with the boys, headed west into the bone-studded, drying grasslands. Grandma and Aurelia stayed home to look after the little ones and to do the work there.

Meg considered the buffalo-killing trade an insidious activity, due to wanton slaughter and so much waste. Professional hide hunters killed buffalo by the hundreds with their heavy Sharps rifles, skinned the animals and left the meat to rot, except for the tongues and humps which they took.

According to the men who had taken lunch and watered their horses that day at the homestead, over a million hides were shipped east in the last year for making leather. She thought the men who ate the meal with them might be buyers, middle men of some sort in the buffalo trade, although they didn't say so.

Even before she talked about it with her guests, Meg had heard that, though much of the meat was wasted, the bones left behind could be harvested, sent east to be made into cutlery handles, harness ornaments, fertilizer and carbon. Aurelia must understand they had to make money however they could.

Grasshoppers clattered in the grass away from their footsteps. The sun beat down on their heads and backs but no one complained as Meg, Lucy Ann, and the boys, Laddie, Joshua, and David John, picked up bones with zeal. The bones went *thump-bump* into her wagon as they inched across the open plains. A hawk circled and kept watch from the hot, endless sky. When the wagon was full, bags Meg had hung from the sides of the wagon were then filled. The next filled were bags that would be tied to the saddles of those who had ridden horseback. After long hunting and picking, they returned to unload beside the dugout. The pile of bleached bones grew.

Day after day, along with other chores, some few of them went out to gather bones from the windy plains, by wagon and horseback.

As they went farther and farther from home on the bone-picking expeditions, Meg could see they would soon run out of bones to find in a day's travel. Spending the night on the plains didn't seem wise, but they would pick their own wide area clean. And then she would take their gather to Dodge to sell.

One day, she and Lucy Ann, Laddie and Joshua, attention on their work, were startled in their bone picking by a rider who seemed to come up on them soundlessly and out of no-where.

The cowboy's face was as black as his hat, a sharp contrast to his pale leather garb and faded brown shirt. He rode a stocky bay. He tipped his hat to them, his grin white-toothed and friendly. "Howdy! What you all doin' way out here?"

"Picking up bones," Meg answered, although she thought that was plain enough to see.

He laughed, wide nostrils flaring, the dimple in his cheek deepening. "I knowed that's what you was doin'. I'm askin' where the hell—I mean, where'd you come from? I thought I was seein' a mirage, women and children with that little old green wagon out here in the middle of nowhere." He laughed again. "Now that's just somethin' I don't 'spects to see."

Meg explained where they lived.

"Haw! You don't mean the place Thorne and McCoy took? Naw. You ain't there. McCoy, he died after bein' gored by a bull. Thorne rode out of here last month, headed toward Montana. Cain't be nobody on that there place. Jack Ambler says he got it back."

"I don't know Jack Ambler or what he's saying," Meg told him, a ribbon of fear cutting through her. "But what used to be the Thorne and McCoy homestead is now ours and we live there." She explained that Lucy Ann's uncle had left Lucy Ann and Laddie half the homestead, and she had bought the other 160 acres from Harlan Thorne. She and her women friends and the children were managing the property; they ran cattle and intended to farm. No, she answered his question, none of the women had husbands, there were no men there.

The cowboy's look of incredulity grew to unbelievable proportions as she talked. By the time she finished, he was slapping his thigh, his head thrown back, and laughing so hard he nearly fell out of the saddle. His horse shifted, churning dust.

Meg was beginning to feel irritated. Lucy Ann sat in the shade of the wagon to rest; she wearied easily these days, to the point Meg worried the girl was sick and failing. The boys had climbed up and now sat on top of the load of white bones, watching and listening.

"This be one good joke on Jack Ambler!" the cowboy said, wiping his eyes on the dirty bandanna tied around his neck. "Only I don't think Jack is a-goin' to laugh much!"

"What do you mean? Explain yourself, please!" Harlan had mentioned Ambler, the cattleman who would make it hard on anyone who tried to settle on land he now made use of for free.

In a roundabout story, chuckling most of the time, the black cowboy explained to Meg that Harlan Thorne and Jack Ambler hadn't gotten along since Thorne and McCoy, both former Ambler hands, filed on their own adjoining spreads. "I don't think Harlan was cut out to be no rancher himself, though. He's a cowboy an' a drifter whether he can hep it or not. But he claimed he didn't like the way Jack controls this country. Didn't seem right to him he could use it all and nobody else could have even a patch of it. He stuck on that little ol' place as long as he did, after Ross McCoy died, just to spite my boss. Haw. He's really got the laugh on Jack now, sellin' out to women and children."

"I don't believe I see the joke!" Meg stood stiffly.

"I'm sorry, miss." He sobered then. "Truth to tell, it ain't goin' to be funny when Jack finds out you're livin' on Thorne and McCoy's place. He knew McCoy died and figgered when Thorne left that was it—he'd won—all this country around here was his alone to graze and water cattle on."

"Well, I'm afraid that's not true. Lucy Ann," she pointed at the girl drooping wearily in the shade, "her brother, and I, own 320 acres and we run our own cattle on it. We need the water from our spring and our sinks for our own cows and for us. Tell that to this Ambler gentleman you speak of, and make sure he knows we're serious about staying. We're not leaving!"

"Miss, I'm plumb sorry I took your bein' out here light. I can see now it ain't half funny. Who shall I say you all, Jack Ambler's neighbors, be?"

"I'm Meg Brennon." She introduced the others.

"My name is Bama," he said, tipping his hat again, in farewell, his horse shifting. "Born in Alabama, headed west 'soon as I got freed. Other cowboys I rode with called me Alabama, Bama for short, an' the name stuck. Don't seem to make no difference what my real name is no more, so I don't use it."

She nodded understanding. But she didn't know whether to call him Mr. Bama or just Bama. "Good day—Bama," she said. "If you're ever over our way, please stop in. You know where we are."

"Thank you kindly." He wheeled the bay and rode away.

Three days later, four whang leather-hard cowboys arrived at the homestead, their horses creating a dust cloud that coated everything in sight. Meg had been at work enlarging the spring pool and lining the bottom and sides with limestone. She fanned dust away from her face, they could have walked their horses in! She got even angrier noting their smirking manner as they looked around them. How dare they look down with such superiority at her holdings, humble though they were!

Chapter Eight

Meg waited with roughened hands clasped in front of her blue calico dress, her weight resting on her good leg and hip, wondering if the riders would be grinning into next Sunday before announcing the reason for their visit.

She looked from Bama to the thirtyish man who appeared to be their leader. Jack Ambler? He sat a leggy chestnut out front of the others. He was solid-built and fairly good-looking although, below his wide-brimmed Stetson, his wet grin and tip-tilted eyes reminded her of a smiling wolf.

"My name is Meg Brennon. You're Mr. Jack Ambler, our neighbor?"

"Well now, I am Jack Ambler." A wider grin cracked his coffee-brown face, though his voice was cool. "But I wouldn't use the word *neighbor*. You are more an interloper, ma'am, say a visitor, just passin' through? You and the rest of these folks can't stay on here." His amused glance took in their scraggly garden drooping in the heat, her crude stone workings at the spring some distance away, Grandma Spicy and Lucy Ann tending the wash at the tubs nearby, the playing children. He shook his head and beamed at her. "Real sorry you wasted your time tryin' to fix up this place."

Before she could reply he continued, "We are gentlemen,

though. My crew here will help you load up to move. Over there is Admire Walsh, we call him Ad." He nodded toward a black-haired young cowboy on a tall, dancing, steel-dust. "Back there is Lofty Gowdy." The young string-bean rider on a dark bay lifted his dusty hat to Meg. "You met Bama already."

Young Lucy Ann, comely in clean, patched pink gingham, her fresh-washed blonde hair pulled back in a ribbon, looked nervously at the openly admiring grins some of the riders were giving her. Placing a hand on Grandma Spicy's shoulder, she whispered something to her and, leaving the laundry soaking, hurried inside. Aurelia came out with floury hands to stand, look, and listen.

Meg finally got a word in. "No time has been wasted except yours, Mr. Ambler, coming here. We don't mind hard work." She told him with determination, frost in her tone, "We own this property free and clear, and we aren't going anywhere."

He nodded, then drawled without particular feeling, "Bama told me the particulars, that you bought out Thorne. That McCoy's niece and nephew came by his half through inheritance."

"All true." It was hard to hide her irritation at his expression of "so what?"

He muttered under his breath, "I'll buy you out. You could all use money to make decent lives somewhere else, a lot better life than you'll ever find hereabouts dirt farmin'."

Aurelia made a small, encouraged sound that might have been the word "good!" She moved closer to Meg. Meg understood the woman's damaged pride, her humiliation, her yearning to leave. The answer Aurelia was holding her breath for, she couldn't give Ambler. To Aurelia, to him, she said, "I believe a good life can be made here. My property is not for sale, not today, not in the future. The Voss youngsters have indicated no wish to move elsewhere, but if you'd like to speak to them—?"

With a small cry, Aurelia wheeled and fled back inside the dugout. Meg could hear her arguing with Lucy Ann, probably thinking the girl might talk sense into Meg. Maybe Lucy Ann stayed where she was because the cowboys leering at her discomfited her. It was just as likely that she had no desire to sell out, either.

Jack Ambler's smile had thinned considerably with the conversation. "Miss Brennon, this is foolishness, your trying to make a livin' out here raisin' a handful of cows an' spuds. This is cattle country and it takes a lot of land to make a halfway go of it. It's a rough, hard livin' that don't suit women and children. You all aren't fit for out here. I'll pay you exactly what you paid Thorne for your 160 acres—"

"Exactly? You can't." Behind her iron stance she was thinking of her father's fiddle and the millinery goods that paid for her property. She enjoyed the private humor, which perhaps he saw in her eyes because he looked about to explode.

"I'll be back in a week with the money. You be ready to clear out and consider yourself lucky at that!" He hard-turned his dust-coated chestnut, then drew up for a minute. He told her, mouth quirked in the ever-present smile, "Anybody else would just run you off, not bother to pay you for this no-account place. In a week you'll know where you want to go."

She swept forward, fighting to control her limp. "In a week—or next year—I'll be as certain as I am this minute that I'm not going anywhere. I don't think you heard me, Mr. Ambler. I own this place, it is not for sale, and I will be here 'til kingdom come!"

One of the Rocking A cowhands snickered and the others gawked, entertained by the word-feud between their cold-smiling boss and the dark-haired woman.

For a minute Jack Ambler looked furious enough to leap off his horse and grab her. His voice was deadly velvet. "You seem to be the one in charge here, Miss Brennon, so I'm tellin' *you:* Little children and women can't survive out here." He looked about to give a litany of reasons, then he shrugged with smiling indication that even a blind man would see why, that he spoke to an imbecile. "You'd be making a grave mistake keepin' these folks in this country. Get 'em out while you can, get out before winter, or some of you won't be alive come spring, I guarantee it!"

She was glad he could not see her shiver under her clothes. Glad her voice didn't shake when she answered, "And I guarantee we will."

The damnable man's deadly pronouncement would not leave her mind no matter how hard she tried to shake it, hard at work, days on end after Ambler's visit. Nighttime worry that he might be voicing the truth kept her from getting enough sleep. One night, aching from exhaustion but unable to close her eyes, she wandered outside. She went to the spring, sat on the rock which shone white in the moonlight, pondered her situation and the fate of those who depended on her.

She had made the right choice for herself, she had no doubt of that. Lucy Ann, Laddie, and Grandma Spicy wanted to stay. Aurelia, though, was barely speaking to her. The children went blithely about their tasks and play, unaware how much her decisions involved them in a life and death matter. *That* weighed heavily on her shoulders.

Beyond threatening her for personal reasons, Jack Ambler's was a truthful prophecy of what often occurred in a place like western Kansas. People lost their lives to accident, to the weather, to starvation—trying to make something good of a wild, desolate land, as she was trying to do. But knowing the possibility of loss, even the chance of death, was not enough for her to give up the dream. Not enough for herself, personally, now she was here.

She had left Teddy Malloy with the sure belief there were ways to better herself other than marriage to a bully. From the moment she ran away, she had worked on that belief, fighting to add finer stitches to the crazy quilt of her life. Coming to western Kansas was the right thing to do, the best chance she had, if only she held on.

But she could not risk the others' lives, not without their say-so, not without their clear understanding of the hardships they faced. She would waste no time making it clear to Lucy Ann and Laddie and Grandma Spicy what they were up against. She doubted, though, the dangers and deprivations she'd spell out to them would seem any worse than what they had already known.

She would do her best to help Aurelia and her children to leave. It was what Aurelia wanted. If Dodge City seemed better to Aurelia than the homestead, she could look for a job there and find a place to live until such time she could move back east to the life she craved and had had to leave behind.

As he said he would, Jack Ambler returned a week later, alone on the beautiful chestnut—except for Grandma sitting sideways in the saddle in front of him, encircled by his arms.

Meg stared at the sight, astonished. Dear Lord, they hadn't even been aware Grandma Spicy was missing again. She'd wandered off a couple of times since they came, but they'd always found her right away.

"One of yours?" Jack Ambler mocked as he let Grandma down to the ground.

Meg nodded but didn't say anything. Grandma mumbled, "Thankee," and hobbled tiredly toward the dugout.

"I appreciate your bringing her home."

"She claimed I stole a baby from her, 'til I set her straight."

"She gets mixed-up sometimes."

"She ought to be in an institution, an old folks' home where she could be taken care of." The way he said it, the fault was all Meg's.

"I don't agree. We're her family. We take good care of her." *Most of the time.*

Jack shrugged off the conversation and confidently laid out his deal for Meg. Although the ready cash he offered was tempting, it wasn't *land.* Once again, Meg stood her ground and turned down his offer. As did Lucy Ann, coming outside to speak for herself and as guardian for her brother. Even after Meg's long talk with them that staying might be a mistake, the Vosses didn't want to leave, either.

Aurelia had joined them in the yard. She stood back, silent, pale, and angry at the other two women. She blurted, "Mr. Ambler, could you use a housekeeper? I am available. I'm a very good cook, I'm clean, and I would see that my four children behave. I would of course, expect a decent salary. My intention—I will be honest and tell you now, because I know you would understand—is to earn enough to take my children and myself back east to *civilization,*" she emphasized.

After a flash of surprise, Jack Ambler studied Aurelia a moment. Then his expression dismissed her, and her four children as they shrieked and laughed, playing wolf-over-the-river nearby. "I have a bunged-up ex-cowboy who cooks and sees to my house. Walker Platt is more than adequate help. I wouldn't hire you even if I did need you," he told her bluntly. "As I keep tryin' to put across to you all, western Kansas is no place for women and children."

Aurelia turned crimson, her eyes averted in furious disappointment as he continued, "No place for you. Not on my ranch, not here, not for any time. Dangers out here are real, and the discomfort is not necessary if you'll just go. Climate's enough to kill you. A woman with good sense would get out now, not wait for somethin' terrible to happen."

Of course a big cattleman like him would not want the plains cut up into farms, Meg thought, hearing more than the surface argument he made. Once that started, once a few such farms showed success, people too poor to buy land, and farmers from worn-out eastern lands, would flock to settle western Kansas's free land like angels to paradise. On the other hand, Jack Ambler could sincerely believe, for reasons of his own, that western Kansas was too hard on women and children, and wasn't a good place for them.

She really didn't doubt that, either. But like herself, and Grandma Spicy, and Lucy Ann, many women had known hard times back where they came from. Such women would see the rigors of western Kansas for what they were, a natural part of life. She saw life here that way.

And difficult situations could change. Given time and hard work, life could improve, get a whole lot better. She liked it where she was too much to leave.

Maybe Jack Ambler, from ignorance, lacked faith in the endurance of women.

"I'm afraid it's no sale, Mr. Ambler, but you're welcome to stay for coffee and plum pie." Meg doubted being neighborly would help, but it was worth a try. Aurelia, who was embarrassed at being rejected yet again and close to tears, looked shocked at her audacity. Not to worry, Meg saw. Jack Ambler was already wheeling his chestnut with a blunt, "No, thanks!"

He said to Meg over his shoulder, lips taut over his teeth, his face hot iron, "It takes ten to twenty acres to support one cow the year around. You're already overgrazin' this place and I can't let you have my grass, not even for that scrub herd of yours. If you insist on stayin' on here, with all I've warned you, you are twenty kinds of a fool."

"I suppose. I've heard that I am, from other folks." She looked toward Aurelia, disappearing in a huff into the dugout.

Fool she might be, quitter she wasn't. Whatever Jack Ambler might do to try and dissuade her from staying, he would lose. It did worry her, though, what he said about her running too many cows on her grass. But shouldn't the surrounding free grass be hers to use, too? He was doing it.

By September, they had added two more mounds of hay to that cut by Harlan. In the evening the women and children twisted tall grass into braids to use for their winter fires if the snow got so deep they couldn't gather chips. As many chips as they could gather were stacked high by the door.

The garden was carefully watched for signs of frost in the early mornings and evenings when it grew cool. They wanted the vegetables to mature as much as possible before they harvested them.

Meg decided she could wait no longer to start hauling their stock of buffalo bones to Dodge to sell. They had to have enough supplies to see them through the coming winter and had to make the trips before bad weather held them home. "I'm leaving day after tomorrow," she told Aurelia. "You're welcome to come with me and look for work in

Dodge. If you find something, we can return for Joshua, David John, and the little girls. I can't take all of you this time, and take bones to sell, too."

Aurelia seemed uncertain, even scared, now that she had an opportunity to leave. "Lucy Ann and Grandma Spicy would have to do all the work, and look after my youngsters, too, while we're gone. I don't know—"

"We'll be awright," Grandma crowed, "you go along with Meg now, Aurelia daughter. We will do just fine."

"Go, Aurelia," Lucy Ann added quietly. "Although if you find a position in Dodge, we'll miss you and the children somethin' awful." Abrupt tears sparkled in her eyes. "Zibby baby, come." Her favorite charge—just learning to walk—waddled gleefully forward to be gathered up into Lucy Ann's arms and kissed.

"Are you sure, Lucy Ann?" Meg touched her arm. "Can you and Grandma Spicy manage 'til we get back? You don't look well. I've made you work too hard—!" She'd been so busy of late herself, she just now saw how drawn Lucy Ann looked, her pallor emphasized by dark blue shadows under her eyes.

Lucy Ann shook her head hard. "Nothing is the matter with me." Her gaze cut away from Meg's. "I'm not sick. It's hard to keep things clean with the wind blowing dust onto everything, but I don't work any harder than the rest of you. You worry too much. Now let's get you and Aurelia ready to go."

"Everything is going to get better for all of us," Meg promised, giving the other young woman a quick hug.

The Dodge City bone buyer was a tall, slope-shouldered man with a sandy moustache that drooped to his chest, and a wily look in his gray eyes. His name was Tog Elsberry.

"If that's the best you can do, Mr. Elsberry." Meg put the

money in her reticule with the two dollars' cash Aurelia had earned from the meal she served the pair of wayfarers.

"Eight dollars a ton is what everybody's gettin'," Elsberry told her. "It's a fair price, costs me a sweet penny to ship 'em east, ya know."

She nodded, thinking about something. "Mr. Elsberry, I would accept less for the rest of the bones piled at my place, providing you'd come out and haul them back to Dodge yourself." She might have a full ton altogether, including the load she'd brought in today. Maybe more. Time was as precious to her as anything; there was so much other work for her to do besides driving back and forth.

"You'd take how much less?" He thumbed his hat back.

She looked him in the eye and gave him a price.

They dickered for another minute and a deal was struck that suited them both. "Thank you, Mr. Elsberry, we'll look for you out at the homestead soon."

He stroked his moustache, then nodded. "I'll send a feller I hired to come get the rest of your bone gather."

The little wagonette felt oddly empty as the women drove to the main part of town where Aurelia would look for work while Meg shopped for supplies.

"Good luck, Aurelia." The other woman gave her a half-frightened smile, nodded, and asked to be let down in front of a boardinghouse called Ma Goshen's.

Meg made her selections carefully at the general store, measuring need against her small fund of cash. When she went out to load her purchases in the wagon, she was surprised to see Aurelia already aboard, mouth pinched, disdain in her eyes.

"Aurelia, what happened? Couldn't you find a thing? Did you try the cafes, the hotel? Surely somebody has work for you."

Aurelia climbed down to help her load the wagon. "I can't bring my children to live in this town," she said with a sharp sniff. "Would you just look? The only women around are—are—well, you know. And a lot of them stay at Ma Goshen's! I've never seen such rough-looking men, either. Buffalo hunters, card sharps, gunslingers. Garbage in the streets, such a smell! Dodge is just not—decent. I want to go back to the homestead. For now."

"All right, Aurelia, if that's what you want. At least you tried." They finished loading. After a stop at the feed and hardware store, where they purchased a crate of hens for fifty cents and a used plow for a dollar, they decided not to stay around town any longer, but to start back.

"We'll eat crackers and cheese on the way," Meg said. They'd have to sleep out on the plains tonight, before continuing on home, stopping by a stream where they could water Butterfield. She wished she had Lucy Ann's gun. She'd asked about the pistol a few times. Lucy Ann always had an excuse for not producing it. Even so, she was sure Lucy Ann had given up the idea of taking her own life.

They were well on the way next day when Meg realized that Lucy Ann had been at the back of her mind all the time they had been in Dodge and since. She spoke to Aurelia. "Does Lucy Ann look well to you these days? She says she's fine, but I don't believe she is. I'm worried."

Aurelia hesitated to answer. "I think I know the trouble, but I've been waiting for Lucy Ann to bring it up herself and, so far, she hasn't." She stared straight ahead, chewing her lip.

"You know? What is the matter then?" Meg asked, a knife of worry running through her at the look on Aurelia's face, where concern mixed with embarrassment. "Is she all right?"

Color flooded Aurelia's cheeks. "A couple of mornings Lucy Ann ran off into the brush to be sick. She hardly eats a thing, but she's getting—rounder. I think she's pregnant, though I don't know how she could be. The few times men came to the homestead, she ran to hide."

"She's—?" Meg began, and then her throat closed and she couldn't speak. The real truth, which Aurelia might not know, filled her with horror. She fought nausea rising in her throat. Poor child, pregnant from the Indian rape, and suffering the knowledge all by herself. She was a farm girl. She would know what caused the changes in her body. Just as she was beginning to forget and get on with a new life. She still had the gun and her single bullet. Dear Lord, she could change her mind about that!

Cold chills chased over Meg. She damned herself for being too busy to see what was happening. She should have guessed the possibility of a baby, been aware. She should have talked long and hard with Lucy Ann.

"Get up there!" Meg shouted suddenly at the top of her lungs, and she whipped Butterfield into a run.

No distance had ever seemed so long as the road stretching before them to the homestead. In spite of trying not to, she reflected on Jack Ambler's prediction that one of them would die. He had to be wrong. Not Lucy Ann because she was with child.

And yet no danger was feared and hated more by women on the frontier than rape at the hands of a savage. When it happened, suicide commonly followed.

Never mind Ambler hadn't named any particular tragedy. She drove on hard until Aurelia protested, "Meg, for pity's sake slow down. You're killing poor Butterfield and we'll be thrown out and crippled."

"We have to get home as fast as we can." Her mind was frantic with the thought: *In time, in time.*

Chapter Nine

In the draw far ahead of them, against a sky of purest blue, a pall of dust hung over the homestead like a dark cap on a poison mushroom. Butterfield had slowed. Meg urged him to move faster down the hill. He swiveled an ear back at her then obeyed, but time seemed to stand still. Finally, they reached the home yard where the chill fall air literally smelled of trouble.

Lucy Ann and Grandma, poles in hand, were struggling without success to raise and prop up the caved-in roof of the dugout. She quickly accounted for all of the children, who were shaking out torn rags and blankets in the yard. Towheaded Baby Zibby sat playing on the ground, so dirty she looked like tar.

The garden that had looked like it might come to harvest and give them fresh food, was shredded to dying bits in the autumn sunlight. "Dear God," she whispered. "A tornado? What happened here?" She spilled off the wagon seat before the vehicle came to a stop.

Helen Grace ran up to catch her hand. "The cowboys crashed us down."

"They what?" she asked in shock.

Behind them, Aurelia's breath caught on an angry, terrified sob. "That ties it! Now we really have nothing. We might as well all be dead!"

Meg gave her a scolding look over her shoulder and hurried to Lucy Ann, whom she'd been so worried about for other reasons. The girl was perspiring heavily. With a tired sigh she released the broken timber she had been using to try and raise the roof back in place.

She was alive; she hadn't done anything foolish with the gun.

"Come away, Lucy Ann." Meg took her arm. She called out to where Grandma grunted and staggered with her lift pole. "That's enough, Grandma Spicy, come now, it's no use. If the roof should fall again, somebody could get badly hurt. We'll try something different later. Tell me now, what happened?" Grandma came to stand nearby, wilting from the effort she'd expended. She was quiet, allowing the younger woman to explain.

"The rancher came back," Lucy Ann said. She dried her face on her dusty apron, leaving a smear across her pale forehead. "His cattle, a hundred or more of them, ran over our homestead."

"No one is hurt then, none of you?" She looked around, wanting to be absolutely sure. Helen Grace was near, chewing on a finger; the boys were poking in the rubble.

"Thank goodness" —there were relieved tears in Lucy Ann's eyes— "nobody was hurt. The boys weren't here then, they were out watching our cattle. The Rocking A herd came charging from the north. They sounded like—thunder. Grandma and me grabbed Helen Grace and Baby Zibby and ran as hard as we could. We thought about waving Zibby's nappies that were out to dry, to try and turn the cattle away, but it was too late, they were running too hard, right at us. Like they were forced, but—"

"*Forced?* But what?"

"Mr. Ambler claimed our ruin was an accident. Said that sometimes during fall roundup a herd will get set off by a snake, even a shadow, or something, and stampede."

"This was no accident." Meg knew it in her bones. She looked at the shambles that had been their home. "Jack Ambler did this on purpose."

Lucy Ann nodded. "He laughed like he was glad of our ruin. The two riders with him weren't any of the ones came here before."

Grandma Spicy, getting her wind back, snorted. "Durn grinnin' fool said now that we're finished here, he could put in a word for us at a Dodge saloon an' get us jobs. Said I was a purty female, old or not. Blast his hide for makin' fun of me. I scorched him with my tongue but he just laughed harder at me."

"Are we leavin'?" Aurelia's oldest boy, Joshua, came up to ask Meg. "Dammit, we ain't goin' back east, are we?"

His wide-eyed mother scolded him roundly for swearing and saying "ain't," but it didn't change his disappointment that leaving could happen. Like a little rooster, he was ready to argue the point. With him were David John and Laddie, all looking defensive, not ready to hear what they considered *the worst:* The bad news that, with no home now, they'd move on again.

They were a filthy, tattered lot, but otherwise unharmed. In those young faces Meg caught signs of independence, confidence, brashness even, that they'd been developing these past many weeks. Qualities that matched the raw frontier. Unlike the adults, the children made games of hard work, competing with each other to get even the most difficult chores done. The dangers of the plains they faced bravely day after day were a grand, exciting lark to them. They were going to become strong, wonderful adults—capable of facing any challenge—if she could keep them alive long enough to grow up.

"Does anyone want to leave?" As one, everybody turned to look at Aurelia. Her face pinked; she shook her head. Meg waited longer, the silence grew. She smiled grimly. "Then we're staying put. We still have the land, we have material to rebuild with, we have our cattle. We're going to be all right."

"Uh, Miss Meg?" Joshua grabbed her sleeve in his grubby fingers, his manner earnest. "Two of our cows, that old brindle and the black one? They got taken into the Rocking A herd when they went charging through. We tried gettin' 'em back, yelled and yelled and rode after the Rocking A cowboys—didn't we, Lad?" Lad nodded his head.

The younger boy, David John, finished with a shake of his dark head. "They was chasin' their own cattle and paid us no mind." He reached down and picked up a small pebble and tossed it back and forth, hand to hand.

"It's all right, boys. We'll get our cows back." *Or someone would pay for them.*

She led the little band to her wagon and showed everyone what she had bought. Food staples—sacks of cornmeal, flour, salt, beans, jugged molasses, lard—were unloaded. Together they lifted down the very rusty breaking plow. A place was found for the crate of hens and the rooster; Aurelia was thrilled with the prospect of cooking with eggs.

They separated into groups. Grass and manure were cleaned from the spring where the cattle had stampeded through. Vegetable plants that had any chance at all—squash, pumpkins, corn, and melons—were replanted and mudded in. Most of the potato plants had been trampled to pieces, and tiny new potatoes were harvested early.

By late afternoon, a makeshift tent had been fashioned from blankets and broken timbers, their supplies and bedrolls placed under cover. Meg announced over a cold supper, "At first light tomorrow we will start a new dugout. Maybe two. It'll be awfully crowded this winter, when we all have to be inside most of the time." Ten of them, counting Lucy Ann's baby. One small dugout would not be room enough to hold them all.

Water was their most important commodity, Meg was reminded all over again when she and Lucy Ann went to the spring together to wash up before bedtime. The water was still muddied, but at least it was refreshing. Reaching for her turn with the soap, Meg spoke cautiously, "Lucy Ann, I'd really like to have your gun if you don't mind. I want to make sure nothing like today ever happens again. Those cattle were driven over us to try and run us out. I should have bought more ammunition. Next time I go to Dodge, I will."

"I'm not sure I can find the gun," Lucy Ann said hesitantly. She splashed softly as she kneeled by the water, then scrubbed and scrubbed. "It's buried somewhere in the dugout. I suppose I can dig it out."

"Is there any reason you don't want me to have it?"

In the dim light Lucy Ann toweled her face and her arms. She spoke with some reluctance. "I felt better having the pistol close to me, after—after something that happened to me and Laddie back home in Nebraska." Briefly, hesitantly, she sketched the Indian raid for Meg, joining up with Grandma Spicy, and finally, the three of them trying to take her wagon.

Meg held her hand tightly as Lucy Ann went on. "I never would have used the .44 on you, Meg, not really. Just to threaten so's you'd take us to my Uncle Ross's place, that's all I ever meant. We just needed your wagon, one way or the other."

"I understand. Don't worry. We'll find the gun. If you

99

trust me, I'll try to look out for all of us."

" 'Course I trust you! Nobody means so much to me, Meg, as you do. Since Mama and Papa—died, nobody has been as good to me and Laddie. The others, they couldn't make it without you either."

"Pish." Meg felt uncomfortable. "I'm here on my own account as much as anyone's." She needed the others as much as they needed her. She approached the subject foremost in her mind. "Lucy Ann, there is something I hope we can talk about. I'm worried— You've been peaked lately and you tire easily. Aurelia says your stomach is upset in the morning. I wonder if—" her throat dried. "Are you with child, do you think?"

The answer came quiet and calm. "I believe I am."

Meg realized, in another moment, that Lucy Ann had begun to cry. Swallowing her own tears, she pulled Lucy Ann into her arms. "It'll be all right," she said, "it'll be all right."

"When I first knew," Lucy Ann said unsteadily against her shoulder, "I wanted to die. I was savin' that one bullet, just in case this should happen from what the Indians done to me. But then, we come and I find out Uncle Ross wasn't alive to look out for Laddie. The baby inside started moving with life and I couldn't hurt my own little one. It's not his fault how he was made, who his father was, a savage. I want my child. He is part of me, too. He's part my mama and papa, and Laddie. He is Nebraska, and he is Kansas, and I mean to raise him the best I can."

Lucy Ann's eloquence, her mother-love practicality, touched Meg so deeply she couldn't speak. They sat on the limestone shelf by the pool for a long time, saying nothing, until both began to droop, weary for sleep. Before they went in, Meg vowed, "It's going to be all right. You'll tell Laddie? He'll have to know."

"I'll tell him," Lucy Ann whispered, "but not yet."

The next morning, the boys were sent to their herding chores right after breakfast. They were told to do a new count of the herd, and as always to watch out for snakes, and now—deviltry from the Rocking A. The women turned to salvaging what they could from the dugout.

A trunk filled with Aurelia's family's clothing was uncovered, basically undamaged. The fireplace, bane of Aurelia's existence though she loved to cook, survived. Broken cupboards, dishes, and smashed tin utensils were sorted bit by bit from the crumbled sod. The rocking chair was brought out, one rocker broken.

It was dreadful work, with bare hands pulling loose the old sod bricks to free the willow roof timbers that hadn't been broken and could be used again. The tin chimney pipe was freed from the rubble, straightened, and carefully set aside.

"Careful where you step, Aurelia. Glass is broken from the front window," Lucy Ann called out, a skillet in her hand. Meg answered, "Save the window frame. We can cover it with hide, or oiled paper until we can buy new glass."

Aurelia sat on a keg sorting broken crockery that might still be usable. Her angry mumbling sounded as close to cursing as Meg ever expected to hear from her and she couldn't help a private smile, in spite of their loss.

Jack Ambler was going to pay, though, for as much of their loss as she could wring out of him. First, though, her clan had to have shelter. By uniform vote they decided to build a sod house this time, and to use the old dugout, to be cleaned out and repaired, for a combination extra sleeping room and bigger storage cellar.

Thank heavens she now had a plow to cut sod for building. A good scraping with a rock rid the implement of rust and sharpened it some, as well as taking most of the skin from

101

Meg's knuckles. After they'd chosen a site for the new house nearer the spring, she picked a wide area several paces on the other side to take her sod bricks from. Next year, the cleared area could be used for a bigger, better garden, minus the sod. With Butterfield hitched to her plow, she began to cut through the sod, weighing down hard on the handles. Slowly, she freed long strips that the other women sliced into twelve-by-eighteen inch blocks with a broken-handled butcher knife and their grubbing hoe.

"Fall be a good time to build," Grandma Spicy said, hacking at sod. "These old grass roots be mighty woody and tough, providin' us stronger building material as 'tis."

"True," Meg panted, pushing down hard with sweaty palms on the plow handles. Her shoulders and forearms ached fiercely after the first hour, trying to keep the blade from bouncing free off the hard ground and pulling her off her feet to land on her face.

"Let's have a pretty house," Aurelia said, staggering under a barrow load of turf brick toward the eighteen-by-twenty-foot perimeter they had marked for the house-to-be. "Lace curtains as soon as we can afford them," she called over her shoulder, her exclamations carried on the Indian summer wind as she moved further away. "Let's have an iron stove. And—an organ. Children ought to be raised with music, literature, the finer things of life. It's so deplorably uncivilized out here."

"We'll see," Meg grunted, surprised that Aurelia had actual plans, however fanciful, for staying. Twice recently she spoke the notion that Harlan might yet listen to his conscience and send for her and her children. In any event, they had to have shelter and soon. They had to get the soddy up before the cold weather hit.

Being careful not to break them, they stacked the turf

blocks in staggered brick fashion, then filled the cracks with loose dirt. By the fourth day, working sunup to sundown, the women had stacked walls eave-high on all four sides, with two framed windows and an opening for a doorway. The self-satisfaction they all felt was of no help in the tremendous effort it took to get the ridgepole onto the two forked support poles on either end inside the house.

Lucy Ann wanted to climb up and lay the roofing of willow poles, but Meg wouldn't hear of it and took the job herself. Teetering on a bench on which she'd placed a square molasses drum, she placed the eave boards to keep the sod from sliding off. She moved like a scared monkey onto the top, adding the willow pole roofing, and lastly, one by one, the heavy sod bricks.

Finally, it was finished. To celebrate, they ate sorghum raisin cake Aurelia had baked in the old fireplace. It was one week and a half after the Rocking A herd had destroyed the dugout. They felt more worn out than ever, but most everything else seemed new and gladsome.

Meg decided her own dwelling could wait until they all had a good rest. But she couldn't put off requesting payment from Jack Ambler for her cows that had disappeared the day of the stampede. Two T Cross critters hadn't been seen since; all of Lucy Ann and Lad's Pocket 7 cows were accounted for.

She set out after breakfast when morning chores were completed. For safety against snakes, wild animals, and any other dangers she might encounter, she wore Lucy Ann's gun—it had finally been unearthed and cleaned—strapped around her waist. She rode bareback on Butterfield, a faster method of getting to the Ambler ranch and back than going by wagon. She had much to do at the homestead, but she was not about to ignore the loss of two cows.

Like a great, rippling gold sea, the grassland stretched out before her. Overhead, a bunting sang sweetly on the wing; a meadowlark sang from a nearby grassy gulch in a strong rich voice. As the sun heated the high plains, grasshoppers clattered up from the brittle grasses, out of the path of Butterfield's hoofs. Once she saw a coyote trotting westward across the wide land.

The further north she rode, the more Rocking A cows speckled the distant reaches. A wealth of cows, both shorthorns, mostly rust-red, and longhorns, some gold, some black, were getting sleek and fat on the rich buffalo grass. Now and then a close-by bovine would raise its head to look at her, before continuing to graze.

The Indian summer sun seared her shoulders through her dress, and envy settled deep in her bones as she traveled. The latter feeling stayed with her, growing as she approached the Rocking A ranch headquarters a long while later.

The fringe of tall cottonwoods growing around the ranch proper indicated how long Jack Ambler had been in the country. Long enough to grow trees! Long enough to trade the buffalo-hide tent or dugout he lived in the first years, for a long, rambling stone ranch house. There was an impressive stone corral where a deep-chested leggy bay rolled in the dust to ease its itchy back. There was an assortment of stone sheds and other outbuildings. A windmill to the south of the house whirred in the wind and pumped water into a tank where several cows drank.

She turned her attention back to the L-shaped ranch house. It surely had at least eight or ten rooms. A matrimony vine drooped in the heat but still managed to shade the veranda that ran the full length of the west-facing front. Empty rockers rocked in the hot wind as she crossed the porch and knocked at the main door.

She felt small, suddenly, and of little account. Turning, she gave the way she had come a long study. Today she had crossed a man's kingdom. Her little spread was a blight on that realm because she and her friends used grass and water the King had for years taken for granted. His fat royal cows needed that grass and water, if he was to keep, and increase, his royal holdings.

She licked her dry lips, then turned back. He ought not to have taken for granted what was never really his. She knocked again.

She hoped the King was home.

Chapter Ten

A towering, well-built man with moustache and hair shaded from brown to grey opened the door to Meg. In his hands was a broom. He wore an apron tied around his middle and an affable but questioning smile on his battle-scarred face.

"My name is Meg Brennon. I'm here to see Mr. Ambler."

He nodded. "I'm Walker Platt, Jack's cook and housekeeper. Come on in." His gray eyes twinkled. In a limping gait, he ushered her through the main door into a spacious, stone-floored entrance hall.

A dining room opened to her left, a parlor to the right. A quick perusal fed by womanly curiosity showed both rooms chiefly furnished in elegant mahogany, with chairs and couches upholstered in silk tapestry. Gun racks and mounted elk horns added an eclectic, masculine touch. Eastern elegance was further warmed and made homey with Indian blankets and baskets.

Walker Platt was saying, "Jack's around the ranch somewhere. Come on in here and make yourself comfortable. I'll get him for you."

"Please."

She followed Platt into the parlor. She eyed the fancy furniture for a moment, then took a ponderous leather-seated rocking chair that stood out as the most comfortable. The stone fireplace was big and without a fire that warm fall day. The room had a musty smell, like dried flowers and saddle leather. A tall walnut clock at the far end of the room ticked off the minutes.

Glancing around after Platt left, Meg's gaze halted on a large gilt-framed painting that hung above the fireplace mantel. The auburn-haired woman in the painting looked very young, fragile, and beautiful.

She couldn't help but wonder who the woman was, if she was responsible for the planting of the matrimony vine that shaded the porch, if she was the one who had chosen the more elegant furnishings of Jack's home. She pulled her attention away, wondering how long she would have to wait. Her eyes went back to the painting. Sister, or wife, to Ambler?

"Knew it had to be you when Platt described my woman visitor," Jack Ambler said a half-hour later when he sauntered in. He flopped onto the sofa to her left, stretched stocky legs out in front of him, folded his hands behind his head, and surveyed her with a daredevil grin, one brow tilted high. "What can I do for you, *neighbor?*"

His hair was still wet, finger-combed back over his handsome brow, and she guessed he'd cleaned up from ranch work before joining her. She found his jaunty, cheeky manner unpleasant, though, particularly in light of why she was there.

In a no-nonsense tone she told him, "As you well know, you stampeded your cattle over my place. You owe me for severe destruction to the dwelling and furnishings shared by me and my friends—"

His slanty gold eyes squinched up as he laughed and slapped his knee. "My God, you talk like you live in a damn castle." He continued to grin, his thin top lip disappearing against shiny teeth, the tips of his teeth pointing inward.

Sweet heaven! What kind of man found a tragedy—a ruined home and misplaced women and children—funny? "It wasn't a castle," she admitted, trying to control her fury, "but it was our home, home to nine human beings."

"Nine squatters where they ought not to be!"

"You also owe me for two T Cross cows caught up in your malicious stampede. I haven't seen them since, and they are worth quite a bit to me."

"Now I'll tell you what caused that stampede, so don't blame it on me." His grin deepened. He leaned toward her, elbows on his knees, chin cupped in his blunt fingers. "Those young herd boys you folks let loose on the prairie spooked *our* herd as we were tryin' to drive 'em by your place, sent 'em runnin' near to hell and gone before we got 'em turned."

"That's not the story they gave me."

"Boys lie. Especially if the truth might get them in trouble."

"They had no reason to lie, you do. You're trying by unfair means to drive us out, Mr. Ambler. We both know that."

He shrugged, grew mockingly sober. "I do what's got to be done. And I don't back down. Remember I tried to buy you off my range, cash on the barrelhead."

"I don't give in easy, either!" she retorted. "Whatever you plan, you can't make us leave!" She didn't like him, and she wanted her business done so she could leave. The gun was uncomfortable against her hip, but she was glad it was there. "If you have my cows, I'll take them back with me, or you can pay me for them in cash."

He chuckled. "*If* those cows were caught into our herd as you claim, they are long gone. My hands took the scrubs like them sorry cows you run on your place, and got rid of them along with a shipment of feeders to Kansas City. Sorry."

"Cash will do then," she said firmly, sliding to the edge of the rocker, ready to flee the moment she had what she wanted.

"Lord, but you're in an almighty rush, sweetheart. That's hardly friendly of a 'neighbor'," he mocked. "We can visit a while. There hasn't been a woman in this house for a long time, and I can tell you it's damn nice. Seein' you sittin' there, all prim, proper, and haughty, but all woman inside, I betcha. Right?"

Heat crept into her face. "I have to go."

Walker Platt came in just then with a tray holding glasses of iced tea and large slices of lemon loaf on delicate china plates. To her dismay, the food looked refreshingly delicious. Jack looked delighted at the chance for delay, thanked Platt and dismissed him to the kitchen.

Alone again with Jack, she wondered if he would attempt force if she tried to leave that minute—which of course she couldn't do, until she was paid. She had the gun, but didn't want to use it. She tried the lemon loaf, took a sip of iced tea, found swallowing difficult. She set the food back on the table next to her chair. Jack's gold, laughter-filled eyes were measuring her every move.

Maybe he wasn't used to having a woman stand up to him, demand recompense for trouble he caused, and her effrontery was high entertainment. The thought made her angrier than ever.

"Now where'd we leave off?" he said suddenly. "Yeah. I want you off my range." He caught her glance straying to the painting over the fireplace.

"My wife, Madeleine." He turned suddenly congenial, mockery leaving his voice. They might have been good friends, conversing, as he told her, "I met Maddie Carlisle when I was eighteen and she was fourteen. I was servin' in the Union army at the time, in Virginia. I got wounded, her family nursed my wounds, fed and clothed me 'til I got back on my feet."

Meg didn't want to be interested, let alone fascinated, but she listened as Jack told how he came west after the war, to make his fortune and give Madeleine a chance to grow up. In four years, he had quadrupled his holdings. His sweetheart with whom he had corresponded over the years had turned eighteen. He sent for her to join him, to become his wife.

"It was this country killed Maddie. She died in childbirth, the child, too, not a doctor to get for them in two hundred miles." From the expression on his face he had loved Maddie a great deal, might still grieve for her and the infant.

"I'm sorry," she said quietly. It would do small good to tell him times were changing, there was likely a doctor now in Dodge, not so far away. Certainly there was a doctor and infirmary at Fort Dodge, west of town.

Still wondering how she might leave without causing a scene, she listened as he went on telling the same story Bama had told her. How he and friends—McCoy, Thorne, and a few others—came to the raw country, fought the Indians, the elements, making the land permanently theirs by their wits and guns. He made the latter point so coldly, so fiercely emphatic, she shivered.

"But I got a deal for you," he smiled widely. "Been thinkin' it over. Women, decent women, are as rare in western Kansas as peony roses. My mother used to grow them around our home back in Rich Woods, Illinois." He surprised her by pulling out a fat roll of bills and peeling off three. "This should get you as far as Dodge or Larned, where you can set up and I can see you again."

His veiled suggestion that she give up her land to become his lady-mistress brought her to the edge of fury. "Your offer is revolting and insulting. I want only what I'm owed: eight dollars for each cow, and twelve dollars for the destruction to our dugout and furnishings."

"Robbery!" he said, then shrugged. "One of those scrawny cows of yours was pregnant with a late calf. Didn't know that, did you, plow lady?" He added an extra bill as he tossed them into her lap.

She put them into her reticule, trying to keep her hands from shaking. She was still outraged enough to want to tap his skull with the butt of her gun, but even unconscious he would probably wear that ridiculous smile.

His obvious contempt for the worth of her two cows, and what they meant to her future, would gall her for a long time, not to mention how he saw *her*. At least today she would have the last word.

"You and the few other ranchers in western Kansas were fortunate to be first, to have no competition for the grass after you pushed the Indians aside and killed the buffalo. But that has changed. The government and the railroads own a lot of the land you speak about, and it's their rule, not yours, that I'll abide by—laws for settlement by people like me, Mr. Ambler." He was scowling, his smile mocking, but before he could say anything, she told him, "I realize we'll never see eye to eye on this and it really is time I was on my way home." She stood up confidently, but so suddenly she weaved from having sat on her bad hip too long.

He was on his feet in an instant, gathering her into his arms while she was at a disadvantage. He burned a rough kiss across her startled mouth. "I can make your dreams come true," he said, gripping her, "some dreams you'd be embarrassed to admit you have."

She jerked away, bolted limping from the house, across the porch and down the steps where, shaking, she mounted her waiting horse. She spanked Butterfield into sudden action, then had a difficult time staying up without a saddle. Her face burned at the sound of Jack's laughter and his words, "We'll do that again, sweetheart, I like the taste of you!"

She was riven with dislike for him, for how he had kissed her like she was a cheap strumpet. She was afraid of his wealth and power, hated to think what he could do to her, to her plans, if he wanted, what he could do to her friends, so easily. If he continued to try and make them leave, they would have to fight back, really fight. And there was no doubt in her mind who was the stronger, who had the better means in hand to get what he wanted.

She was so preoccupied thinking about Jack Ambler and how she might stand up to him, she wasn't aware that he followed until she heard a faint sound. A quick look over her shoulder showed him about a quarter-mile behind, on the tall bay she'd seen earlier in the Rocking A corral. She felt her scalp tighten.

Each time she looked, he was there, coming on at a steady pace, dust stirring under his horse's hoofs. Although she could not see his features from that distance, she knew he smiled. He was playing with her of course, rattling her nerves, making her wonder if he meant to take the money back, and more.

It would be a mistake to underestimate how far he might take his malicious sense of humor. Paying her the money she demanded was nothing to him. He was seeing in her a way to have fun. She knew his kind—wild, irresponsible. Crazy for self-gratification and excitement, and let the chips fall where they may. He had had a good time running the herd over her place, even if it meant risking his own cattle, his hired men's lives.

On the other hand, making the situation even worse, he

was dedicated to the core to the Rocking A, to keeping all he had fought for and considered his alone.

She was afraid of him, very afraid.

A buzzard glided in circles overhead, then slanted toward the horizon and prey, likely a small prairie dog. Jack was like that buzzard; she was his prey.

She tried to hold Butterfield to a steady trot, sometimes a walk, and not show her fear. To the left of the trail a jackrabbit zigzagged away in bounds, but otherwise she was alone on the prairie with Jack. She couldn't help a peek over her shoulder now and then. He came on and on, relentlessly, mile after mile.

In the last golden sweep of sunlight their soddy was a welcoming lump in a shallow dip in the big land. A tightness in her chest eased somewhat. But Jack was not far behind her, and she heard him coming hard and fast, his bay's hoofs pounding like a drum. Jack's laughter rolled on the wind as he rode by, so close she had to jerk Butterfield aside or be run down. Caught in a swirl of dust, her throat dried at the same time curses burned through her mind.

He was yelling something at her over his shoulder; he'd slowed, then halted. It sounded like he said, "See you in Dodge, darlin', or Larned if that's your pick," among other things she couldn't—didn't want to—decipher.

She rode up to the soddy in a fury, determined to *never* leave, to fight him his way, with land and power. Of course it would only make Jack Ambler angrier, but she was going to get hold of as many acres of western Kansas as she could lay hands on! He had his fight now, confound him!

Her encounter with Ambler, her fear and worry, had left Meg so unsettled that everything that happened that evening at the soddy was like a file sawing away at her raw nerves.

Aurelia carped about not having a proper stove to cook on, about the wind that had blown the laundry off the elk rack into the dirt. Lad let Aurelia's boys cheat him over and over in a shell game played with a tin cup and badger bone, rather than use his tongue to tell them off once and for all. In the corner, Grandma Spicy sang "Green Grow The Lilacs" in a sad monotone to her empty arms while she rocked. The repaired rocker creaked as horribly as off-tune singing.

Suddenly, Meg had had enough. She exploded, turning on Aurelia first. "Aurelia, you're so bitter about your poor husband's dying and leaving you, you couldn't taste the sweet in a bucket of honey! You're as well off as any of us, so stop your complaining!"

A slow burn crawled into Aurelia's face. Abrupt tears filled her eyes. "How dare you, you can't know—!"

Meg hardly saw her. She breathed hard as she went over to Grandma Spicy. "Grandma, your little grandbaby is gone, gone for good. But it isn't your fault. Realize that once and for all, and you'll be fine, just fine." She grabbed the scrawny shoulders and shook them. Grandma Spicy looked up, eyes rolling in fear, but she stopped singing.

They stared at Meg in shock, but she wasn't finished. "I haven't got time for everybody's craziness. Lad, you speak up and stop letting Joshua and David John overrun everything you do. If you'd just try to talk—!" His mouth struggled with an effort to speak, his eyes were wide on Meg's face, but no words came. Lucy Ann was furious.

The expressions on their faces was like a dash of cold water to Meg's senses, jolting her from a bad dream. These were people she cared about, who cared about her. "Oh, dear heaven, what's gotten into me? I'm sorry. Everybody, I'm so sorry." She dropped onto a keg-chair, covered her face with her hands to block out their alarm, their hurt. Grandma came over and after a timid second, squatted down and stroked her arms. Lucy Ann moved closer and put her arm around Meg's shoulders. "We're the ones sorry, we lean on you too hard, expect too much."

"No, no, it isn't that, it's—everything else. None of you are the problem. I had no right to take out my frustration on any of you. Aurelia, I'm very sorry. You're right, I haven't lived in your shoes, and I can't know what you've gone through."

"It's just the stove," Aurelia sputtered her usual refrain, though apologetically, pink with embarrassment. "Cooking is such a trial. I just wish I had a real stove. I'm sorry I complain so much, Meg. It isn't your fault I'm here, you did me a favor to let me stay." She shrugged, bit her lip. "I suppose what's really ailing me is that—that I loved the children's father so." She looked at her youngsters. Her eyes filled with the shine of tears. "And I—I miss him—'til I could just die!"

Together, all of them shared a brief community cry. When it was over, Aurelia made molasses candy to cheer everybody, still complaining she lacked a proper stove. The children's shell game was taken up again, Lad as usual allowing himself to be cheated. Grandma Spicy didn't sing, but she still held a child the rest of them could not see.

Giving up changing any of them for the time being, and hoping to do better herself, Meg showed the others the money she'd gotten from Jack. A fresh wave of optimism filled the small soddy by bedtime. They weren't defeated, yet.

Jack had suggested Larned. She would go there, to the land office.

Chapter Eleven

As weary as she was from the long trip to Larned, Meg felt euphoric as she left the land agent and lawyer's office in the chill of a late October morning. They had had a heavy rain, and her steps were quick and careful in the street's mud and dung as she crossed to the general store, smiling to herself.

Her bill of sale showing she'd bought the homestead Harlan Thorne had proved up on was in proper order. With a practiced eye, the lawyer also approved Thorne's final certificate, the land patent. He would see that the transaction was properly recorded in district court.

She had brought with her a description of the quarter section north and west of that she already owned. She had staked out the piece and begun perfunctory improvements before coming to Larned, in the hopes that the quarter section was available for homestead. It was free of claim, according to the land lawyer's large book of surveyed lands. He accepted her filing fee for the additional 160 acres which would be headquarters for her holdings. She would build her sod dwelling there, and her main corrals. Those plans carried out, she would prove up in five years and the additional acreage would become legally hers.

The biggest and most pleasant surprise—Meg smiled at a

thin bonneted woman in gray and stepped back on the board-walk to let her enter the general store first—was the agent's news of the Timber Culture Act.

By paying a second small filing fee, and agreeing to plant forty acres to trees, she had come by another 160 acres! The Tree Claim Act had originated in Nebraska. A law was passed there that taxpayers would be exempt from paying a certain amount of taxes in return for planting timber, such as cotton-wood, elm, ash, hackberry, walnut. A second act exempted the landowner a certain amount of taxes for planting fruit trees, too. Nothing, of course, was so valuable in a treeless land as thriving timber and orchards. A body didn't have to live on a timber claim.

She could hardly wait to tell Grandma Spicy and Aurelia that they should each file on property for themselves. To-gether they would have a ranch as big as Jack Ambler's!

Inside the store, which was overheated by a potbellied stove and smelled of tobacco, coffee, and vinegary pickles, Meg chose her purchases carefully. Filing fees and the law-yer's fee, she realized with a touch of guilt, had taken most of her ready cash, including that received from Jack for her lost cows and damage to the dugout. A room and supper last night at a boardinghouse down the street had taken a pre-cious fifty cents. But she had an idea.

Smiling and giving her best sales pitch, she managed to trade the last of her millinery goods to the storekeeper in ex-change for outing flannel to make baby clothes, for needles and thread, and for a bolt of woolen yardage to make warm winter clothing for the other children. There would be gar-ments for the women, too, if the cloth could be made to go far enough.

Her remaining small amount of cash went for food: dried apples, cornmeal, and vegetables to replace what was destroyed by the Rocking A cattle. She bought candles and, finally, canned milk. Sweet heaven, but she wished they had a regular milk cow, a nice Jersey!

In short order she was headed toward home in her wagonette, her breath and Butterfield's making small puffs in the chill air. She huddled into her coat, her mind going over the reasons the trip to Larned had been delayed once her decision had been made to go.

Old Joe Dillard, the squint-eyed, barrel-built man Tog Elsberry had sent to pick up her gather of buffalo bones had been waylaid by masked riders on one of his trips, and been warned not to help the women at the springs. The riders were hired by Jack Ambler, Meg was sure. The children had found Joe, beaten bloody, on one of their forays for fuel chips. She had brought him by wagon to the homestead where he was laid up a couple of days with cuts and bruises.

Joe Dillard had no sooner recovered enough to stubbornly haul off the last of her bones as ordered by his boss, when four of the children simultaneously came down with dreadful sore throats and fevers. Delicate little Helen Grace suffered the most. Pneumonia was feared, or one of the other child-killing diseases, but all of the youngsters had rallied under strong doses of onion syrup, hot broth, and the constant care of the four women.

Today's success erased a host of worries, or at least whacked them down to size. Of course, the new claims she'd obtained brought their own set of fresh problems.

The land agent had given her fair warning about "claim jumpers." Now that word of the opening of free lands in western Kansas was spreading, there would be shady types who liked to acquire improved land the easy way—by force or by fraud. The dollar-chasing scalawags he spoke about had no desire to work the land, their intention was to grab and then to sell the land off fast for ready cash. She would have to be on guard until she held clear, indisputable title to all her properties.

She would put up a fight like a body couldn't believe before she would be cheated or bullied out of her land. She felt for the .44 riding her hip, glad for the feeling of security it gave her. She wasn't sure she could kill another human being, but she wouldn't hesitate to wound them, to stop them from taking what was hers.

It was well into the night of the second day since she had left the homestead when she drove Butterfield into the yard under a high moon, skirting the elk rack, and the huge pile of cow chips. She had fallen asleep on the way, but had gotten home. Hardly able to keep her eyes open, she unloaded the wagon into the shed. She unhitched and rubbed Butterfield down with an old burlap bag, watered him, and staked him to graze. She headed in the dark for the soddy, found her spot in the crowded room where the others snored softly, and crawled into bed. She was eager to tell what she had done, but the good news would have to wait until morning.

"You're as insane as Grandma Spicy!" Aurelia railed at Meg when she told her about the acquisition of additional lands over breakfast. "We can't take care of what property we have; we can't afford seed or proper implements. Why on earth would you think we need more land?"

To begin with, Meg protested, Grandma wasn't crazy, her poor old mind just slipped a cog now and then and Aurelia should lower her voice. Grandma had gone to gather eggs, Lucy Ann was at the spring. The children, having eaten breakfast first, had gone to their cattle work, the youngest ones playing in the yard.

But Aurelia stormed on, "That money could have gone for

a new stove or a cow, which the Lord knows we surely need."
Tears filled her eyes. "It would have paid for train tickets out
of here."

"Aurelia, I thought you wanted to stay. You and Grandma
Spicy could take up land yourselves, next time we have
money for filing fees. We have a golden opportunity here."

"You're not listening to me, Meg Brennon." She shook
her finger. "You are the one who wants land and more land,
not me. I'm leaving here as soon as my good-for-nothing
brother-in-law comes to his senses and returns for me and my
children. I wouldn't stay in this godforsaken country if they
paid me all the gold in the world to do so!"

Meg silently suspicioned Harlan was never coming back,
any more than Aurelia would get up the gumption to leave on
her own as long as she had a roof over head, even a sod roof
she hated.

Grandma Spicy came in from outside carrying three eggs
she'd found in the hen coop they had built for the chickens.

As it turned out, she wasn't interested in Meg's proposal,
either. "Don't care to live alone, like I'd have to do if I
homesteaded my own place. I got serious doubts I'd live long
enough to prove up anyways." She shook her head, dis-
missing the whole idea. "There ain't no use atall of me filin' a
homestead."

Meg thought her reasons for building up their holdings
were sound, but she couldn't make the others understand
that they needed the land for security. In her mind, she saw it
as a fortress, a wall against invaders, against Jack Ambler's at-
tempts to drive them out, in particular. "The land agent says
we're wise to take land now, that others will be flocking here
to western Kansas like crows to a corn patch, by next
summer. I know in my soul, too, that it is only a matter of
time before Jack Ambler wakes up, stops taking for granted

that we will leave here on his orders. Once he catches on that we aren't leaving no matter what he does to us, he will take up land all around us, by some legal fashion or pure outlawry, and try squeezing us out like a python killing a frog."

Her discussion of the Timber Culture Act, and the land she had taken under it, set Aurelia off worse than ever.

"Trees? That's just jim-dandy! How are we to work that much land, and plant trees anyone with good sense knows won't grow? You really have taken leave of your senses, Meg! Don't you think that if trees could grow out here, that God and nature would have taken care of it already, there would be trees growing here?"

The truth to these last remarks of Aurelia's made Meg uncomfortable. "I don't expect to make it happen overnight, for pity's sake. The first year will be spent mostly to get the soil prepared for planting. Another crop could be grown on it the next year, to pay for the tree seedlings to put out the third year. The requirement just calls for a grove of healthy, thriving trees to be growing over eight years' time."

"Which is impossible. Precious little rain falls in this part of the country. There's no way to keep water on that many trees from the springs, no way. They won't grow." Aurelia dried a plate so hard Meg was afraid it would break.

"Well, I'm going to try anyway." The land agent indicated it was unlikely the timbersteads would be officially checked on. A nosy neighbor, or a claim jumper wanting her property, might make a report if she failed to live up to the rules. Not that that mattered. She was going to do everything possible to live up to the requirements so that in eight years all that land belonged to her. If it wouldn't work, and she had to relinquish the timber claim, she would still have her purchased land and her homestead claim. Three hundred twenty acres to be exact, and a lot more than she arrived there with.

* * * * *

Lucy Ann had let out the seams of her dresses to accommodate her expanding girth until they couldn't be let out any more. She was a chunky girl to start with; the children didn't seem to notice her expanding girth. In private, Lucy Ann and Grandma and Aurelia sewed tiny soft white garments. A couple of wrappers were made for Lucy Ann when her other clothes no longer fit. She found it more and more difficult to get around and was excused from heavier work as her time drew nearer.

Lad needed to be prepared about the coming baby. They all agreed that the arrival of his sister's half-Indian baby was going to be an awful shock to him. Lucy Ann, dreading the moment, continued to put it off.

Most of November Meg bundled up against the cold and went out to work—cutting and stacking sod, building her own soddy, calling on the others for help as she needed it. She built close to the corner of her other property, and the corner of the Voss youngsters' claim, so she wouldn't be far away. Slowly, the soddy went up, followed by an open-sided shed to provide shelter for Butterfield. As her buildings were added to the others already there, they began to resemble a small village.

Days turned into weeks, weeks into months. Autumn chill turned into frigid winter cold. When Meg wondered aloud why Jack Ambler had not bothered them of late, Aurelia retorted that it was because the rancher *knew* they would kill themselves by freezing to death or by starvation.

Meg did worry about Lucy Ann, and her birthing time to come, but Grandma Spicy insisted she had delivered so many babies back in Missouri she'd lost count. She'd bring the baby, there would be no trouble.

How long ago Grandma had midwifed was anybody's

guess. She was old and could get confused. If it came to that, Meg hoped she and Aurelia could safely deliver the child.

Days passed, mostly uneventful. Thankfully, they had food and fuel supplies to see them through 'til spring, providing they were careful.

They splurged for Christmas, which was celebrated with quiet joy. Each child got a precious lump of sugar with their breakfast oatmeal. Aurelia served a delicious dinner of fried rabbit, potatoes, creamed hominy, applesauce, custard pie, and pumpkin pie.

Using kitchen knives, the boys had carved small wooden dolls for the little girls, wooden spoons for the women. In turn, the boys were made silly-headed with pleasure over real jackknives Aurelia had bought the one time she went to Dodge. Frontier boys ought to have them, she had conceded, having hidden the pocketknives away for that special day.

By remodeling old clothes and using the new fabric Meg bought in Larned, each person had at least one new garment. It was not a bad ending to what had been a rough year for them all.

Believing she had done enough to antagonize Ambler by taking additional lands and building herself a soddy and outbuildings he wouldn't expect to see, Meg was careful to keep her cattle and the Vosses' on their own property. On the coldest days, she told the boys to stay inside and help Aurelia keep the fires up, while she took on the herding chores.

Snow had been spitting off and on most of the winter, sometimes piling up several inches, to be burned off by a bright sun next day. Late in January, it began to snow in earnest, the wind blew fierce. Looking out at the gale, the depth of white over everything, Grandma Spicy announced they had a sure enough blizzard and had better be ready.

Piles of hay were brought in to be twisted into braids for additional fuel. Cow chips were stacked high in the Arbuckle box by the fireplace. Ice on the spring pond was broken to keep the water running free. Every available container was filled with water and brought inside. To make sure they did not run out of food, it was decided to make do with two meals a day, or one hot meal if it came to that. Candles were conserved for times when they were most needed. They went to bed early, soon after sunset.

From the day the blizzard began to blow, Lucy Ann had been having mild pains. Grandma said the baby wasn't coming just yet, but they better be ready for that, too.

Other than being mentally and emotionally prepared, there was little the women could do but wait. The infant's clothes were ready. Grandma had prepared antiseptic lotion from boiled soapweed root and goldenrod leaves. She had a cache of herbs, such as green-thread plant, for making a soothing tea should Lucy Ann need it for pain.

Meg was at the main soddy thawing their drinking and cooking water. The buckets of water had frozen only two feet from the fireplace!

She held her breath as Lucy Ann, who had had a bad night, drew Laddie aside to explain to him that she was about to have a baby. Because of what the Indians had done to her, she told him softly, the infant would likely be dark-skinned, an Indian baby.

For an eternity, Laddie stared at his sister, his face puckered in a terrible frown as he absorbed what she was telling him. Then he jerked aside from Lucy Ann's reaching hands and bolted through the door, letting in an icy blast as he raced out. Lucy Ann grabbed her shawl and started after him.

"Stay here!" Meg ordered. "I'll go after him."

"No, he needs me!" Lucy Ann shook free of Meg's grip and rushed outside.

It was only seconds before Meg followed into the blinding white, but already the two of them had disappeared from sight. She could hardly see as close as her hand. Frantic to know which direction to take, she called out, "Lad? Lucy Ann?" A thick quiet was her only answer.

With effort, she made out Lucy Ann's path in the snow. It was fast being changed by the swirling wind. She plowed after her, Jack's words a chant in her mind, "Some of you won't be alive come spring."

She pushed on against the cutting wind, her water-filled eyes straining for some sign of Lucy Ann or Laddie. She called out, again and again, the wind forcing her words back down her throat. She had so little time before the tracks ahead of her would be filled, erased. Anybody could get easily confused with no landmarks to go by.

Finally, she made out a shadow ahead through the white. She caught up with Lucy Ann a few minutes later. She grabbed her shoulders, shouting above the wind, "Lucy Ann, you have to go back! Think of the baby!"

"No, I have to find Laddie. Oh, dear Lord, which way did he go?" She gripped Meg's arms as they both peered into the swirling snow. Suddenly, a spasm of pain caught Lucy Ann and she dropped to her knees, arms wrapped around her body.

Meg pulled her up, held her. She gave a silent prayer of thanks moments later when she saw that Aurelia had followed close behind her. "Take her back, Aurelia, she's in labor. It's your time, Lucy Ann, you have to go back by the fire. You have that child out here and you'll both die of this freezing cold!"

Lucy Ann, shivering, whimpered, "Find him, Meg, please

find Laddie. Don't let him die, please." Her voice broke on a sob which ended on a whistling breath as she was caught by another contraction.

"I'll find him," Meg promised. "Aurelia, get her back to the house, fast. Let Grandma know it's her time. I'll keep looking for Laddie before he gets too far. Take her, go—!"

Meg searched on, coming back every so often to the soddy as a starting point in a new direction. She found no trace of Laddie; her shouts against the wind brought no answer.

She was losing time. She went back and got Butterfield so that she might search greater distances. It was impossible to see. As she plowed through the deepening snow on horseback, she told herself that there wasn't a lot she could do except hope her calls would bring Laddie in her direction.

Finally, returning a second or third time to the area near the sinks, she heard terrible ripping screams, rambling words of fear and rage. "No! I hate them! I'll kill 'em, kill 'em!" bounced from a wall of deathly silence. He had to have wandered all over the place before coming here. Icy shivers traveled her spine as she halted Butterfield to listen.

She squeezed her eyes shut, let the biting snow whip her as the screams, the tearful shouts raged on and on. In spite of the cold, she felt relief so intense her blood warmed with it. She wanted to shout, but joyfully, herself. She had found Laddie. And Laddie had found his voice.

Trauma robbed Laddie's ability to speak and trauma, again, had given it back. "Lad, are you all right? Where are you?" The muffled reply came a long moment later: "H-here" brought glad tears she had been holding in check. She whipped Butterfield through the drifts toward the sound. "I'm coming, Lad!"

Chapter Twelve

When they got back to the soddy, Meg pulled Laddie's heavy outer clothing off him. "Go over to the fire," she said, giving him a little push. "I'll bring a pan of water to thaw out your poor hands and feet. Don't touch your ears or they might break off; they are likely frostbitten." He was a bluish color and shivered so hard his teeth clattered. "How is Lucy Ann?" she asked the other women, her glance darting to where Lucy Ann lay on the cot under a buffalo robe.

"Pains have let up a little," Grandma told her, "but they'll be back fulsome."

"I'm all right." Lucy Ann struggled up off the cot to embrace her brother. Deep concern filled her eyes as she held him away to study him. "Laddie, you listen to me. You ought not to've run out in the cold that way, you could have frozen to death. We're lucky you're alive. What if Meg hadn't found you? I told you that other time, don't run off from your troubles. We got to stand our ground."

He looked up at her, shaking, tears spilling from his eyes. She went on, "It's not my fault what happened to me, and it isn't the baby's fault, either. No more than it's your fault half your hair and your speaking voice is gone. I'm going to be brave about this, an' I need you to be brave, too,

Lad. It'll mean so much to me."

He nodded, wiped his nose, and gave her a hard hug as a sob caught in his throat.

He was still visibly shivering and Lucy Ann said, "Go on now, get yourself warm. Pray you don't get pneumonia from being out in the cold so long."

Meg watched the boy closely, waiting for him to speak. She didn't imagine that he seemed different. There was resignation in his face, his body movements, in response to Lucy Ann's speech. But beyond that, a knowing eagerness emanated from him. She was sure he wanted to speak, but was afraid to try in front of the others. When she had found him, he had told her in a shivering young voice, husky and halting from disuse, that he was okay and wanted to go home.

"Laddie got his voice back," she declared, rubbing her hands together in front of the fire, looking from Laddie to the others.

It took a moment for her announcement to register. And then Lucy Ann was on her feet again from the cot, waddling to Laddie as fast as she could. "You can? You can speak?"

"I—I think so," he said, and everyone laughed.

It was hardly noticed that Lucy Ann's contractions had begun again as the children closed in on Lad, getting him to say his ABC's, asking him to answer riddles, sing lines to songs. He laughed with them, and in a while began to talk nonstop, just to hear himself. He talked about the snowdrift that nearly buried him, a big black crow he saw riding a cow's back. About ice thick enough to skate on at the sinks, but that had better be broken up soon so the cattle could drink.

Meg took note of the lines of pain in Lucy Ann's face, while the others continued to marvel over Lad. "Can you get to my place, dear?" she asked her quietly, sitting on the edge of the cot. "You'll have privacy there. I can take care of you, and Grandma will come, too. The children—will need their sleep over here, later."

Lucy Ann nodded, let herself be bundled into shawls, and then a blanket. As they went out, Lucy Ann told Lad over her shoulder, "You save some of that gab for me, hear?"

He looked at her with a frown. "Lucy Ann—?"

"I'll be all right, I'll be all right," she told him. "I haven't," she told Meg, "heard him say my name for the longest time. It's pure music." She gave a little jerk, catching her breath, as a pain passed over her.

After Lucy Ann was put to bed in her soddy, Meg went to the spring for fresh water which Grandma set on the fireplace to boil. Lucy Ann claimed she didn't hurt much, except for her back, although the contractions were coming closer together, and were more intense with the passing of time.

Grandma placed a knife under the bed. "That'll cut the pain," she said matter-of-fact. She had Lucy Ann sit up so she could massage her back and her thighs.

Aurelia came to the soddy occasionally to check on Lucy Ann's progress. She brought necessities: a stack of clean cloths, another blanket to keep Lucy Ann warm, the layette Lucy Ann had prepared for the infant's first clothes.

"If we had a proper stove with an oven," she lamented, "we could sterilize the birthing cloths and the thread for tying off the navel."

Grandma answered without looking up, "Take everythin' on back then, an' hang it over the fire. But not so close to burn. If it'll make you feel better, that'll do for sterilizing." She added, "We got time."

Aurelia sniffed, gathered up the cloths, layette, and spool of thread. "Maybe if I put things a few at a time in an empty clean kettle," she said over her shoulder as she departed with them.

"The children are all asleep," she said on the fourth trip over to Meg's soddy. "How is Lucy Ann?"

Meg spoke from where she sat by the bed, wiping perspiration from Lucy Ann's forehead. "I hope, if I have a child someday, I do as well as this dear girl." Lucy Ann breathed hard, unable to speak. Her contractions were coming hard and fast, one on top of the next with no time to rest in between. She didn't complain, but she held Meg's hand so tightly her hand felt broken and it was going numb.

Grandma took a peek under the blanket that covered Lucy Ann's knees. "Goin' to be anytime now, girl." She looked at Lucy Ann, who was white as a sheet, her eyes rolling up as though she might faint. "You hang on, darlin', don't give up on us." She spoke very loud, to penetrate through Lucy Ann's pain, her near-unconscious state: "I want you to push when I tell ya and push good."

Lucy Ann nodded, gave a quivery little moan.

" 'Bout time," Grandma said, rolling Lucy Ann's chemise up around her waist. She slipped a birthing cloth under her to absorb the blood and covered her again. She gave Lucy Ann a piece of leather. "Bite down on that, daughter; bite it in two if you have to."

Lucy Ann took the leather in her teeth, bit down in a grimace, and groaned deeply.

"Now!" Grandma said in a few minutes from her position. "Push, honey." After a few seconds she straightened up, looking at Lucy Ann whose eyes were shiny with pain. "Whoa, just rest now. Yes, sweetie, breathe deep. There." She looked under the blanket. "Push again, push! Lay back now, take a passel o' deep breaths. There, now."

The other women worked with Lucy Ann, breathing almost as hard, pushing at least in their thoughts, fingers crossed against her pain.

"Push again! Push, darlin', push!"

Meg's eyes filled with tears for Lucy Ann's struggle. Aurelia stood by, eyes wide.

"Consarn' little youngun, anyhow," Grandma exclaimed suddenly, smearing her hands with the soapweed-goldenrod lotion. "This is goin' to hurt like hellfire, Lucy Ann, but I got to help this baby along." She ducked under the blanket, mumbling to herself.

Lucy Ann let out a cry, a moan, and bit her lip, drawing blood. Meg wiped it away, blind with tears, giving her the leather that had slipped away.

"There we are, our little one's a-comin'!" Grandma crowed, coming out from the blanket with a wide smile. "I seed a little head, lotsa hair. Push, Lucy Ann, honey, push!"

Lucy Ann half-raised, pushed so hard her face was mottled and distorted out of shape. She threw her head back, wailed, took a deep breath and pushed again, and pushed, and pushed.

Meg's flesh popped out in goosebumps when Grandma shouted, "Got us a child! Got us a little 'un. There, baby, there." She held the tiny cinnamon-colored morsel up, gave the bottom a swat. The baby's cry—quivering, sweet, life-affirming—filled the room.

Lucy Ann lay back, laughing, crying, sucking air into her lungs. "B-boy—or g-girl?" Her wadded chemise was wet with perspiration and her hair hung in damp ringlets. Meg stroked back Lucy Ann's hair from her temples, covering her again temporarily against chills.

"Got us a girl," Grandma chortled, "an' she's pretty as a picture. Gimme the knife and thread. I got to cut the cord, tie it off on the babe."

In another minute, Grandma Spicy handed the slippery infant to Aurelia who waited with a baby blanket. "Keep that little 'un warm," Grandma directed, "while I see to her momma." She tossed back the cover, massaged Lucy Ann's abdomen, gently, over and over. In a while she caught the afterbirth and handed it to Meg in a pan. "Take it outside somewhere, but first bring me that other pan of warm water an' a clean cloth, so I can clean this girl up. She's plumb tuckered, but she did a good job, a good job."

"So did you, Grandma." Outside, Meg stood in the freezing cold and wept. For the new life, for the fact that Jack Ambler was dead wrong. Lucy Ann and her baby were going to be all right. Laddie had been found before he froze to death. They would all make it through this winter, and many other winters to come.

Two days after the arrival of Lucy Ann's baby girl, whom she named Rachel Marisa Voss, Meg overheard Lad telling Joshua and David John: "If my sister's baby turned out to be a boy, I was goin' to teach him to hate Injuns. I was goin' to teach him to help me *kill* Injuns when he growed up. But a girl—a girl ain't good for nothin'."

Meg wanted to scold, to correct him, to point out that what Lucy Ann had been through was hardly "nothin'," that women's part in sustaining humankind was a miracle to beat miracles. But he was a boy and, in time, a man grown, he would know that truth for himself.

She loved Lad. He was obedient, mostly smart, sensitive, but she thought he would bear watching. Even a normally good youngster could think of mean things to do to another child they didn't like. And Lucy Ann's infant, tiny Rachel, was helpless.

To save fuel as winter wore on, Meg spent most of her indoor time at the original soddy with the others. She was there, brushing little Helen Grace's lovely hair, the day a "hullo the house" sounded from outside. "Wait," she said, when Joshua went to open the door. She waved him back to the game of tic-tac-toe he and the other boys had been playing in front of the fireplace with charcoal on a shovel blade. Grandma, seated on one of the cots, looked up from her mending, poked her needle in the pair of overalls, and laid them aside. Aurelia turned from trimming candlewicks at the table. Lucy Ann, in the rocker, held her nursing infant a little tighter.

They hadn't seen another human being for many long wintry weeks and had felt isolated from the outside world.

A peek through the window showed nothing but a snowbank. Cautiously, Meg opened the door a crack. A Rocking A cowboy stood there; she remembered him from his unusual name. "Hello. You're Mr. Admire Walsh?" He was maybe twenty-two, twenty-three years old.

Deep blue eyes beneath burly dark brows lit up at her remembering who he was. "The same," he said, "but call me Ad. Howdy." He nodded and waited, Adam's apple bobbing in his throat. He smelled of fresh cold air, and something else. A blood smell. Snowflakes clung to his thick black moustache and beard, and his tall, wide-brimmed hat. There was fresh blood on the front of his coat.

"Is there something I can do for you?" Meg hung tight to the door, ready to slam it. The red smears on his heavy coat were worrisome, although his expression was friendly.

He motioned with his head back over his shoulder. "Shot two antelope, drug one this far, but I can only take one back to the ranch on my horse. Figured you folks might take one?"

"Goodness, yes, if it's only going to waste. Thank you!" Meg opened the door wider and saw the buff-colored animal lying in the snow just to the side of the doorway. The other one lay across the cowboy's tall steel dust, off to the left.

Aurelia joined her in the doorway. "We have hot coffee on,

Mr. Walsh, if you'd like to come in for a cup."

" 'Deed," he said, after a moment's thought. "I'll put my horse in your stable if you don't mind." A few minutes later he was back. He stomped snow from his boots, brushed it off his clothes, then came inside. Immediately, his eyes hunted for something in the room. He nodded and spoke to the others, seeming to find what he was looking for when his glance fell on Lucy Ann seated in the rocker nursing baby Rachel. A corner of Rachel's shawl covered her breast. He looked at the small bundle in her arms a long time, shock in his face. His high cheekbones and broad forehead, the only skin visible above his black beard, turned beet-red.

Recovering some, he went to the table where Aurelia had set out a cup of steaming coffee, a plate of sliced bread, jam, and beans. He thanked her shyly and slid onto the offered keg-chair. He ate quickly, his eyes traveling every few minutes to Lucy Ann and the baby. Finally, he and Lucy Ann smiled shyly at one another.

Trying to sound as if it were only a neighborly question, and nothing to do with her worry about Jack's next move against her, Meg asked after his boss.

"Jack got into a fracas over a woman and he's been cooling his heels in the Dodge City jail. Luckily, there ain't a lot of work on the ranch this time of year, so no harm done there. Most of the hands went back to their homes for the winter, only takes a small crew of us—me, Bama, Burch, and Tidwell—to look after the cattle. Not a lot to do midwinter," he repeated, " 'cept hunt, when the weather allows it."

Meg was grateful that Jack's money and influence in their part of the country still hadn't gotten him off punishment. His time in jail provided her further respite from his plans to drive them out. It was news she was very glad to hear. Relaxed, she returned to fixing Helen's hair, braiding it into silky pigtails.

"We appreciate the meat, Mr. Walsh," Lucy Ann spoke up from her chair.

She might have honored him with knighthood, from the smile that wreathed his face turned toward her. "Mighty welcome," he said, "be pleased if you'd call me Ad." He was looking at the baby again, no longer nursing but asleep. Lucy Ann had buttoned up her bodice. Nothing showed of the infant, wrapped in white flannel, but her tiny dark face and a sprig of black hair. "Boy or girl?"

"Girl." Lucy Ann smiled, her heart-shaped face glowing with pride in her infant. She raised the baby to her shoulder, patted its back. A soft infant burp sounded.

"What'd you name her?" The cowboy tossed back a big swig of coffee and wiped his mouth.

"Her name is Rachel Marisa."

He got up, came closer, squatted down. "Mighty pretty name for a pretty child." But he wasn't looking at the baby, he was looking at Lucy Ann who turned prettier under his gaze. "Your mister must be proud a' you both," Admire told her.

"There's no mister," Lucy Ann answered him quietly. She added, "He's—dead."

Witnessing the scene, Meg could only think, *My goodness. My goodness.*

The cowboy got ready to leave soon after. When he asked if there was anything he could do for them, Meg thanked him again for the meat but told him they needed nothing else. They were women and supposed to fail—she didn't want them beholden to anyone from the Rocking A.

For the second time, Lucy Ann surprised Meg by speaking up. "The younguns say the wind blew some young willow trees down, yonder by the river. Maybe if they had help, they could bring them here and cut them up for fuel. Don't go to no trouble, but if you happen to be by this way again, Mr. Walsh, maybe you could give the boys a hand. We can pay you with supper, Aurelia is a fine cook. Maybe next time there will be pie. Her dried peach pie is the best in the world."

Lucy Ann, who usually fled from the sight of strangers, was getting as talkative as her brother! Meg decided. And not a bad thing, either.

When she spoke about it later in amused, private conversation, Lucy Ann answered, "Admire Walsh is a good man. When those Rocking A cowboys come here, I saw that about him, right off. *He* didn't laugh at what we're tryin' to do here. I saw him frownin' at the others for making fun. An' he wasn't one of them run the cattle over us, either."

Meg nodded slowly.

Lucy Ann's face turned pink. Blue eyes cast downward, she said, "I ain't claiming him, nothing like that. He probably wouldn't have me, but that don't mean we can't be nice to him when he's been nice enough to bring us fresh meat."

"Of course," Meg said. "You're right, Lucy Ann." What she didn't say was that she wouldn't be surprised to find Ad Walsh on their doorstep a lot. She hoped he would understand about Baby Rachel, if and when Lucy Ann told him the truth. He had eyes for Lucy Ann, clear as day, and Lucy Ann, whether she would admit it or not, fancied the dark-haired cowboy as much. What would be would be. And how could a sweet romance between two good people stir up any worse, the troubled waters between them and the Rocking A?

That night, lying in bed, Meg remembered what Ad Walsh had told them about how Jack was spending the winter. He hadn't backed down, or given up his intention to drive them out of the country as she might have hoped. He was still out there, with heaven knew what ideas for getting rid of them.

Best she remember that a lull was just that and not a finish to a battle.

She brought her Indian blanket up closer around her chilled face and, shivering, tried to relax and sleep.

Chapter Thirteen

Thin sunshine leaked from the sky. Spring rain and a hard hailstorm had made sod at the place Meg called "The Rocks" soggy. Perfect conditions, she told herself, wiping perspiration off her forehead with her sleeve, to dig limestone.

With her spade, she scraped the sod away from an outcropping, marked blocks, then began to chop them free with her grubbing hoe. Precious hours had been used last year just keeping cows away from the garden and spring. Stone fences would make a difference. This year's bigger garden was just poking through the ground in tiny green shoots, and she wanted a decent harvest, or else. She couldn't even consider what else.

She straightened and rubbed her aching back. She looked around, enjoying the morning serenity and being alone for a change. There were times over the long winter just past, cooped up with the others, she had felt spring would never come. She smiled, puffing a little with pride that they were still there, Jack Ambler be hanged.

As far as she knew, he was still serving time in Dodge.

Maybe he didn't know that his hand, Admire Walsh, was courting Lucy Ann on a fairly regular basis.

When Ad first expressed his wish to court her, Lucy Ann

had told him the truth about what happened to her at the hands of the Sioux, and that her tiny Rachel was half-Indian. They didn't see him again at the homestead for weeks. Sad as they felt, it was not as cruel as the case of a man they'd heard about, who shot and killed his wife after "a buck got to her."

Then Ad was back, asking Lucy Ann's forgiveness, telling her that he couldn't forget her. He understood that she had nothing to do with what happened to her, nor did her child. He had given the matter plenty of thought, and he hoped Lucy Ann would let him continue to come around.

The pair were a sight to see. Watching them together, seeing their shared happiness, gave rise to envy in Meg's own heart, but she put those feelings aside. She was already married to a man she had no use for and never intended to have truck with again. She might feel free of him, most of the time, but legally she was in no way free. Not free to think of another man, a happy marriage, children. Best to be content with her own form of single blessedness.

She sighed, stood straight, and looked around her. That's when she saw the man. Actually the crouched shadow of a man on the rocks where they spilled together above and several yards to her right. Her breath caught sharply, wondering who it might be, and how long she had been watched. Was he a claim jumper?

Or Jack Ambler?

The figure, now he'd been spotted, stood up and stepped out into clear view. Not Jack, the man was short and stocky, and he wore a dust-covered brown suit and derby.

She began to tremble and it was hard to stand, as she recognized the plain square face with its stubbled, sagging jaw in the shadow from his hat. It seemed a century ago that she had studied that face from hiding so as never to forget the man following her. Now, however he had managed to find her; he had caught up. Her terror drove deep, her heart seemed to stop, she wanted to run and couldn't move.

Finch. In a tired but hurried shuffle he came toward her through the rocks, his eyes boring into her. The desperation and determination in his movements were like spikes nailing her to where she stood.

She gripped the handle of her grubbing hoe tighter while her thoughts ran frantic and accusing: she'd been careless, brought this on herself. Wisely, last year she had left the homestead as little as possible. But this spring she'd already made several trips to Dodge. The first trip, before winter was really over, she'd taken Lucy Ann to a doctor there when she became seriously ill with milk fever. Another trip was made to replenish supplies depleted over the winter. A third, desperate journey was made just weeks ago to take out a mortgage on her Thorne property so she could buy seed, a milk cow, and, finally, an iron cookstove for Aurelia. She had hated to borrow money, but Aurelia had been right last fall when she said Meg had taken on too much by filing on more land.

Unfortunately she was now known by any number of people who could describe her as well as reveal where she homesteaded.

Because she'd gotten lax, almost forgetting her past, it had caught up with her. Frank Finch had found her.

In a gentlemanly gesture he removed his derby with his left hand while his right hovered near his vest, where he probably carried a pocket gun. He looked wildly satisfied that she was within reach, caught at last. He clapped his hat back on.

She could smell him. His sweat sharply overrode his stale bay-rum cologne. She could hear his puffing, excited breathing.

"So you've found me, Mr. Finch?" At his look of surprise,

she informed him, "Of course I know who you are. You've been trailing me for a long time. I know your name because I doubled back one time, after you'd almost caught me. Your name was on the hotel register. The hotel clerk guessed you were a bounty hunter and I was obliged to agree." *Sent after her by her husband and his family.*

He appeared relieved she knew the facts. "You're comin' back with me to St. Louis, to Malloy." He smiled, inching toward her. "Don't give me any trouble and we'll get along fine. We'll take your horse. I left that nag I hired in Dodge back there in the damn rocks and it run off. We'll ride double." He surveyed her in her raggedy dress, her muddied boots with holes in them.

She shook her head, answering him quietly. "I am not going anywhere with you, especially not back to Teddy Malloy. This place is my home now. Nothing, and no one, can drag me off it. Be warned, I'll fight you tooth and toenail." Pray God, she thought, to give her the strength to lift the damn grubbing hoe high enough off the ground to whack him unconscious, if she had to.

He looked surprised at her animosity, and his own face swelled with anger, like filled air pockets on a frog. "You are Ted Malloy's legal wife! You've got to go back, by law."

Two-handed, she held the hoe menacingly in front of her. "The law didn't prevent Teddy Malloy nearly killing me once and won't again. The law says a man can do that to his wife, if he wants. But I won't have it that way. I swore back then that I'd never give him a second chance to finish what he started. I won't go back to St. Louis, or to Teddy Malloy. Tell him to divorce me on grounds I abandoned him. Tell him I'm dead and buried, or you couldn't find me, or whatever else you want to tell him. But I won't go back."

A divorced woman was considered in nearly the same light

as a prostitute, but even that was preferable to being beaten, perhaps to death, by Malloy—or at the very least having her dreams, the chance to be herself, killed.

He stepped closer, threatening, his mouth white-rimmed with rage. "You gave your vows to obey! You're a woman, his wife; you've got no say in this!" His right hand clasped the bulge of the pocketed gun.

"*I* say I do have rights. And I choose not to go back to Teddy Malloy, ever." Angry desperation made her perspire at the same time fear gave her chills, and the grubbing hoe wobbled in her grip. She doubted Finch would listen to reason but she tried. "I made a mistake believing I loved Teddy Malloy. I take the blame for marrying him. But I don't intend to pay the rest of my life for a misjudgment made because I was young, inexperienced, and alone. I am free of his maliciousness, and I intend to stay free."

He was losing patience; his dark eyes glittered. "Don't none of that matter to me. That's between you and Malloy. Deal with him when I get you back there."

"I said," she jerked away as he grabbed her arm roughly, "I'm not going back!" She held the grubbing hoe in front of her, knowing at the same time what little protection it was against his gun.

Her continued defiance unnerved him and he suddenly snapped. With a crazed growl, he yanked the grubbing hoe out of her hands. He tossed it aside like it was no more than a matchstick, leaving her feeling vulnerable. Before she could move he grabbed her again. With all the strength she could muster, she fought, scratching and kicking. It was useless against his arm-breaking grip. He brought out his derringer, struck her across the face with the butt of it, nearly sending her to her knees as she stumbled. She gasped with pain and tried to cover her face. He struck her with the gun twice more.

Blood spilled into her eyes. Dizzy with pain, she dropped to her knees. She grabbed at his gun, felt her fingers slide over it, over his legs, as she went down. She closed her eyes to blot him out standing over her, his gun pointed at her face. A shot rang out and she jerked at the sound. Frank Finch dropped across her.

Bleeding, sick at her stomach, fighting not to lose consciousness, she struggled out from under Finch. She sat up, and looked around in a daze. Lad stood some ten to fifteen feet away, Lucy Ann's .44 hanging from his hand.

Speechless, she motioned him over, her trembling arms outstretched. Tears spilled from her eyes to mix with the blood on her face as she found her voice. "Oh, Laddie, come here." She shook hard. "Th-thank you." Her face pained so much, it was going numb. Nausea rose in her throat, and she fought it back.

He ran over, kneeling beside her. His young face was white with shock, with worry for her. "Aurelia thought she saw a stranger skulkin' around. We saw a horse headin' back to Dodge but couldn't catch it. She said to bring you the .44 just in case you needed it. There wasn't no time to give it to you, that feller just kept hittin' you. He was goin' to shoot you!"

"It's all right, now," she said huskily, "all right." She drew him to her, needing desperately at that moment to feel his closeness. She said, choking, "You saved my life, Laddie."

They sat rocking in one another's arms while above them birds sang, a pocket squirrel came out from the rocks, saw them and dashed back out of sight. In a while she felt her strength flowing back, but she was still shaking. She wiped blood from her face on the hem of her dress. She crawled to where Finch lay, her bloodied fingers trying to find a pulse in his neck. "He's dead."

"Who was he? Why was he tryin' to hurt you?"

She thought a moment. With Finch dead, her past might be forgotten for good. She trembled. "He—he was a claim jumper, I think. He wanted to take our land." In a way it was the truth. As sure as sin, he would have parted her from her beloved land, maybe hurt the others in the process, if they tried to stop him.

"What we gonna do with him?" Lad came to crouch on his heels beside her. His hand sympathetically touched her shoulder.

She shook her head to clear the rocketing pain, the fuzziness that blurred her thinking, that edged her close to passing out. Should she report what happened? She supposed there was some kind of law governing the unorganized lands of western Kansas, she just didn't know what it was. Charlie Bassett was a law official, but she thought his jurisdiction was Dodge and Ford County. And why bring the law into the matter, anyway? Lad was justified in shooting Finch to save her. Any judge or jury would clear Laddie, and her, of wrongdoing.

"We have to bury him," she answered, "and might as well do it right here, dig down, put him under some rocks." If she reported Finch's death in St. Louis, it would be an open invitation to Teddy Malloy to find out where she was. God only knew what he would do to her for having had the gall to leave him, for not "learning her lesson" as he tried to teach it.

The knowledge that she truly was alive, would not have to leave with Finch, added to her returning strength and resolution. Weaving, she got to her feet, steadied herself, and asked Laddie's help. "Up there." They grabbed Finch's heels and dragged his body, bumping over the rocks, after them. After a few minutes' rest, they took turns digging his grave below the farthest limestone ridge on her property.

While she sat on the ground, watching as Lad took a turn

digging, she saw that some of the stone was different from the rest around them. Her overwrought mind registered a second on the fact that it looked like magnesia marble, and then she forgot it. They had killed a man; that, and his grave, must be kept secret forevermore.

If not—

When they were finished, she caught Lad's shoulders in a tight grip. "I don't think anyone will ever come looking for him, he was a terrible person. But if they do, *I* shot Fi— the claim jumper. Do you understand?" She shook him. "Do you promise to say what I'm telling you?"

"Sure." Laddie nodded. His eyes crinkled with worry. "Your face is awful cut up, Auntie Meg. We need to hurry home so Sister and Aunt Aurelia can take care of you."

Maybe, because he was young and had experienced savage violence firsthand before, he didn't seem overly bothered by the killing. And it had been to save her.

She thought briefly about the saddle horse Finch had hired. There would be curiosity when the horse returned without him. The livery stable owner might surmise Finch had been thrown and was on foot 'til he got aid. She doubted they would investigate, as long as they got their horse back.

"Lad, if . . . what happened today ever bothers you, worries you, come and talk to me about it. All right? It was a terrible thing to have to happen. I wish it never had. But I won't ever forget what you did for me."

He looked at her, his face solemn. "I wish somebody would have killed them Injuns before they killed my family and hurt Lucy Ann and took half my scalp. But that time, there wasn't nobody to do it. I'm glad this time I could save you."

She nodded, blinking away tears. She put her hand on his slim shoulder for support, and they started for her horse and home. From time to time she mopped her face on her sleeve. She would have to continue the lie about Finch to the others.

"He was a claim jumper," she explained later. Aurelia clucked over her, cleansing her face with soap and water. "Things got out of hand. He tried to kill me, so shooting him was the only way to stop it."

Gauging the seriousness of the situation as soon as they arrived, Aurelia had sent the children out to play, except for Lad, who refused to go and sat quietly in the corner, examining the callouses on his slender palms.

Grandma Spicy and Lucy Ann stood by, listening in silence, grabbing things for Aurelia as she needed them.

Aurelia spoke up as she applied homemade antiseptic lotion to Meg's face. "We need to tell somebody. We have to take his body into town."

"He's already buried." Meg shook her head. "What's done is done."

Aurelia gave Meg a long, disbelieving look. "You can't just kill another person and forget about it. Just like that."

"I didn't *just kill him,* the way you put it. And I won't forget about it as long as I live. What happened will plague me forever. What would you have me do, Aurelia? He tried to kill me, I defended myself."

"Perhaps so. I'm not saying you were wrong. I believe you were within your rights. But his death must be reported. There are laws, for goodness' sakes! Or ought to be, even in this dreadful country."

"I reckon there are laws. But sometimes a person has to settle things for themselves, when there is no law nearby at the time it's needed." She stole a look in Lad's direction; the words she'd used were nearly identical to the boy's earlier ones about his family's tragedy in Nebraska. "If you aren't satisfied with this, Aurelia, then you go dig him up. Find yourself a judge and jury to make sure everything is fair and square and socially proper. But as far as I'm concerned, what's done is done."

Grandma Spicy spoke up. "Meg is right. We know she wouldn't hurt no one, lessen she had to. Nothin' we do now will bring that feller back, an' we all know he was a bad 'un or he wouldn't've done what he done to her. Look at her face. Couple of them cuts is goin' to need a stitch or two."

Lucy Ann staunchly agreed. "Meg did what needed doing. The man might have killed her, and maybe Laddie, too. I couldn't stand to lose no more of my family. Sorry as I am somebody had to get killed, I'm glad it wasn't one of ours. I say we put it behind us."

Aurelia was eventually resigned. "It doesn't seem right, but I guess if the rest of you feel we should just let the matter go, so be it. An investigation would only take time and be a nuisance for us. And then no doubt we'd be found within our rights. If he had family, though, shouldn't they be told?"

"If he had family," Grandma snorted, "they'd be plumb ashamed of him, that be the truth of it. But his kind usually don't have no folks." She went for her needle and thread, and whiskey to help with the pain.

The women all looked at one another, hoping that to be so.

But Meg found the matter hard to set aside. For weeks she went around with a cold hollow at the pit of her stomach. She felt responsible for Finch's death, even if she hadn't pulled the trigger. She didn't like it that another human being died because of her. Nor, if she could turn back the clock and change what had happened, would it have been Laddie who did the actual killing. She hated that fact most of all. Lad was just a boy. He shouldn't have had to act on such a violent need, shouldn't have had to save her.

The bond begun earlier between the two of them, on the other hand, was even stronger. He showed her so much loving compassion after the beating it often brought Meg close to tears. He would always be her hero. He was not a killer. He had done what had to be done.

He had grown up some, too, in other ways that had once worried her. Now that his baby niece could coo, smile, and show two dazzling teeth, and especially reach for him, he'd become devoted to little Rachel Marisa.

Still, she personally couldn't forget that awful day anymore than she could change what had happened. It would be a heavy burden she'd carry forever.

The corn was in the ground, as was the wheat. Meg was in the garden cultivating, the earth crumbly warm beneath her bare feet, the day she heard the muffled footfalls of a horse approaching from behind her.

She turned and shaded her eyes with a dirty hand against the warm spring sunshine. "Admire!" she exclaimed, surprised to see him there, instead of hurrying to the house to see Lucy Ann. "Hello!"

He tipped his battered Stetson to her and grimaced slightly as his eyes took in her facial wounds, now healed but still showing pink scars and yellow-green bruising. He told her soberly, "Hoped I'd find you alone to talk a bit."

"Of course." She put aside her hoe, waved at a patch of grass, motioned for him to join her, and sat down.

"Thought you ought to know Jack's out of jail and back home," he said as he swung down out of the saddle. "He been by here?" She shook her head and he went on, "He ain't gonna like all this when he sees it." Sitting down, he waved around at her newly planted fields, the second soddy and outbuildings, and, further away, the ground she was turning for her tree patch. Ad, who had seen every bit of her building, plowing, and planting taking place, seemed to have a fresh, worrisome view of the results. As if from Jack's eyes.

"I warned him we women would be here 'til kingdom come. Bettering what we have is part of the picture. We can't make it any other way."

"I know that, and nobody wants you ladies to succeed here more than I do." He blushed slightly, brushed at his gangly dungareed knees, and looked out at the big blue sky.

"Because of Lucy Ann?"

"I got strong feelin's for her, couldn't bear to see her have to leave these parts," he admitted, meeting Meg's eyes and speaking earnestly. "I want her here 'til the two of us—" He fell silent. Finally, he went on, his voice low and savage, "I'd like to kill the Injuns what hurt Lucy Ann. I'd like to kill the bushwhacker that raped and cut my mother's throat and left her to die when I was a boy, too. But I cain't; those awful things is over and done."

He choked up for a minute, his eyes shiny, then he went on, "Lucy Ann told me about wantin' to die, that she purely intended to kill herself, after what the Injuns done to her. She says that would have been the easy way out. That ain't like her, though. Lucy Ann is strong. She kept herself goin' for her brother, for her little one. An' now, though I can scarce believe it, she cares for me, too."

"You are lucky, Ad, and Lucy Ann is lucky, too."

His face broke into a wide grin. "Now that's the truth, I am plumb lucky!" He stroked his coal-black beard. "That ain't what I come here to talk about, though." He pulled a piece of grass and gnawed on it for a second or two. "Jack heard something while he was doin' his time. Something about you."

She shook her head, hiding her rising alarm. "What did he hear? Are you sure it concerned me?"

"A feller was lookin' for a woman whose description fit you, Meg, durn close. Dark hair, gray eyes that look silvery. Pretty."

"I doubt if it was me, though."

"Well, it wasn't your name, Meg, they was mentionin.' Cass or Cassie or somethin' like that, the name was. The man who told Jack the story," he went on, "was servin' time for bein' drunk and unruly. Said a bounty hunter was offerin' money around town to anyone who could tell him how to find this woman he was describin' to 'em."

She shook her head, forced a smile. "Bounty hunter, looking for me? Not hardly. Do I look like a criminal, Ad?"

"Well, no!"

"And for heaven's sake, who would believe the story of a man sotted with drink?"

"Maybe a mix-up," Ad nodded, shifting uneasily. "I didn't think that it was you, that you committed any crime. I thought the man might be after you for somethin' else."

"No. Thank you for coming by to tell me, though." She spoke from the heart, then lied some more. "This has to be a mistake."

"Yeah," he said, without conviction, then added, "Watch your back, anyhow, Meg." He seemed to be weighing another thought before finally uttering it. "Sometimes they's things in a body's past that needs clearin' up, Meg. Like a boil on a cow's backside, ain't nothin' goin' to be right 'til it's took care of—opened up, aired, and put to healin'. Know what I mean?"

In his crude but gentle way, and without knowing the full particulars, Ad was advising her to face her past and take care of unsettled matters there, and soon, before Jack could use them as ammunition against her.

He was right, unfortunately. From the day of Finch's death, the idea had been in the back of her mind that she should return to Kerry Patch, face Teddy Malloy once and for all, and insist on a divorce. But it would take more than gumption. There was no money for a journey to St. Louis and to pay a lawyer. And how would the others manage without her for the time it would take to make the trip and be gone long enough to obtain a divorce?

Chapter Fourteen

Ad's advice, as good as it was, presented more questions than answers. Meg decided she *would* return to Kerry Patch and ask for a divorce as soon as it became possible. In the meantime she would hold back Jack Ambler however she could.

The women took a vow of silence on the matter of the man buried on their land. Even so, the grave by The Rocks was never far from Meg's mind as she labored only paces away at her stone work. The terrible event probably dwelled in the minds of the others only a trifle less.

Two days after Ad came to warn her, Jack arrived as she worked at The Rocks in bright spring sunshine. He dismounted and climbed toward where she stood watching him, stone hammer in hand. He stopped a few feet away, smiling. In spite of the fact that she was dirty and sweating, his gaze on her was probing, sensual and caused her to feel edgier on top of the reason that brought him.

"There was a man askin' about you around Dodge," he got right to the point. He stood with one booted foot in front of the other, balanced on the rock. He thumbed his hat back on his head, his gold eyes glittering. "Ad Walsh says you're not the woman, but I don't believe that. The description the bounty hunter gave fit you, exact. Was the bounty hunter by here? He seems to have up and disappeared." His gaze trapped her.

Months behind bars had left him a little gaunt, his tan faded. A freshly healed scar not there the previous fall traveled his jaw. "You're trespassing," she said finally, quietly, hefting her hammer a little higher to make the point, "and I don't know what you're talking about."

His smile widened as he seemed to look through her and see that she was lying. "You're sure? The bounty hunter was looking for a dark-haired woman your age, and some folks thought he rode out this way." He was enjoying himself immensely, toying with her.

Chills traveled her spine. "You're on a wild goose chase, Jack. That description could fit a dozen women around Dodge, hundreds in the state of Kansas."

"Or it could fit you."

She said quickly, "Don't you feel a little bit the fool, believing stories born from your jail companion's whiskey-soaked mind? He was probably delirious."

His expression grew serious, calculating, his tone much cooler. "Believe me, I'm no fool, so listen to me a minute. I may not have proof, but I know the man was after you, and he has disappeared plumb mysteriously." With a toss of his head, a smile, he finished, "With me, you wouldn't have to worry about that."

"I beg your pardon?" She was dumbfounded by the turn his words had taken. Was he going to pursue that ridiculous idea of his that a woman, hard up, would consent to be his mistress, just like that, rather than choose another route?

He moved nearer. "Listen, I'd take care of you, whatever your troubles. Buy you the finest clothes, a nice house. You're goin' to ruin yourself" —he nodded at her hammer, her appearance— "keepin' on the way you are."

153

Because he felt he had something on her, he believed she would admit defeat, would do exactly what he wanted? Be his mistress, marry him, or whatever other absurdity he had in mind? "And in exchange for your generous offer—which I don't need, because you are mistaken about this preposterous notion that I'm the woman being sought—I must get off my land? Send my friends packing when they really have no other place to go? Put myself and my land in your hands, hmm?"

"I fancy you, Meg, I swear I do, no matter if that's not your real name or what it was you did. Underneath those rags," he smirked, "you've got to be a fine-looking female. Sittin' around in that damn cell, I got to thinkin', in the right clothes, the right place, you—"

"You are truly insulting me, do you know that? I want you off my land, right now."

He stood there, staring at her for a long time before yanking his hat down over his eyes, but she could see that they glinted with anger. "You'll change your mind about this," he growled, "you'll have to. You might as well make it sooner as later."

"The word, Jack, is *never*. And please stay off my land. I will arm myself if I have to."

He shrugged, climbing on his horse. The wolfish grin returned. "We're in no way done with one another, you know that, don't you, Meg? We're not finished, not by a long shot."

She gripped the hammer in her hand, wanting to throw it after him.

For weeks, she drove herself: at stone work, at breaking more sod to eventually plant cottonwood seedling-switches on her timber claim. At bedtime, she fell into exhausted slumber only to have thoughts held dormant by work return in the deep of night to torment her. Hard labor was becoming less and less of an antidote to worry.

Jack returned twice more. But he learned nothing from her for his prowling, nothing from the others, either, or he would have used it. She knew better than to believe he had given up, however.

During May and June, a trickle of land-seekers that looked to become a possible flood, came by the homestead. At first, the sight of a stranger approaching filled her with dread. Suppose someone other than Jack came to investigate Finch's disappearance? Or what if Finch had time to notify Teddy Malloy of her location before he had approached her? Somehow, she had to find a way to get back to St. Louis and see to matters there.

As the visitors continued to come—mostly families looking for free land and a better way of life—she became less guarded. She welcomed them, offering drinking water for them and their animals. Sometimes they took a meal. When they needed a place overnight, pallets for women and children were provided in the soddy, the men given beds in the dugout cellar.

For the poorest families, meals and feed for their animals were free. But many folks were able to pay, and insisted on doing so. The sugar bowl in the box cupboard over Aurelia's stove filled encouragingly with coins and paper bills.

Meg continued to relax. Along with the other women, she relished the idea of having neighbors, however distant. People needed neighbors' help in times of sickness and disaster. Needed them for trading work and tools and ideas, and for sharing good times to keep up spirits. In truth, self-preservation depended on community aid. Alone they likely could not last, a fact Jack Ambler could count on.

Summer came on hot, dry, and windy. They had no rain for weeks. Meg watched their crops with a worried eye, praying they wouldn't frizzle to nothing in the heat.

Every day there were weeds to hoe out of the fields, but the grueling toil was worth it. They had lots of fresh corn to eat, tiny new potatoes, and early juicy melons. The wheat would soon be ready for cutting and stacking. Everything had to be done by hand, even the threshing of the grain. But someday she would have all the proper implements.

In mid-July, a tall, straw-haired Scandinavian and his blonde, blue-eyed wife and children spent three days at the homestead. The Hesslers had somehow missed the road to Dodge, where they expected to re-stock supplies and rest up. They were worn out from the heat and weeks of travel, were lonely for company, and they were more than willing to pay for bed and board.

It wasn't until the end of their stay that Mr. Hessler revealed his assumption that they were an established road ranch. Another traveler had told him of their fine hospitality and good food, leading him to believe Meg's and her friends' main intention out on the plains was to serve the traveling public.

"Not really," she corrected him with a smile of thanks for his compliments, "although I suppose that's what we've become. A road ranch." He was packing up his family to leave. She handed him a quarter-full gunnysack of fresh roasting ears he had purchased from her. He'd also bought early melons, several loaves of Aurelia's bread, and a precious cake of butter.

"What do you call this place," he asked as he climbed up beside his plump little wife, "if I was to mention it to other folks?"

A name sprang so quickly to Meg's mind it startled her.

The name had to have been there from the start, or at least for a long time, without her being outwardly aware. A bit fancy, maybe, for a dusty watering hole on the high plains, home to a handful of women and children, less than a half-dozen horses and a small herd of scrawny cows. For all that, this was a special place, a standard for everything meaningful to her. She told him, "Paragon Springs. The name to tell them is Paragon Springs."

Two weeks later, Ad came on one of his courting visits to see Lucy Ann and be treated to Aurelia's delicious pie and coffee. He told them that Will and Bethany Hessler had taken a claim ten miles north and west of them, and Will was busy breaking sod for his house while his family lived in a tent.

"Some west of that," he said, "a couple other families have taken land. Last time I was in Dodge, there were four, five wagonloads of folks, asking 'bout land to settle." He leaned back, a frown creasing his brow. "Jack Ambler ain't none too happy the way the wind is blowin'. 'Ceptin' you all here, so far he's managed to discourage folks off range considered the Rocking A's, sayin' there's been plenty of Injun trouble in these parts, that it never rains, the land won't grow nothin', that the only sure thing is starvation. With you all still here, and now others comin', he is real worried. An' worry don't do no good to his ornery streak."

"There is enough land in western Kansas for everybody," Meg said stoutly. "It's Jack's own fault he took the wide-open, unsettled range for granted. Just because he and others like him have grazed their huge herds on it for years, doesn't make the land theirs. Even if they think they paid the price fighting Indians." She considered, "No one has been hurt, have they? Any of the home seekers?"

"Not yet, though Jack ain't above wavin' his pistol under a nester's nose to encourage him on down the road. Mostly, he's been gettin' more land. Spreadin' out the boundaries of the Rocking A however and every which a way he can."

She'd worried about that, had imagined the Rocking A as a large python bent on squeezing the life out of a frog, *them*.

Ad continued, "Jack has now paid legal for a big chunk of land he's always used. Then he got as many as would of the Rocking A cowboys to homestead, preempt, and take timber claims. For Rocking A holdin's, of course, the way he tried with Thorne and McCoy. Jack had some tent shacks built on runners for his hands to sleep in. The sled shacks are took from claim to claim, so's to appear the claims are bein' proved up on, legal." He looked down at Lucy Ann, sitting quietly on a chair beside him, mending a shirt of Lad's. "I told him *no* to that. I want my own place, I want to get married."

A smile tugged at Meg's lips. "That's understandable," she said, watching Lucy Ann's face turn rosy.

"Well, it ain't understandable to Jack. I been fired."

"But that's not fair!" Meg protested.

Lucy reached out and touched Ad's arm as he went on, "Jack says he hates to lose me, but he only wants cowboys loyal to the Rocking A. And of late, I guess I ain't been." He grinned sheepishly. "I told some folks from Indiana where a good piece to settle on was, not far off the Rocking A range, and they took it. Jack found out and he was mad as hell. That's only the second-best piece I know about," he boasted, his grin widening. "The best one I want for myself, and my family." Again he looked at Lucy Ann, his dark eyes shy. She looked up and their glance caught, hopeful, yearning.

"You'd better file your claim right away, before Jack finds a way to take it up, too." Meg went to the stove for the coffeepot and poured their cups full again.

"I reckon I will. It ain't that far from here. It's a little south, on that year-round crick that flows from the Pawnee River up north." He raked fingers through his black hair, his manner worried. "Course now I ain't got no job, I got no way of payin' for improvements."

From the expectant way he was looking at her, Meg realized that he was asking her for a job. She could use more help, especially a strong, male hand, to help run Lucy Ann's place and her own, but she had little to pay him with unless they could turn a real profit.

She was thoughtful a moment, finally saying, "If you want to work off and on here at Paragon Springs, I'll pay you what I can." She told him about Mr. Hessler, how he had assumed they were running a road ranch. Taking her time at first, she began to reveal a plan that had been yeasting at the back of her mind.

"Besides selling an occasional meal and produce, I would like to stock supplies to sell to travelers who come through this way. General merchandise like beans, flour, medicinal whiskey, canned fruits and oysters. We could put up a bakery sign for Aurelia's baked goods; we could make and sell cheese and butter and smoked meat. We could sell hay and grain if I had help putting it up."

Aurelia listened from where she had been putting bread to rise. Grandma sat forward in her rocking chair. Meg told them, "I would like to be in a position to trade stock, our fresh horses and oxen for wayfarers' footsore, half-starved animals plus a few dollars in cash. A few weeks on good grass, the stock we take in trade would be in good flesh to trade again. We could even" —she took a deep breath— "if needed, repair wagons and shoe horses. You know, do blacksmithing."

"You done hired me!" Ad exclaimed, slapping his thigh.

All of them began to talk excitedly, making plans for the venture.

That same night, by the light of the summer moon, while Baby Rachel slept in her cradle, Ad Walsh—with fine new prospects under his belt—asked Lucy Ann Voss to become his wife.

Lucy Ann explained to her women friends next day, "I know Ad loves me. He cares for Baby Rachel. He says he won't let it be no never-mind who fathered her. He'll be her pa from now on. He's fond of Lad, too. But it's also for his ma, that he's doin' this. He's felt bad for years about what happened to her."

She went on, telling them, "He and his mama had a little farm up at Elwood, Kansas, on the Missouri River. There was only the two of them to do the work, his pa was dead of consumption. One day bushwhackers came."

She sighed. "Ad didn't know they was there right at first, he was hid out under the porch from his ma. He didn't want to weed the garden in the scorchin' heat, an' she was doin' the work alone. He'd gone to sleep an' didn't know what was happenin' to his mama 'til it was too late for him to help her."

Lucy had difficulty continuing. She closed her eyes, took a breath, then continued, "His mama had been raped and her throat cut. Those Rebel marauders ransacked the place and burned down the house and barn, while Ad escaped to hide out down by the riverbank. He was ashamed that he wasn't there in the garden to protect his mama. He took that shame to Missouri to the closest fightin', walkin' all the way. He lied about his age and signed up on the spot to fight for the Union."

She finished telling them, "He's a good man, through and through, and I know how lucky I am to have Admire Walsh to care for me and mine."

A week and a half later he was back with a stout little

preacher, the Reverend Van Wormer, from Larned. While there, Ad had also filed on his claim, just barely missed in Jack Ambler's land grab.

In spite of straitened circumstances for all of them, Meg wanted her dear friends' wedding to be as lovely, as memorable as could be managed. During Ad's absence, the children had helped her create a bower of willows by the spring, where the nuptials would take place. While the women sewed, cooked, and cleaned, the children had scoured the surrounding countryside for wildflowers. On each side of the bower, now the day had come, were arrangements of yellow goldenrod and spikes of white evening primrose in shiny sorghum-tin vases.

Baby-white asters and pink bush morning glory had been located, the blossoms picked the last minute and tied with ribbon for Lucy Ann's bouquet.

At the appointed hour, there was a flurry as the wedding party and guests found their places on boxes and barrels, the rest standing. The Hessler family had been invited, and claimed they would have traveled five times as far to attend the merrymaking. Ad had invited several of his old friends from the Rocking A. Lofty, Bama, Flan, and a half-dozen others whose names Meg couldn't remember, waited at the fringes, well-scrubbed, hats in hand, spurs jingling softly when they moved. If Ad had invited his former boss, he had chosen not to attend.

Aurelia, helping everyone to their places, looked elegant enough for a ball in spite of her chapped hands, weathered face, and sun-streaked hair. Her children, as she lined them up to watch the ceremony, looked like strangers. They wore their Sunday best, their faces were washed, hair slicked down—they were uncommonly well-behaved. Grandma Spicy, worn out from the work of the wedding, was asleep in the rocker brought out for her to sit in.

In front of the bower, Lucy Ann waited, her face rosy, eyes radiant. In her arms she held Baby Rachel; one hand clutched her nosegay of flowers. She had never looked more beautiful, more clean and sweet, with her cornsilk-yellow hair parted in the middle and formed in curls on her shoulders. She wore a made-over dress of Aurelia's, of pale blue china silk, with a draped overskirt trimmed with Val lace.

Admire, spiffed up in humble but clean cowboy garb, hat in hand, stood beside his bride-to-be. His black eyes snapped with a mix of pleasure and seriousness. His shoulders were boxed so square he could have held up a house on them. On the other side of him, looking just as proud, if a little nervous, stood his best man and brother-in-law to be, Laddie. They looked like a portrait, a little family already.

Meg, her throat thick with happiness, moved to take her place as Lucy Ann's honor attendant.

The cherub-faced preacher removed his plug hat and tossed it aside. Bible in hand, he spoke to Lucy Ann and Admire about the sanctity of marriage. About their duties to one another, to their future and present children—a few glances skittered to the dark little baby in Lucy's arms—and most of all to God. The rest of his patent phrases as he droned on and on, sounded culled from camp meetings.

It didn't matter. Having a wedding at Paragon Springs gave the place a sense of permanence like nothing else had. Already it felt like they were growing and prospering.

All at once, the good Reverend Van Wormer was pronouncing Lucy Ann and Admire Walsh man and wife. Ad turned and kissed his bride so lingeringly it brought hoots and hollers from his friends. He kissed and cuddled his new baby, gave her back to Lucy Ann, and hugged the shoulders of his young brother-in-law.

Then with a loud whoop, Ad tossed his hat in the air. Everyone laughed and woke up Grandma.

Meg took a second to console Grandma for having missed the ceremony, but told her the best was yet to come. She turned back to the couple. "I'm so happy for you all!" She hugged Lucy Ann, Ad, and Laddie. She planted a kiss on the baby's forehead. Then she hugged and kissed them all again for good measure. She stood back, waving others forward to congratulate the newlyweds. Ad's friends shoved in, clapping him on the back, shaking his hand. One by one, following custom, they snatched the opportunity to kiss a girl. Lucy Ann was like a rose in bloom from blushing.

With a smile at the scene, Meg joined Aurelia and Grandma in carrying out the food to the large, sheet-covered, makeshift table in the yard. The table literally groaned under the feast they laid out. There were antelope roasts, baked prairie chicken, deviled eggs, and the customary beans. Hot roasting ears, boiled turnips, squash. Mountains of sliced bread, decorative mounds of butter, bowls of jam. Pumpkin pies, custard pie, raisin pie, pitchers of sweet milk, and hot coffee. The wedding cake, a towering buttermilk cake with boiled white icing, centered it all.

After the feast, frenzied dancing to music from fiddle and harmonica went on for hours. It was as if, Meg thought, as she danced the Virginia reel, too happy to notice the stiffness and pain in her hip, the homesteading women and their friends were stomping out bad times for good and all. At least for the time they could feel it to be so. Tomorrow would come soon enough.

Chapter Fifteen

Lucy and Ad had only recently completed, with the others' help, their new soddy on his claim. Meg chose to walk the two miles to see Lucy Ann, for their first real visit in Lucy's new home.

Although everyone worked, Ad's help at Paragon Springs had been a special godsend in past weeks. Today was an opportunity for a wide view of the results of their labors. Normally, she only saw what was immediately at hand and underfoot as she worked.

Although it had been a hot, dry summer, crops were better than adequate. Most of her wheat and a small patch of rye were in shocks. Beyond the grain fields, stacks of fresh-cut wild hay dotted the prairie. Buffalo grass was abundant, her cows in good flesh as they grazed between the stacks.

Late garden crops—squash, turnips, potatoes, watermelon, pumpkins—were almost ready to harvest, to be added to the staples already stored in the dugout cellar. This second winter, they would be well-fed!

In spite of the heat shimmering over the land, she walked fast and before long arrived at the Walsh homestead. She waved at Ad and Laddie at work on a stone corral some distance from the soddy, then to Lucy Ann waiting in the open door with Rachel in her arms.

"I don't have anything real special to serve," Lucy Ann apologized, leading the way inside where she offered Meg a glass of spring water.

"This is just what I wanted." She admired the pretty goblet in her hand. "Wasn't this a wedding present from Will and Bethany Hessler?"

"They gave us a whole set of them," Lucy Ann said with shy pleasure. "I don't know what Ad and me would have done without folks' generosity." She looked about her at the tidy, sparsely furnished room.

"You and Ad fixed things really nice, Lucy Ann." She nodded toward the crude but useful furniture Ad had made, the stone and mud fireplace.

Aurelia's wedding present to them was a set of tea towels she had made from flour sacks and embroidered with pretty flowers and birds. Lucy Ann used one of them as a tablecloth, spread on a box table and centered by a bottle of wildflowers and grasses. There was a nested set of willow baskets Grandma Spicy had woven for them. The buffalo hide being used as a carpet was from one of the Rocking A cowboys, as was the hand lamp on the bureau. Meg and Aurelia had thinned out what cooking and eating utensils they could spare for the couple. Meg's other present was a blue enameled coffeepot and matching preserving kettle she'd bought on credit with promise of good crops. And of course Lucy Ann had blankets and a few other things inherited from her Uncle Ross.

"You're happy here, aren't you, Lucy Ann?"

"Oh, Lord, yes!" Then, for a few seconds her face clouded, and she said softly, "There was a time I thought I never would be, again." The shadow gradually lifted from her expression. "Ad is a true miracle in my life, the best thing that could ever have happened to me." A tinge of color came to her cheeks, and she looked down at the top of Rachel's head in her arms. She brushed her lips across the small head. "We want a bigger family, but God will see to that if it's to be. We feel blessed to have what we have."

Meg nodded and smiled wistfully, without admitting that at times she yearned for children of her own. Before such a thing could happen, she would have to divorce Malloy, and find a man she could love and trust. A tall order, to say the least.

Because Meg had much work to tend to, their visit was brief. Walking back, she noticed a darkening, cloud-like smoke, or dust, off to the northwest. As she watched, the cloud filled the sky and turned silvery, like an approaching snowstorm which of course it couldn't be, in August. She picked up her steps and hurried along with a hammering heart, her mind pricked with curiosity.

By the time she reached home, the cloud had completely blotted the sun and sounded like a roaring broad river.

When small objects began to drop from the sky, she thought it was hail, then on closer look she saw that it was *grasshoppers*. She stopped in her tracks, stunned, as hundreds, thousands, of grasshoppers showered down. They crunched underfoot as she broke into a run; she could hear their jaws chomping as they fell thick and fast to swarm over every green living thing.

She screamed and beat them from her hair as she ran.

Aurelia burst from the soddy, chunky Zibby on her hip, fair-haired Helen Grace at her heels. She looked aghast at what was happening all around them. "I thought it was hail, popping on the roof. Joshua, David!" But the boys, out with the cattle, were already riding their horses hard toward home through a veil of flying insects. "Grasshoppers!" they yelled at the top of their lungs as they rode in. "Grasshoppers!"

"Quick," Meg told Aurelia, and the boys spilling off their horses, "we've got to do something to get rid of them. They are everywhere, eating everything!" She hurtled into the soddy and began throwing bedcovers, blankets, buffalo skins, shawls, coats, at the others. "Take these and cover the garden plants." She asked where Grandma Spicy was, not seeing her, but Aurelia's mumbled answer was hard to understand. She snatched up their willow broom and ran for the cornfield, where she began beating the munching insects off the stalks.

She moved down the corn row like a mad person, sweeping the voracious grasshoppers off the valuable corn. When she looked behind her, she saw the hoppers were more numerous than ever. The stalks began to bend under the weight of the insects that sounded like a herd of feeding cattle.

She hurried to help Aurelia and the boys with the garden truck, seeing the potato vines flattening to the ground with devouring hoppers. Within minutes, hoppers wormed under the spread blankets to the squash and melon vines beneath. Everything in sight was covered with insects; on the ground they were several inches deep, in sickening motion. She swatted her skirts as they crawled up around her ankles, her knees. In horror she saw that the insects that had been crushed under her feet were being devoured by a fresh on-slaught of hoppers.

The chickens, at first scared, now were eating the grass-hoppers as fast as they could gag them down.

Racing for a potato fork, Meg began digging potatoes, small as they were, as quickly as she could. Aurelia and the children furiously picked up potatoes, put them in buckets and sacks, then lugged them toward the house on the run.

Aurelia, screaming their names, herded her children into the house and slammed the door. Meg went after her, bringing the last of the potatoes and turnips. In the house, she ordered, "Make sure every bit of provisions is protected in wood boxes, or in tin containers, or we won't have a bite of food left. Fast, now!" In shock, she saw that the hoppers were eating their way up the curtains, leaving them in shreds. Helen Grace was shrieking, tears of terror flowing, as she batted them out of her hair and off her dress.

Meg helped her for a moment, then rushed back outside, wanting to protect their stores in the pantry dugout. The salt, flour, sugar, and beans, seemed to be safe underground as long as the hoppers could be kept out. Aboveground again, she saw that Ad, Lucy Ann, and Laddie had arrived in their wagon. Ad shooed Lucy Ann toward the house and, taking in the situation, told Meg, "Maybe fire will drive them off. We'll try smudges of dry hay and litter."

For the next hour and more, they worked at top speed to plow and dig trenches for fires around the garden and the grain shocks. But it seemed to no avail. The hoppers continued to rain down like a snowstorm that would never end.

Meg, coughing from the smoke when the fires were well-lit, remembered that she still hadn't seen Grandma. Back in the house, Aurelia told her, "I think she went to the spring for water awhile ago. I expected her back before now."

Lucy Ann, holding Rachel protectively and bouncing the whimpering infant, added with a worried frown, "But you know how she wanders off to look for that lost baby when she gets confused."

Meg went cold all over. "You two stay here and do what you can," she ordered solemnly. "I'll go look for her." She strapped on her gun as a means of signaling if she needed help.

Outside, whipping the pests and smoke away from her face, she told Ad what she was going to do.

"I'll go," he said as he tried to hand her the pitchfork he was using to feed debris to the line of fires.

"No, please stay here. Grandma doesn't know you as well as me. I'm the one to go, she must be scared out of her wits."

Leaving the others in charge of battling the insects, she struck off toward the spring through a blinding, whirring wall of grasshoppers.

Meg had no idea how far she had traveled. The storm of insects nearly blinded her, and it would be so easy to miss seeing Grandma. She carefully scoured each area she came to then moved on. Every brief while she called out, listened for an answer. Nothing. Nothing.

Passing the rocks where Finch was buried, she felt only enormous worry about Grandma Spicy.

Another mile and she found her. Through a curtain of swirling hoppers, she saw Grandma sitting up, her back against an outcropping of limestone. Meg gave a glad cry, ran to her, and kneeled down. She recoiled when she saw that the grasshoppers had eaten at Grandma's clothes. They clustered around her closed eyelids, her mouth, and ears. Her gray, straggly hair was brownish from their excrement. With a cry of rage, she brushed frantically at the insects crawling on Grandma's face, arms, apron.

"Merciful God! Oh, Grandma, are you all right?" She gathered her close, but Grandma was lifeless in her arms. She pressed her ear against her chest to listen for her heartbeat. There was none. For a long while she sat and held her, numb with shock. Then gently, she rested Grandma's body back against the rock.

Tears prickled her eyes, then streamed down her cheeks. She sat doubled up, hugging her knees as she rocked, but she couldn't escape the pain. "Grandma . . . Dammit, Grandma!" Eventually, she got to her feet and fired the pistol as a signal she had found her.

"Maybe it was Grandma's old age that did her in," Meg told Ad when he arrived with the wagon, "but I think she was so scared her heart simply quit." *How could the dream continue?* Grandma was one of the most loved, most helpful members of their Paragon Springs family. "I have no idea what we're going to do without her. She knew how to do so many things, taught us all—" She wiped her nose, brushed her hair back. "Let's take her home."

Two days after the grasshoppers arrived like a snowstorm, they left in the same way on a high wind.

The scourge to their crops couldn't have been worse, Meg saw in her survey afterward. Even parts of her fresh-cut haystacks were gone. Plainly, they going to feel losses from the devastation far into the future.

As far as the eye could see, the world had been turned a dreary winter-gray in August with every green plant devoured. Their source of water was as brown as coffee, the hoppers' pollution making it unfit to drink. Even at the sinks, her cattle drank only when pushed to the extreme limit of thirst. Ad helped her clean the spring by draining out the holding pond. During the wait for the return of fresh water, all of them went dirty and were nearly driven to distraction by thirst.

Sweaty objects, wooden pitchfork handles, broom handles, leather harness, blankets and clothing, had been gnawed by insects. A chicken killed and prepared for a meal tasted so strong of the insects they couldn't eat it.

One hot, gray day, Meg went to sit by Grandma Spicy's

fresh-turned grave up on a knoll beyond the spring. She was too numb to cry, but needed to think. With their crops for the year almost depleted, how were they to live? She had counted on the extra crops to trade for supplies: for clothing, household needs, and for food staples they couldn't produce themselves. Gone was her plan to sell excess vegetables to travelers.

Wracking her brain—staring down toward their crude soddy and the activity around it but seeing nothing—she wondered if they should use the money earned from travelers before the devastation, to pay the mortgage soon due, and risk starvation? Or should they buy food and other goods they needed and risk losing the roof over their heads and their land, to the Dodge bank?

She set her mouth grimly, and pulled herself to her feet. She would try and assess the little *good* the pestilence had left them and determine the ways and means, if there were any, to survive the coming winter.

In some ways the grasshoppers were laughable, she noted during her examination. While they would eat an onion or turnip from the top right down into the ground, leaving a hollow shell, they didn't care for the castor beans Grandma Spicy planted to keep bugs from the garden and also to make the children's castor oil. Tears for Grandma joined Meg's twisted smile at the crazy sight.

Thank the Lord, although every green and succulent plant had been consumed, the umber prairie grasses had been left alone. There was graze for her cattle, although winter storms could change that burying the grass deep under layers of snow.

Skirts in hand, she started back to the house and the chores there. It was dashed bad luck that the cash that had seemed such a tidy sum, before the devastation, amounted to far too little to meet their needs, now. There was not even enough to leave the country on, if they wanted to go. Nothing for a St. Louis journey.

Still, besides the small amount of cash, they had managed to salvage some potatoes and cabbages; they had flour and cornmeal. And as long as they could hang onto it, they had the land. She shooed three hopper-sick chickens out of her path.

There was no real choice. They would stay and try again. But she would have to sell off a large number of cows, maybe half of her herd. The decision hurt, but it was the only plan she had. *If* she could find a buyer.

With Ad and Laddie's help, she drove the cattle to Dodge in early October, the last possible minute. She was hardly surprised to find that the tall, slope-shouldered bone buyer, Tog Elsberry, was now head over teakettle in the cattle business, buying from those destituted by the grasshopper scourge. Some sellers would use the money to pay their way out of western Kansas for good, to go home to families in the East.

Grimly, Meg accepted half what the cows were worth, all Elsberry would pay. He had her over a barrel, and he knew it.

As they were leaving the stock pens for the bank and general store, Meg spotted Jack squatting on his heels, smoking a cigarette by the sod livestock barn. "What's he doing here?" she asked Ad. "I didn't see any Rocking A cattle in those pens."

"Buyin'."

"What?" She whirled to face him, accidentally shoving into Laddie in the process. He gave her a worried, cockeyed grin and rubbed his ribs she'd poked with an elbow. She touched his arm in apology, while her face burned with anger.

Ad told her, "I said he's here to buy livestock, like as not.

It's a good time for a smart rancher with any money to increase his herd. Can't fault nobody for that."

"Buy *my* cows, cheap as dirt? No! I won't stand for it! I don't want my cows on Ambler land!"

Her raised voice caught Jack's attention. Over by the barn, he grinned, tipping his hat to her in a manner of personal rejoicing. *Damn him.* He knew better than to try and buy directly from her. She'd rather sell to the devil.

Ad caught her arm and steered her down the street. "Don't be a fool, Meg. Don't let pride get in the way of good sense. 'Sides, your cattle is already sold. Ain't yours no more. Was nothin' else we could do." He hustled her along toward the business area of town, leaving Ambler laughing.

She concluded bitterly, "I know selling to that money-lusting Elsberry was the only thing we could do. But I don't have to like it, Ad Walsh, so don't ask me to!" She snatched her arm away.

For weeks after her return to Paragon Springs, she would recognize a few of her old cows wandering back onto Paragon land, with her T Cross brand nearly obliterated by the Rocking A. She sometimes wondered if Ambler deliberately headed them toward her place, to rub in the fact of her desperate straits.

She wouldn't be alone if she did give in. Several area homesteaders had pulled out of the country right after the scourge, desperate to reach their eastern destinations before winter set in. Jack and his men would have plenty to see them through, of course. The Hesslers also meant to stick it out. Will and Bethany's relatives in the East were already sending them aid: barrels of beans, flour, rice, and boxes of dried fruit and salt, with a promise of crop and garden seed to come in the spring.

The Paragon Springs family had no such relatives to ask

for help, and although Will and Bethany begged to share, Meg deferred their offer for the time being. They would manage on what they had as long as possible. The forthcoming seed was another matter. Come spring she would accept the loan of seed if they had plenty, and repay as soon as she was able.

She moved back to the original soddy with Aurelia and the children chiefly to conserve fuel, although by legislative act homesteaders were allowed to vacate their claims without penalty following the grasshopper plague. They did their best to conserve, but their food stores vanished at an astonishing rate. A noon meal might consist of a baked potato each, supper one serving of hot, cooked cabbage. The cabbage was portioned especially carefully so that it might last the winter and prevent scurvy.

The hoppers had devoured a 250-mile-wide swath across the Dakotas, Colorado, Nebraska, Missouri, Iowa, and Kansas. Government aid was asked for, but it was generally believed that thinly settled western Kansas would be ignored, in favor of help to more heavily populated areas.

Then, Army action toward hopper relief was set in motion late in November. President Ulysses Grant gave the Quartermaster's Department at Jeffersonville, Indiana, authority to distribute several thousand forage caps, sack coats, jackets, boots, greatcoats, and blankets, to settlers in hard-hit Nebraska and Kansas. Other help, food, and seed could be forthcoming from other departments.

Ad drove to Fort Dodge the middle of December for their share of coats, caps, and boots distributed by the Army. Although Meg's boots didn't fit and she nearly got lost in the huge coat she wore when she went out to check on her few remaining cattle and the horses, the army goods were a blessing against the bitter winter cold. Those goods, a batch of sorghum taffy Aurelia made, plus stories and songs by the fire after a supper of watery cabbage soup and cornbread, made up their Christmas Eve celebration that second year.

Because of deep snow, the Hesslers weren't able to share Christmas; Ad and Lucy Ann, Laddie and Baby Rachel, barely struggled through.

Late Christmas day, Jack plowed in on horseback, carrying a basket of oranges for the children and gloating at what he saw as her total ruin in that country. She snatched the oranges for her charges, let him know she was far from through, and sent him packing as quickly as possible.

To worsen matters, Aurelia scolded her for not showing an iota of interest in Jack. "If you'd encourage him, properly of course, he might decide to marry you! All of us ought to have husbands. It's not natural the way we live. Look how happy Lucy Ann is!"

"I'm glad for Lucy Ann's happiness, and you should marry, too, if you want to, Aurelia. But I have other things to think about for now, lots of things. I don't believe Jack has any interest in marrying me and I could never fall in love with him! That's that, and I don't want to hear anymore."

She would have liked to tell Aurelia that she was already married—and tell Jack, too—but that would open up a smelly kettle of fish. Problems she wasn't prepared to handle.

One night in February, Meg woke to the sound of one of the children coughing severely against the howl of a blizzard outside. She got up and wrapped herself in her blanket against the sharp cold. Aurelia was kneeling by Helen Grace's bed.

"What is it?" Meg whispered, seeing that Aurelia massaged the child's pale little throat and chest at the same time Helen Grace's crowing, breathless cough increased, filling the room with a frightening sound.

"I fear that it's croup," Aurelia answered in a panicked voice, "but it came on so sudden. She was all right earlier today, I swear she was, but now she's burning with fever, breathing so fast and hard. I'm trying to dislodge the congestion that's ch-choking her."

True croup, then, Meg thought, closing her eyes for a second in pained dismay. She kneeled beside Aurelia next to the bed where the child was fighting for every breath. She remembered talk of true croup in the old Irish neighborhood. A more innocent croup often had to do with teething—there was little or no fever, no quickened pulse, the child recovered. This was far more serious. Her voice falsely confident, she said, "We'll take care of her, Aurelia." She put her hand on her shoulder and squeezed, then got to her feet. "Tell me what you'd like me to do. I can ride to Dodge and fetch the doctor."

Aurelia's face was pale as she looked up at her; she shook her head, and her voice broke, "In this awful weather you couldn't get through. I want you here to help." She put one hand behind Helen Grace's head and lifted, gently massaging her throat with the other. "Would you stir up the fire and put some water on to heat, please, Meg?"

"Of course! Vapors from a steamy bath should help. You stay there with her."

They worked frantically in the next hours, making use of every remedy either could remember. They gave Helen Grace hot, steamy baths that seemed to help, but only for a minute or two. They coaxed her to swallow the white of an egg; she would vomit the choking phlegm, but still she coughed and choked, grew weaker, convulsed. They held a hot cloth dipped in a combination of salt and vinegar under her nose, but she couldn't inhale the strong vapors enough. The sound of her croupy cough and strident breathing finally woke the other children, and they lay watching wide-eyed from their beds.

176

Chapter Sixteen

The next afternoon Helen Grace was worse, strangling on each feeble cough. "I—I'm going to lose her," Aurelia said on a broken sob.

"No, Aurelia, no!" Meg protested. "Here, I've brought a few drops of kerosene on sugar. Like Grandma Spicy gave the children for sore throat last winter. Keep massaging her throat, Aurelia. We can't give up." She handed over the treated spoon of sugar and rushed to the window. "She needs fresh air—that will help her get her breath." She nearly broke the window, getting it open. Outside, foot-long icicles hung from the eaves. "Fresh water, if we can just get her to drink a few sips—"

The cold winter sun was just spilling through the window the second morning when Helen Grace gave a final gasping cough, strangled, and was silent. "Oh, dear God, no!" Aurelia wailed, "no!" With deep, tearing sobs, she held her child to her breast and rocked. Meg knelt behind them, her face pressed against Aurelia's shoulders, her arms grasping her friend and her child, seeking to take the loss, the pain, into herself.

They padded a wooden box with Helen Grace's baby

quilt, washed and dressed the child, and laid her inside. Aurelia took a long, loving time arranging the little girl's blonde curls just so around her still, white face.

No grave could be dug in the hard frozen ground. They carried the child in her padded box to the old dugout. Only last summer, wayfarers had slept there among the stores of vegetables and staple goods. The dugout was now nearly empty except for the cot holding the small coffin.

Aurelia went so often to the dugout, to sit by the little coffin in the cold, that Meg was afraid her friend would catch pneumonia and die. Life seemed to have left Aurelia. She went through her daily tasks a husk of the woman she had been.

In mid-March the weather broke. The snow melted, the ground softened under a chilly rain. Ad and Lucy Ann came with their little one and Lad to attend Helen Grace's funeral. There were no flowers for the tiny grave they dug near where Grandma Spicy lay. But Aurelia had woven a wreath of straw pulled from her mattress. She tied it with a piece of lace from her petticoat.

They stood with bowed heads, all of them somber. Lucy Ann whispered reassuringly in the midst of the heartache, "God lives."

Meg had her doubts. First Grandma, and now little Helen Grace, were gone, the rest of them on the verge of scurvy and starvation. Jack had said this would happen, if she didn't leave, or become his and let him take over. She hated him for that. Life was hard enough. People doing their best needn't be given a road map to pain.

A better way for folks in a hard country would be to stand together to build the land. Really care about one another, not segment off. If she had a say, it would be that way yet, but Lord, she felt gutted and beaten.

* * * * *

Spring flowed into summer. Hard work on the plains was again the order of the day. Meg saw less and less of Jack. She hardly dared hope that his absence meant he had given up attempting to break her down. She guessed that he was considering some other devious plan to get her off the land, and she watched with dread for signs of trouble.

Leaving Laddie and Aurelia's boys to help Ad shock the last of the wheat, and Lucy Ann to feed any travelers who might stop at Paragon Springs, Meg had encouraged Aurelia to accompany her to pick wild plums by the river one day, believing an outing might do her dear friend good.

From the time of the tragedy six months ago, Aurelia had refused coddling, didn't shirk her labor. Today she'd picked most of the two large baskets of plums she and Meg had gathered, but she showed not one bit of enthusiasm. No anger, either, or complaints when there was just cause and griping would have been her usual way.

"The temperature must be over a hundred degrees! But what else can we expect from July?" Meg slapped at an insect that nicked her neck, shoving her sweat-damp hair behind her ear.

Aurelia's response was a quiet nod. Mechanically, she continued to pluck plums from the thickety branches. Grief had left deep lines in her face.

Zibby played in the wagon with her corncob dolls, talking to them and to herself. Once in a while Aurelia looked toward the child, checking in a calm, dazed manner that was eerie.

Meg moved her half-filled basket deeper into the thicket and scratched her arm in the process. Bees and flies swirled up around her head; she bit back strong words that flew to the tip of her tongue.

"Some of the plums have worms, but we'll cut them out

and dry the plums anyway," she ventured.

"Yes," was all Aurelia had to say. Meg wanted to shake her. It was as though Aurelia was in some kind of numb sleep that would eventually obliterate her.

She remembered how Aurelia had spent an obsessive amount of time in April and May, engraving lettering and the figure of a little lamb and flowers on the simple magnesia marble monument Meg had cut for her from the stony acres of her land they all referred to now as The Rocks.

Aurelia's artistic talent had surprised everyone. Lucy Ann and the children had persuaded her to make a second monument for Grandma Spicy's grave. Grandma's marker, engraved with a sheaf of wheat, a beaming sun, and the words "At Rest," had taken a fraction of the time but was as beautifully done. And it had finally broken Aurelia away from constant labor—reworking, refining little Helen Grace's stone—when she couldn't seem to stop herself.

Because of her own penchant for privacy regarding her past, Meg had never probed into Aurelia's affairs. But she thought it might help her friend to talk about *anything*, really talk. Somehow, she had to be brought back to normal, to *life*, for her own sake and her children's.

Meg wiped her sticky fingers on her apron and took the plunge. "Aurelia, I wish you'd tell me about your husband. We've never really talked about the two of you very much, your marriage and life, but I've often wondered." She bit into a sour plum and made a face. "It seems all we have time to talk about are immediate things like what to have for dinner or what to plant, how to fix extra beds for travelers who stop for the night. How to stop the grasshoppers next time—"

Aurelia turned slowly and looked at Meg. "With all your work, I've been a trial to you, haven't I, since Harlan abandoned me for you to look after?" She went back to work without waiting for an answer.

"No more a trial than I have been to you." *Me, and this place, my big ideas.* "Come, we have all the plums we're going to find. Let's get Zibby and sit by the river and cool our feet."

When they were settled on the riverbank, bare feet dabbling in the water, Meg continued, "Go on, tell me about your husband. Where did you meet?" She smiled encouragement.

Aurelia's winged brows and her forehead puckered. She seemed to have difficulty remembering, as though she was pulling herself away from somewhere deep inside. Some wintery place with Helen Grace. Her chapped hands smoothed her faded skirt.

"I—I knew John Thorne from childhood. We were sweethearts even as youngsters." She sighed, the words coming weighted, difficult to form. "That was in Spencer County, Kentucky, a few miles north of the town of Fairfield. Those were very happy days—I suppose I was somewhat spoiled." Her mouth quirked in a pathetic smile.

She shook her head as if to clear it. "My father, Emmett Allen, wanted the best for our family and worked hard to get it. He had a small tobacco farm and, later, a furniture manufactory in Fairfield. My mother, Charity Allen, was what you'd call a 'gentle, southern woman'."

She was quiet a moment, remembering. Meg waited, patient. Zibby giggled as she kicked her feet up and down, sending a silvery spray of water over the women's legs, dampening their calico dresses clear to their laps. Aurelia reached out and touched the child to stop her splashing, then went on:

"When I was seventeen, my family sold everything and headed by wagon train to California. All but me: I stayed behind to marry John Thorne. He looked something like Ad Walsh—black-haired and handsome, I mean—although he was an educated man, a teacher." She looked at Meg. "Not anything against Ad, of course. Admire is a good man, for a cowboy."

Meg smiled. "Yes. He's very good to Lucy Ann and Lad, and to Lucy's baby. I don't know what any of us would do without him."

Aurelia nodded. "John was like that." The furrows in her brow smoothed out, and a softness came to her eyes, her mouth. "I loved him with my very soul, Meg, I was *crazy* in love with him. I was also very young. My" —she cleared her throat— "my parents and my brothers and sisters . . . all died of cholera on the way to California. I was devastated not to ever see them again. I clung even more tightly to John, he was all I had."

Meg reached out and covered Aurelia's hands with her own, understanding her better. They ought to have had this discussion long ago. She was ashamed that they hadn't.

"My husband was a man of honor, very loyal to his friends. Both John and his best friend Karl—they'd known one another from boyhood—raised fine blooded horses; the horses were a sideline with John that sometimes brought in a little extra money. Karl lost one of his finest horses to theft and it infuriated him, plus they were afraid it would happen again. He asked John to go with him to hunt down the thief."

She bit her lip, again turned her pain-clouded green eyes to Meg. "I was pregnant with Zibby, just a few months along. I had three other small children. Karl wasn't married—he had other friends, not family men, who could have gone with him. So I begged John not to go, I was afraid to let him out of my sight. I had a premonition that something terrible would happen." Her lip trembled. "I also knew I could never make it without John; he was everything to me and the children."

"What happened?" Meg had a hollow feeling. She turned

182

to look at Zibby, who had gone back up the bank to play.

"John went with his friend, of course. There were six bullet holes in his poor bloody body when they brought him home to me. He and Karl were both shot to death, and the thief was never caught."

Meg released her balled fists slowly and put her arm around Aurelia. Her mouth had dried; it was hard to speak. "I'm so sorry."

Aurelia acknowledged her sympathy with a nod, blinking back tears. "I was close to penniless after I sold John's horses to pay our debts. But still I had a thread of hope. John's brother, Harlan, had written many boastful letters trying to convince John to join him in his ranching venture here in western Kansas. With nowhere else to go after John was killed, I came out here to Harlan. I expected to keep house for him. In return, I expected him to take care of me and the children." She finished on an angry, explosive breath: "I nearly died when I saw this country, when I saw that Harlan lived in a dirty crude hole in the ground. I couldn't go back, I had no funds. And—" Her expression finished her thoughts: *then Harlan deserted me, too.*

"We can still find a way for you to go back to Kentucky, Aurelia, if that's what you want. Our crops look very good this summer; Ad says our wheat will average eighteen bushels per acre; the corn may run as high as thirty-five bushels an acre. Travelers coming through are bringing some income from our road ranch venture. Aren't there neighbors and old friends of yours in Fairfield who'd help you get established there again, if you went back?"

"It doesn't matter now." She looked at her hands. "I wouldn't leave my little Helen Grace—now she's . . . buried here." She wiped her eyes on her apron. "I'll never go far from this place. I'll just have to do the best I can for my other children, right here, from now on." She looked over her shoulder at Zibby, whose little skirt swirled as she danced about on bare feet trying to catch a white butterfly in her chubby fingers.

Aurelia's expression grew even more bleak as she turned her head first one way, and then another, to look further beyond them. She said of the rough, rolling prairie stretching away for miles in every direction, "I suppose this godforsaken piece of nowhere is all there is for me, all there will ever be. A big, ugly, empty nothing that grinds one down."

"Nonsense! Out there," Meg waved an arm, "isn't *all* there is, and it's not so bad anyhow. Life *is* harder for women alone, I don't have to tell you that. But we can *make* whatever it is we want, I really believe we can. So many things are going to change, Aurelia. This country is going to be settled fast according to the land agent at Larned. There will be other folks to visit with, share our problems with to make them lighter. Heavens, you may meet someone and want to marry again. And as soon as possible" —she took a breath— "we're going to have a real school for the children." All of the youngsters knew how to read and count, but they needed so much more book knowledge, a formal education. "We'll be as civilized as anywhere in the world if we work at it and don't give up."

Aurelia shook her head, her wry smile shiny with tears. "I envy you your unflagging optimism, Meg. I don't have the determination, the grit, that you do. We'd all be better off if I did. Maybe that's the real problem."

"Fiddlesticks! You're stronger than you realize, Aurelia. You're doing far better here in western Kansas than you let yourself believe. Think on it and you'll see what I mean!"

But Aurelia's expression of doubt didn't change. "It's always bothered me, Meg, to be dependent on your charity."

"My charity? Goodness gracious, you have as much to do

with running our place as I do! When we turn a profit beyond our needs, a share will be yours and your children's." Meg had a plan for another source of income, but until she had the details thoroughly worked out in her mind, until she was sure Aurelia was going to recover, she wouldn't bring it up. She would need Aurelia's help toward some of the success she envisioned.

"I suppose I don't get over things easily, either," Aurelia was saying. "Please be patient with me, Meg."

Meg grasped her friend's arm and said softly, "I've lost neither a husband nor a child, so there is no way I can know, or judge, what you're really feeling, Aurelia. Take all the time you need." She realized that now would be a good time to tell Aurelia about Teddy Malloy. She opened her mouth to speak, but the ugliness, the shame of all that, stuck in her throat and she said nothing. She drew her feet from the water. She stood up, shaking out her skirts. "Let's get your little girl and take her home before she stirs herself up an anthill and gets stung."

From the time she and Laddie had buried Finch, Meg's mind had returned again and again to The Rocks, but of late that had nothing to do with the grave there.

She remembered Papa's work as a stonecutter outside St. Louis. She'd been aware, then, of the many uses for stone. Here on the ranch she had built watering troughs and fences, lined the spring pond, and someday, she meant to build a stone house. If she could find a way to quarry the stone on her property, and sell it by the wagonload, they would all be better off, make real progress at last.

Once the grasshopper scare subsided—the scourge was still publicized in newspapers across the land—western Kansas would again be looked upon with favor. Even with the bad stories, a few folks had come to take up claims again recently, and their numbers would increase. Immigrants would need stone for permanent homes and outbuildings; they wouldn't stand for crude dugouts and soddies forever.

Even now, she guessed that building stone would be welcomed in Larned and Dodge City for permanent construction. Those towns were not going to disappear, they were there to stay. Freighting over the long distances wouldn't be easy. They would have to have a freight wagon, a team of oxen or mules, maybe more than one outfit. She'd see what Ad had to say about that; she would have to have his help. For now he helped her with the crops, cattle, stock trading. He did blacksmithing for travelers stopping in. They might need more help than his.

She would like to be the first to provide building stone for this part of the country. The demand, in this near-timberless country—she was now facing the fact that her timber claim would likely have to be relinquished—could only grow as the population expanded. They had to be ready.

Stone could be used for sidewalks, hitching posts, and fencing, for monuments and statues made to order. She believed she recognized some of her stone as magnesia marble comparable to the finest marble anywhere. The stone had been used for the monuments Aurelia had carved for Helen Grace's and Grandma's graves. They were beautiful markers and would stand forever.

Quarried stone could provide means to a better life for all of them, compared to the bare existence they were now leading at Paragon Springs. She was determined to end the constant threat of failure hanging over their heads.

One evening after supper, she called Ad, Lucy Ann, and Aurelia together for a meeting, to discuss the venture she had in mind.

She began cautiously, "We'll have to mortgage my land, and Lucy Ann's, to buy proper quarrying tools, a freight wagon and team. We might even have to hire help, if business is such we can't handle it all ourselves. Stonecutting is heavy work."

Ad looked dubious, and as anxious as she was feeling. "We'll do the work alone 'til we're sure we're on solid footin'," he said.

Lucy Ann burst into a nervous giggle. "Ad, there isn't any more solid footing than stone."

All of them laughed. Meg said with renewed good feeling and excitement, "I believe his remark is true, both ways."

"If you want to make monuments to sell," Aurelia spoke up, showing the most interest she'd expressed in any matter in a long time, "I'll carve the designs. If we could find a way to ship our products across the country, yard and garden statues are very popular in the South. I'm sure they are popular in eastern gardens, too, and eventually will be desired here in the West."

Meg could have kissed her.

Two weeks later, Meg and Ad had lined up encouraging markets: stone to build three small outbuildings and a new jail in Dodge, stone for a new Larned bank foundation, plus chimneys for six new houses being built there. Two housewives in Larned also contracted for clothesline posts.

They returned from the same trip driving a freight wagon for which they'd forfeited thirty-five borrowed dollars, a team of oxen that had cost sixty-five dollars. In the wagon was an assortment of tools: wood augers, feathers, and wedges, four-pound hammers, a stone drill they'd ordered specifically made by the Dodge blacksmith. Meg felt toward the implements as another woman might toward a cache of rare jewels. Even then, she prayed fervently that she would never again

187

have to borrow money on her precious land.

As though he read her mind as they rumbled along, their horses tied to the back of the big wagon, Ad said, "Lord, we fail at this I don't know where it'll leave us."

"I do," she answered honestly. "We'll be left with nothing but the clothes on our backs, worse off than when any of us came to this country. Which is why we can't fail."

Chapter Seventeen

When they had first come there, Meg had sledged out stone as needed. But quarrying to meet orders called for improved methods, using drills, feathers, and wedges. It helped to remember how Papa worked. The rest she and Ad guessed about, made up, and made do.

As she worked at the top of a ravine one day, she dropped her hammer to the ground, straightened and rubbed her back, and surveyed the day's work thus far.

First they had strip plowed and shoveled away the shallow soil overlay from a fairly level twelve-inch-thick rock slab, the slab running twelve feet wide and twenty feet long. They then used a straight edge to measure off the post lengths they wanted.

Newly exposed stone was fairly soft, but would dry and harden in the air and sunshine. With the stone hand drill, an elongated brace and bit made for them by the Dodge blacksmith, they bore a hole every ten inches in a straight line. A pair of feathers—two short metal rods curved at the upper end—were driven into the hole and were then forced apart by a wedge hammered between them, in order to split the rock.

According to Papa, splitting stone with feathers and wedges was known to the early Egyptians, whose slaves used them to quarry rock for the pyramids. She supposed the method would be used to the end of time.

Trying to ignore the pain in her back, she went back to gently tapping with her stone hammer, alternating with Ad as he tapped from the other end the feathers and wedges in the line of holes. With each tap she listened for the *ping* that meant the pressure of the wedge had started cracking the stone. That wedge was not tapped again, but the others tapped until each had *pinged*. When all had, they had a post. Rock that broke in lengths too short for posts was laid aside for building block.

While still soft, the post, or block, was shaped with hammer and drill.

Loading five-foot-long posts, each weighing around three hundred pounds, was the heaviest, hardest part of the work, but Ad had found a way to make it possible, if not easy. When they had a pile of posts ready, they would dig into the slope, back the wagon in, and push the posts onto the wagon bed. When that method wouldn't suit, they used a block and tackle to get the posts up off the ground and into the wagon.

Regardless, after a twelve-hour day of cutting and loading stone, some ten posts to a wagonload, Meg knew every muscle in her body by the relentless aches and pains.

In the ensuing months, word about the developed quarry got around, and they had no shortage of orders. Most of that late fall and winter—the easiest, best time to cut and stock-pile stone due to moisture—Meg was too tired to think, or care about very much other than the progress they were making.

Sometimes, dizzied by the work and heat the following spring, their third at Paragon Springs, she saw a whole village built of stone coming to life on the plains, but that was only in her mind. Cold reality was endless distances of rocky strata, chalky limestone ledges, slowly being broken into piles by their drill, hammers, and chisels to fill the many orders. She couldn't complain. They were eating well and chipping away bit by bit at the bank loan.

There were rumors that Jack had left the country; other stories indicated he was still around and getting into trouble as usual. She hadn't the time, or the inclination, to find out the true facts, as long as he stayed away from her and her land. Ad learned that Jack had gone on a trip of several months to Texas to round up longhorn cattle to increase the Rocking A herds.

But Jack wouldn't stay away forever, and when he returned she'd still be at Paragon Springs.

One noon, Meg stopped work to take up her canteen nearby. She swished the water around in her chalk dust-coated throat, spat, then took a long, fresh drink. Her eye was caught by a long line of cattle to the west, moving north toward Ogalalla, Nebraska.

Quarantine lines had moved the latest cattle trail across Kansas to just beyond their lands, about as far west in Kansas as a cattle trail could be. The quarantine was meant to save Kansas cattle from Texas or Spanish fever. Texas longhorns were immune to the disease, but carried the tick that would drop off the longhorns and infect domestic cattle in Kansas and Missouri. After more than ten years of Texas cattle trade through Kansas, Dodge and Caldwell were now the only cattle towns not inside quarantined lands.

She'd instructed the boys to keep watch for the disease in their cattle, but so far there was no sign of it. Luckily, the ticks were killed by Kansas winters.

The trail herds passed by against a distant blue sky all that spring and summer, one gigantic dust-stirring herd on the heels of another, headed for market in Nebraska. The muted bawling of the cattle, the shouts of the cowboys, became an accepted, natural sound.

Grass beyond the Paragon Springs ranches was eaten to the ground. The sinks were visited by herd after herd, and although the water level stayed low—not as ample as during the rainy months of early spring, or when used by their cattle alone—the sinks didn't dry up.

Fortunately, there were benefits to having trail herds come through their area.

Small calves that were dropped by their mothers on the trail, that were too young to keep up, the cowboys turned over to the Paragon Springs settlers. The calves became the responsibility of the children who bottle-fed them. Fattened and grown, the critters could be sold or become part of the brood herd.

It became a regular thing, too, when the cowhands spotted the homesteads in the distance, for them to ride over and buy fresh milk, butter, eggs, bread, and pies. Meg bought a second milk cow. Lucy Ann and Aurelia were kept busy churning and baking, while Meg continued quarrying stone and doing other outside work with Ad's and the boys' help.

The cattle herds' bedding ground, after they moved on, provided a trove of cow chip fuel. It was a godsend, now that most of the buffalo were gone. The children were constantly busy, gathering and stacking the dried cow chips in the shed.

One evening, Lad, Joshua, and David John were working off excess energy by racing their ponies on the plains to the south. Meg had just returned from the quarry after a day's work that left her feeling like the dregs of death. She wasn't ready for the news the boys brought on their rushed return.

"We saw Injuns!" Lad yelled as he spilled off the pinto Ad

had given him. Lad was pale under his tan, he'd grown a foot since coming to Paragon Springs, and his voice broke in a squawk. "They're camped in that third draw south of here, by the creek!"

When Meg heard that the Indians were a "squaw-woman who spoke English," an old white man, and two youngsters, she guessed the campers to be harmless. Normally only mission-schooled Indians spoke the white man's language.

Lad maintained that the dirty, dog-eatin' Injuns should be run off their land anyhow. He focused wild-eyed on the gun Meg strapped around her hips as she prepared to visit the campers.

"We'll do no such thing!" She gave him a stern look. "I'm taking the gun simply as a precaution." Maybe she only imagined that after the run-in with Finch, Lad sometimes too easily saw a gun as an answer to a problem. At the same time, it wasn't surprising he would hold no love for Indians, his small half-Sioux niece being the exception. "I want you boys to stay here while I investigate." They argued until Aurelia came to her aid by giving them a stern reprimand and chores to do.

Meg found the strangers' camp where the boys said it would be. A thin trail of smoke rose from their small fire. There was a wagon, a tethered horse, a tent. A woman in calico cooked over a fire, a gray-haired man lay on a pallet. As Meg approached quietly on Butterfield, she noted the unhappy state of two young people seated on a blanket on the ground.

Whatever the woman had in her cookpot, it smelled to high heaven. The ravishingly beautiful girl and the handsome boy were tasting the food, making faces as they set their plates aside.

"Hello," Meg called tentatively, riding forward. The

woman jerked about, staring warily from almond-shaped eyes. She wore her raven-black hair in a plait down her back. Her skin was the color of creamed coffee, glowing and flawless. Her nose was blade-like. Shiny earrings pulled down the lobes of her rather large ears. She was very full-breasted for a woman so short; dressed in flowered calico, she reminded Meg of an exotic Bantam hen.

She gave Meg a guarded smile. "Hello. This is your land? We only mean to be here a short while, but if you want us to go—?" She spoke in hesitating but warm, dulcet tones—perfect English.

"No, you don't have to leave 'til you're ready. I'm Meg Brennon." She slid off Butterfield, led him forward, and held out her hand.

Slender fingers met hers. "Emmaline Lee. These are my twins, Selinda and Shafer Lee." The youngsters got up off the blanket, greeted Meg politely, and stood aside. Emmaline Lee nodded at the pale old man lying on his side on the pallet. "My father, Whitcomb McCurty." Her black eyes grew velvety with tears as she explained that her father had wanted her to bring him to the land of his youth to die. "Old age," she whispered in explanation, "he suffers from ossifying bones and organs. The Lawrence doctors said we might as well grant him his wish to see the buffalo again."

Meg nodded. "The buffalo are almost gone."

"Yes. It upset him to see the hides in Dodge City, and we've seen few buffalo herds. But he doesn't want to go home. I will make him comfortable and happy as long as we stay, if I can't make him well. But we were robbed in Dodge. Our poor dog, Bruin, tried to protect us, but got hurt in the fracas, and now I'm afraid he's dying, too, over there in the wagon."

She sighed heavily. "We're out of food." She nodded toward the cookpot, wrinkling her nose. "I understood from my Cheyenne mother that the boiled young fruit of the devils-claw plant is tasty. To me, it smells bad and tastes worse. My children," she nodded at them, "would rather starve, I think, than eat stewed devils-claw plant."

Meg smiled; she didn't have to think twice. "You'll come home with me. Your father will be more comfortable at my house and we've food to spare."

While the two young people eagerly put out the fire and gathered their loose gear, Meg helped Emmaline lift the old father into the wagon next to the ailing dog. The old man moaned, opened his milky-blue eyes briefly, but settled down once he was covered with a quilt.

Emmaline whispered, "We looked at bringing Old Professor west as a summer adventure, but the journey has been hard on all of us. I'm afraid my youngsters and I are very soft."

Meg nodded, smiling. "It's a hard country, that's for sure."

"Your husband wasn't able to accompany you?" she asked as she helped Emmaline hitch up and load the last of their belongings.

"I believe my husband, Simeon, might be dead." With a sad and wistful smile, she explained, "He was a journalist by trade and a teacher like my father, but also like Old Professor, he had a strong taste for adventure. During a lull in his life, he was teaching at the same school as my father and we met. Soon after the twins were born, Simeon headed to Montana to strike it rich in the goldfields. I haven't seen nor heard from him since. He cared very much for his children and for me. He wouldn't have forsaken us, so I'm certain he must have met his death in Montana."

"I'm sorry," Meg said, touching Emmaline's arm. They

were ready to leave, and she mounted Butterfield to lead the way.

"Please understand," Emmaline said, when she sat at the table with the others that night after a filling supper, "that I want to earn our keep. The Professor might not be able to travel any further. I'm not sure any of us can. And for now we have no way of going back."

Meg said, "I saw a crate of books in your wagon. We have several children here at Paragon Springs who desperately need books to study and a teacher."

Emmaline laughed in relief. "Oh, yes, I brought many books with me. Writing papers, too. I could no more do without such things, even on a journey into the wilderness, than I could do without air to breathe or water to drink. Selinda is the same; she must have her paints and papers with her at all times."

"You'll teach our children then?" Aurelia's voice quaked with excitement.

"Of course I will!" Emmaline laughed again, then closed her eyes in ecstasy as she took a last bite of Aurelia's pumpkin pie. "It's my regret that I didn't inherit more of my mother's practical skills. I must be satisfied that I'm my father's daughter. Teach the children? Oh gladly, gladly."

Nothing gave Meg more pleasure than recounting to herself the changes and civilizing influences added to Paragon Springs little by little. Then, afraid her vanity would bring a return of misfortune—when it could happen with no help from her swollen pride—she would immediately halt her thinking and turn her mind to other things, practical matters.

First of which was to settle in the new family and set up a school. The newcomers moved in with her, but though she invited them to stay on as long as they needed to, Emmaline wanted a place of her own. And she needed it, with two children, an elderly father, and their big dog, Bruin. The dog was recovering, thanks to Aurelia's sewing needle and thread, and administration of herbal medicines as taught by Grandma Spicy.

Meg allowed a portion of her acreage for the new schoolhouse, which would also be living quarters for Emmaline, her elderly father, and the twins as long as they stayed. The third soddy at Paragon Springs was raised by September, and school started two days after the house went up. Word had gone out early about the new school, first to the Hesslers, then to other families on surrounding claims.

Not every child could come every day, but on average ten other youngsters joined the home group, which now consisted of three thirteen-year-olds—Lad Voss, and the twins, Selinda and Shafer Lee—plus ten-year-old Joshua Thorne, nine-year-old David John Thorne, Zibby Thorne, age four, and little Rachel Walsh, almost three. Helen Grace, had she lived, would have been six years old.

In the midst of sadness thinking of Helen Grace, Meg was so proud of the school she could have burst. She reminded herself of a self-satisfied sage grouse, it being hard not to preen and strut.

One early morning on the way to the quarry—she had missed far too many days' work there—she whistled the happy "tsee-titi" of the lark. The birdsong died on her lips when she arrived at the work site.

Chapter Eighteen

"Ad! Oh, dear God!" Meg dismounted on the fly. She scrambled over rocks to Admire's inert body. He must have struggled under a heavy load of stone, fallen, and hit his head. Or his heart could have given out from the deplorably hard work. Either way, he was either unconscious or dead.

As she reached him, she saw that he had been beaten bloody by human fists or a club. She knelt by him, her heart racing. Carefully she lifted his head onto her lap, found his pulse throbbing in the side of his neck. Her eyes stung as she stroked the side of his blood-matted head. "Ad?" He didn't stir.

His face and arms were covered with welts, cuts, and bruises. Identical mutilations showed under his torn and bloody shirt. She bit her lip to keep from crying out her fury at the person, or persons, responsible.

As she bathed him with her kerchief and water from his canteen, she could tell by the irregular feel of his side, as well as from his torn breathing, that some ribs had been broken.

He moaned and opened his eyes.

"Ad, what happened? Who did this to you?"

It took effort for him to speak. "Didn't—know 'em. Snuck up on me, I was makin' noise, poundin' rock. Ain't got a doubt" —his breath whistled as he breathed through a pain from his attempt to move— "was Jack h-hired 'em."

Jack. With all the busyness at Paragon Springs, she'd paid too little heed to the fact that Jack had returned from the Texas trip. He had come home to find the Paragon Springs people still there, at a time when he needed even more land for Rocking A cattle.

It was hard to keep her voice steady and calm. "Lay still, Ad. Let me look at you." She pressed him back, wiped his battered mouth with the damp cloth. She tried to shush him, but he talked anyway.

"Them two that ambushed me—made the same threats Jack's been makin' against me. Same wordin' almost exactly. 'I wasn't to help the woman and her tribe at the springs.' Said in time you'd get up and leave on your own, if nobody helped you."

"That's not going to happen, but, oh, Ad, you've had threats before this?" Her heart was crushed that Jack would try to ruin her by hurting Ad. "I had no idea Jack has been threatening *you.* I wish I had known." She picked pieces of debris out of his bloodied beard. "You should have told me. Lucy Ann hasn't said a word about it—"

"She don't know," he panted, grimacing with pain as he tried to sit up again. "Don't you tell her, neither!"

"She has to be told. She can guess from one look at you that somebody beat you to within an inch of your life. Whatever's been going on, Ad, you should have told me! This whole fuss is about me—I'm the one keeping the others here."

He tried to say something about Lucy Ann, but she couldn't make it out. He lay silent. After a moment his words came in jerky puffs. "I thought—Jack was just a big wind. Didn't pay him no particular mind. Didn't figure—he'd hire out his dirty work, but I shoulda guessed. Them two what beat me was—pond scum I've seen hangin' around—the dives of Dodge. They wasn't Rocking A hands did this. Damn glad. Most of 'em been my friends a long time." He gasped for breath, wincing with pain.

"I'm going to bind your ribs the best I can with my shawl." She pulled it from her shoulders. "Do you think you can stand when I'm finished? We've got to get you into the wagon somehow and get you home."

She bound him tightly, then drove the wagon as close as she could to where he lay in the tumbled stone. Kneeling beside him, she put his arm over her shoulder and whispering "Easy now," she inched him gradually to his feet.

She brought him along slowly. Ad sucked his breath through his teeth at every unavoidably sharp movement, exploded cusswords in Meg's ear she had never heard before. She got him through the rocks and up into the wagon where he lay down in back, panting.

She drove toward his claim, trying to avoid dips and bumps that would jar him. "Hell," he said, behind her, "hell. I'd like to kill the bastards—" She looked back when he fell suddenly silent, and saw that he'd passed out again.

Lucy Ann stepped out into the yard, her delighted expression turning stricken when she saw the inert form of her husband in the back of the wagon. "Admire! Oh, dear heaven, what's happened to you? Ad?" Frantically she clambered over the side of the wagon and was kneeling beside him, making a whimpering sound as her fingers hovered over his battered face.

"He's alive, Lucy Ann," Meg told her quickly. "He's going to be all right. We have to get him out of the wagon and into the house." Together they brought him around, eased him feet-first down to the ground. They braced him between them and headed for the soddy.

Rachel toddled worriedly after them, her rag doll clutched in her arms. Meg smiled reassuringly. "Your papa will be fine."

They struggled to place him on the bed. Lucy Ann undressed him while Meg heated water. Lucy Ann called after her, "In the cupboard there is some extract I made from black samson root. That will dull his pain. There is leaf extract from goldenrod for an antiseptic, too."

Meg brought the heated water, medicines, and clean cloths, and Lucy Ann took over, cleaning his wounds, then blotting them with a pad dipped into the antiseptic, another into the extract of black samson root. With utmost care, she used one of her own shawls to rewrap his ribs, asking Meg's help to make the binding tight.

"I want to know what happened."

Meg told her.

"We'll get the law after them. They can't do this to you or Ad," Lucy Ann said, her voice husky with unshed tears. He watched her from pain-clouded eyes as she finished and drew a bright-patterned quilt up and over his bruised shoulders.

Even cleaned up, Ad's face was hardly recognizable. Lucy Ann brought him a drink of whiskey in a tin cup and held his head while he sipped it through purpled split lips.

After a while he responded to Lucy Ann's remark. "No law out here, honey, that would do nesters like us any good. Law is the big man, like Ambler. We got to take care of ourselves."

Meg nodded agreement, and he told her, "You got to forget about filling that Spearville order for posts for now, an' for the buildin' stone they asked for to build them a new newspaper office. Takes both of us and then some to get that rock out, an' we ain't got enough stockpiled. If the Spearville folks won't wait, we'll just have to let them orders go by."

Absolutely not. Not only was the income a dire necessity, they had a reputation to maintain, Meg thought to herself. That order had to be filled as close to schedule as possible. Maybe she could hire someone to help her, one of their far-flung neighbors. It was about time to take on someone else to work with them, anyway. Jack had put Ad down to halt their quarry business, but she would keep it going or else. "This is my fault—"

Lucy Ann shook her head as she went to gather her child up onto her hip. "Laying blame just to yourself is wrong, Meg. Have you forgotten it was me and Laddie and Grandma, made you come here in the first place? You think you're the only one wants to stay here bad enough to fight for what's yours? Why, Ad and me are willing to do what it takes, anything at all, to keep our land and our home. Nobody has a right to try and push us out! This is our country, too."

So this was what Ad had tried to tell her about Lucy Ann back at The Rocks: that his wife was every bit as strong of a mind as Meg to be there, and no more apt to turn tail and run away. Of course. She always had been. As glad as she felt about that, Meg still worried. "But—"

"Gimme a few days," Ad drawled, mouth tight, eyes closed, "and I'll be back to help out."

Lucy Ann shook her head at him. "You, Admire Walsh, aren't doing any stonework 'til you're properly healed."

"They could have killed you, Ad," Meg agreed with Lucy Ann. She'd been wrong to think of her friends as simple-minded, follow-the-leader sheep. At the same time she was relieved that Ad didn't want to bring in outside law. Not only did she agree with his reasons, but because of the grave up at The Rocks, she'd like as little to do with law officials as possible. She asked solemnly, "Aside from the matter of the quarry business, any ideas what we should do about Jack's hired ruffians in case they stay around to finish the job?"

Ad was beginning to look better. "Be armed, whether we want to be or not," he said, "and all the time keep an eye out. If Jack keeps the same two on his payroll, they'll be a tall fella looks sickly but is strong as an ox, and a stout, sawed-off runt with a head bigger'n a melon an' fists like hammers. We can't let 'em catch us off-guard like I done today. They mean business. But when I'm on my feet again we keep doin' what we been doin'." He reached out and caught Lucy Ann's hand. "Sooner or later they'll get it through their thick heads; us and our kind are here to stay."

He was right, but there was so frighteningly little to support the plan. Just one man, four women, a passel of youngsters, a fistful of legal papers. Yet what else could they do, but stick like starving fleas on a cur dog's back?

Meg smiled at him, but it was a fleeting smile.

For several days, she worked at the quarry alone, scraping off topsoil, marking her post lengths, drilling holes, splitting stone with feathers and wedges, then using block and tackle to drag her posts to the waiting pile that wasn't near big enough. It was slow and backbreaking work, but she was determined to fill their orders even if she had to be late with them.

At supper one night when Meg could hardly hold her head up, Aurelia cautioned, "You're killing yourself, Meg! You can't continue quarrying alone. Maybe Mr. Hessler would come help you. Would you like me to send the boys for him?"

She shook her head. "Will is busy with harvest, he couldn't come if I asked him. All our neighbors are head over teakettle in harvesting."

"All right then, hire someone from town. Or let the boys,

Joshua, David John, Lad, and Emmaline's son, help you."

"Yes," Emmaline nodded. "I'll come help, too."

Meg shook her head, her tongue feeling numb, her throat thick and dry when she spoke. "I considered hiring someone else, but at the moment we can't afford it, even if I had the time to look for another man to hire. I'll manage alone 'til Ad is on his feet again. The boys have all their other chores to tend to—keeping watch on the stock, gathering fuel, harvesting our gardens both here and at Ad's, on top of their school lessons. That's enough. Thanks, Emmaline, but you have other things to do, too."

Emmaline had pitched in from the first, helping in the house and garden in addition to teaching, but she wouldn't last more than a couple hours at stonework, Meg thought.

She worked a few more days alone, and just when she felt she couldn't lift a four-pound hammer one more time, or do a single thing to move a post, Ad showed up to work, driving their big wagon. He tried to act normally, but she saw how stiffly he got down from the wagon, how slowly he moved.

"Good grief, Ad, what are you doing here?" She went to meet him, catching his work-roughened hands in her own calloused palms. His hands so much preferred ranching that she hated to think about it. "Please, Ad, go home. You can't do this. You'll end up a cripple and I'd never forgive myself. How could Lucy Ann let you out of the house? She wouldn't want you here!"

"We're in this together, Miss High 'n Mighty," he said fiercely, "and I'll say when I can work and when I can't. We got an order that's got to be filled, since you didn't cancel it!"

They argued for five minutes before she finally gave in. "You're to do nothing heavy, Ad, do you hear me? You can mark lengths, maybe drill holes, but nothing more!" Even that much would help her; the Spearville order was due in eight days. If she managed to fill it, maybe there would be other orders from the new little town east of Dodge.

Every few minutes as she pounded and chiseled newly cut stone into finer shape, she stole peeks at Ad. His forehead dripped sweat; he gritted his teeth each time he had to move. He couldn't last and she couldn't let him try.

At the creaking sound of a wagon and rattle of traces in the distance, they both looked up. Meg stared. She straightened, rubbing her back. "Lunch coming, Ad," she said, "although it's early yet and I don't know why it's taken all of them to bring it. A picnic, I guess." She watched as Aurelia, driving Emmaline's wagon, pulled up at the far side of the quarry. Beside her was Emmaline. Piling from the back of the wagon were Lucy Ann with small Rachel, and next, Lad, Joshua, David John, and Shafer. Selinda, whispering happy secrets to Zibby, helped the youngster out, then grabbed up her paint box and sketch pad she was seldom without.

"Heavens!" Meg grumbled aloud. Back at the ranches their stock would be wandering off to kingdom come, there would be nobody picking corn, digging the potatoes. She wiped the grime from her face, then took a few steps forward on stone-bruised feet. She rotated her shoulders against the permanent ache there.

"Show us what to do, Meg," Aurelia said firmly. One of Zibby's old, oft-washed nappies was tied over her hair; her fancy gloves were stained from several seasons of garden chores.

Meg didn't answer, staring openmouthed.

Lucy Ann confronted her husband. "I'm taking your place, Admire Walsh." She put Rachel down on the quilt Selinda spread, and kissed the toddler's cheek, handing her her doll. She pointed a finger as her glance bored into her astonished husband's. "I want you resting on the quilt, playing with Rachel, like as should be. Take care she doesn't wander off. Zibby will help you. Boss us, if you want, but that's all the stonework you're doing 'til I say otherwise."

He looked to argue, then sagged in the direction of the quilt, mumbling, angry, but pale with fatigue and pain.

Looking terribly out of place in fresh-starched calico, and as pretty as a parrot, Emmaline lined up with the boys. Her own Shafer and Lad were taller than she was, Joshua was up to her shoulder, and David John almost there. "We're ready, aren't we, boys? Come on, Selinda, you're helping, too."

Trying to take in everything at once, Meg asked, "What about your father, Emmaline, was it all right to leave him?" The Professor was a little improved since they came, able to be up and around some, but he still required care.

"He'll be all right." Emmaline smiled.

Selinda said, "Grandpa wanted to come, too. But someone had to stay home to keep a fire under the beans and make sure the pot doesn't boil dry. He'll put the bread in to bake after it's raised."

Shafer added with a joking smile, motioning with his head, "Besides, the quilt over yonder is a bit crowded."

"All right," Meg gave in finally, managing a smile herself. "This is how we'll do it. We'll make three teams: One team— Aurelia, Emmaline, Shafer—will scrape topsoil off the next stone to be cut. I'll show the second team—Lucy Ann, Selinda, Joshua—how to measure and drill. David John and Lad will be the hammer crew with me, to break the stone after we place the feathers and wedges."

Working in force on each task, maybe they could do it.

Over the next days Meg watched her troop inexpertly, clumsily, but surely, cut stone. In the beginning, they joked among themselves, telling stories, singing as they worked. That stopped when they realized they were expending energy needed to cut and load stone. Ad grouchily helped Meg give instructions and orders to do over a job not going right, but he didn't like being left out of the actual work and would chafe until quieted by a strong frown from the woman who loved him.

Meg had to ask twice for extensions, but the day came when she started making her deliveries of posts and building stone to Spearville. Driving to and from town, it amazed her how many claims—marked by a tent or wagon or crude shelter—had sprouted on what was once wide empty plain. Ad, afraid of ambush, insisted on riding shotgun with her.

They made several deliveries without being harassed and were not sure what that meant. Maybe Jack thought that having Ad beaten nearly to death had put her out of business, and he hadn't bothered to check to be sure. Jack probably still had no idea what a batch of women and children could accomplish together. They would cure him of that bit of blindness.

One day in Spearville, shopping from a list Aurelia had sent, then eating a meal in a nice restaurant, watching people going about their business, Meg arrived at a way she could beat Jack for good, if she could bring it about.

Actually, the plan had always been there on the fringes of her mind and the first steps already taken. *Permanency* was the weapon she would use. Already, she had the makings of a small community—a road ranch, a school for the children, a quarry business—each indicative of permanency. All brought about in spite of Jack's warnings that failure was around the next corner, and his cruel, underhanded tactics to make them quit the country.

From now on, she decided with strong determination, every traveler who thought they were only passing through, each drifter who stopped to simply water his horse at Paragon Springs, would be encouraged to take up claims still available in the vicinity!

It would be no trouble to reveal that Jack held hundreds of acres in illegal claims using his cowboys' movable sled shacks. It was land that could be made available for honest settlers. Along with folks already settled thereabouts, it would be numbers against might.

Staying folks like the Paragon family would, of course, be particularly welcome.

"You're doing what, you want me to—what did you say?" Aurelia asked in a hushed tone.

With the Spearville order filled, Meg had taken a rare day off and sat outside with Aurelia, each doing their own work. It was a pleasurably warm Indian summer day. Aurelia sorted beans from a basket into a bowl, picking out debris; Meg sat with a sheet of paper and pen and ink on a board in her lap.

Through the open window of the soddy nearby they could hear Emmaline conducting a series of recitations from her pupils.

"I said I am writing to apply for a post office appointment for Paragon Springs." She held the corner of her paper down with one hand when a soft breeze threatened to blow it away. She wrote with the other hand in flourishing sweeps.

"This is a petition. I asked folks in the post office at Spearville how to go about getting a post office in one's own community and they told me all I need to know. I will take this petition to other settlers in this region, for their signature that we need a post office. I hope that they, and the government, will agree that the post office should be named Paragon Springs."

Insects sang in the dry grass around them as Meg went on

to answer Aurelia's question. "I want you to be postmistress, Aurelia, because you'd be perfect for the job."

She was thoughtful a moment, rubbing at an ink stain on her finger. "This area needs more convenient mail service. Think how many folks who stay the night with us request that I carry their letters to Dodge or Spearville or Larned for mailing, when they learn I'm going there with a load of stone. Or ask that I pick up their mail in Dodge. Some folks have to wait weeks or months to get their mail and packages, or to send a letter. We might as well be a legitimate post office right here and make income off stamps as well. Folks would come here for their mail and buy supplies at the same time."

"It makes sense." Aurelia looked pleased. "Postmistress, hmm?"

Meg nodded, dipped her pen, wrote another few lines. "I hope you can run the store, too."

"Good heavens, what *store?* Unless you mean the shelves of goods we already carry for travelers stopping in?" She looked perplexed. "I've done that all along."

"I'm not talking about those few shelves. I'm talking about a real store, a genuine mercantile. I'm going to build two back rooms onto my soddy for my living quarters. Out front in the main soddy we'll have the store. The Paragon Springs General Store and Mercantile. I want to carry things like window glass and plows, and maybe lumber. Remember when Hessler had me bring back window glass for him on one of our stone delivery trips to Dodge? The price was exorbitant. I'd charge less and still profit."

"It's true we're always running out of things or don't carry them in the first place. Every Tom, Dick, and Harry that passes this way has come to think we ought to have whatever they are without and must have. In winter folks are particularly desperate, when they have to travel so far for what they need. A mercantile is a good idea, Meg. The post office, too."

Meg nodded, "And the freight line." Laughing out loud, she told Aurelia, "Close your mouth, dear, before you catch a fly." She explained. "It's a waste for Ad and me to freight stone to Dodge, Larned, and Spearville, and return with an empty wagon, except for a few groceries for ourselves or window glass for Mr. Hessler. This fall and winter we'll bring supplies for our store back with us, plus whatever larger needs settlers have from the outside. They can order by mail, or through us, and we can pick up their farm implements, furniture, whatever they've ordered, and haul it here to Paragon and be paid for it. I looked into the freighting business, too, while I was in Spearville."

Aurelia had totally lost interest in sorting beans. "I suppose you'll be talking about having a newspaper next."

"With a post office to mail them from, why not? Emmaline and I have already talked about a paper and she wants to be the editor, the publisher will be me. I am going to buy a printing press and the necessary supplies on my next trip out." She laughed at the expression on Aurelia's face. "Think *permanency*, Aurelia. Didn't I tell you things would get better? We're the ones, our funny little misfit band, who'll civilize this country for others to come. Don't you know, don't you see it?"

"It sounds wonderful," Aurelia sighed. "But you know what happens when a body goes out on a limb with too heavy a load? The limb breaks! As much as I admire your ambitions, Meg, I think you may be whistling in the wind, just like the birds you mimic. Jack Ambler isn't going to just bow at the waist and say 'go ahead, ladies, take my country, bring the rest of the world to my doorstep, and help yourselves.' Nosirree, he won't! He's just panting to see us fail, if he doesn't run us and the others off first."

By way of reply, Meg began to whistle softly under her breath as she finished drawing up the petition and drafting her letter to the post office department. In a few moments she sobered and fell silent. Aurelia spoke strong truth, unfortunately. If she went ahead, it would again be all or nothing. But if a person wasn't willing to gamble on a worthwhile dream, what chance did they have to win?

Chapter Nineteen

Getting their post office was easy to talk about, but not so easy to accomplish, Meg soon found out. But by stopping to talk to folks on her stone deliveries, and taking evening rides after long working days, she finally had enough signatures. There wasn't a settler not excited about the prospect of having a post office nearer than Dodge, Larned, or Spearville, *and* a newspaper.

Gravely disturbing, on the other hand, were stories she heard of others beyond Paragon Springs who had suffered attack of some kind. Description of the perpetrators who committed the violent acts fit that of the two men who beat Ad almost to death.

A man out on the plains hunting a missing horse, was caught and beaten nearly senseless. He lived only because his son went looking and found him in time. The injured man had been given the message to leave the country, but so far he had no intention of buckling.

Some homestead wells had been dosed with saltpeter—rocks of potassium nitrate—to render the water unfit for use. Luckily, the owners were able to haul water by the barrel from nearby streams to fill their needs.

Two farmers had been shot at in their fields, and told to

take their families and get out of the country while they could.

They too, had no intention of leaving, but now went about their fieldwork armed with weapons.

To date, no one had been killed, but they had a war on their hands as surely as any officially declared. She worried, but knew that nothing could make her leave.

She was carrying Lucy Ann's loaded .44 the late night she went out to have a quiet bath at the spring. She was thinking more of the wolf tracks she had seen in the mud at the spring a few evenings before, so she was surprised to see two shadowy riders approaching the pool. Her heart beat fast as she moved into the shadows thrown from a haystack.

One rider was tall and thin, and from what she could tell he wore a frock coat. The other sat his horse as squat as a toad, his head almost as big as his broad shoulders. The latter carried a fat round bag in front of him.

"Get it done," the tall one ordered, and the other man swung down, taking the bag with him. He headed for her pool.

"Hold it!" she commanded, staying in the safety of the shadows. As long as they couldn't see her, she might have the upper hand.

One of them cursed. The toady one took another step toward the pool. She spoke loudly, "Nobody comes here without invitation, especially carrying salt rock." Two-handed, she aimed the pistol at the ground in front of the moving figure and pulled the trigger. He yelped sharply and dropped the bag. For good measure she fired a second shot.

She ordered, a lot more strongly than she felt, "On your horse! Both of you clear out, now!" The man with bullet-burned toes flew onto his horse, but neither of them made a move to go. They could tell from her voice that she was a woman, and maybe thought they could still overpower her and do their dirty job.

The taller one pushed his horse a step toward the other rider and muttered, "Jack ain't going to like this. Go on, Hammett, you empty-headed runt, and salt that water. She ain't goin' to kill you. Get it done so we can get our pay."

She intervened, loud and clear, "I don't think you want to try me. Make me mad enough and who knows what I'll do?" She added, "I've got a bead on your chest, tall one." She wondered if she really could pull the trigger. She thought she might. She couldn't let their water source be destroyed.

A long tense silence was broken by a muted click as she thumbed back her gun's hammer. Maybe the soft noise was as loud in their ears as in hers. As she watched, the pair grumbled to one another. Then they swung their horses around and thudded off into the dark. She slipped to the ground and sat there, the gun still pointed in the direction they had taken.

The two had no stake in the trouble they were making, except the money they were being paid by Jack. They had named him. Very soon, she was going to use that knowledge to stop him from harassing folks. She just wasn't sure yet how to go to the law without putting herself in serious trouble with her far-off husband.

It was a late, blue-sky October day when she headed to Dodge to mail her request for the post office, and to see to other errands. As Ad was using their freight wagon, she had borrowed Emmaline's large wagon for the day. Soft splats of dust flicked back from her team's plodding hoofs as they followed the wagon trace. She sat back on the hard board seat, impatient, but with the lines loose in her hands to allow the team—Butterfield and a black nag they called Crow—their way.

In Dodge, she drove her team and wagon toward the train depot. The train wasn't long in arriving, whistling its arrival, blowing steamy fumes when it halted on the glittering tracks.

A couple of fancy women, plume-hatted and satin-gowned, a blonde and a brunette, were first to step down from the train. Meg eyed them, feeling plain and dowdy although she wore her best.

Prostitutes were a common import to Dodge. The prettiest ones often married cowboys within a few weeks of their arrival, necessitating sending for others. Cy Watts, one of Jack's riders, had recently wed a saloon girl, and had settled down here in town.

She took careful note of other debarking passengers. A young couple in farm clothes with a baby got off. They were met by a man she recognized as the owner of Dodge's largest mercantile. It could be they were family, or possibly he'd offered the young man new opportunity, working as a clerk for him. Two drummers in fancy duds and carrying sample cases got off. Due to her trade in the old days, she could recognize a drummer every time.

Suddenly, she perked up.

The Easterner who'd just got off the train looked so ill at ease in his surroundings, she was positive he was the man she had come there to find. He was different from the traveling drummers, gamblers, and gunslicks, the usual male type that alighted in Dodge. She wanted an honest man, willing to work.

He was shorter than average, but looked strong enough to load a stone wagon or haul a cow out of a snowdrift, if he had to. He was a little thick around the middle, perhaps in his late thirties or early forties. He was nicely dressed in a black suit, white celluloid collar, his cravat tied bow-fashion. He had a sincere, earnest face behind a silky dark moustache.

Although he seemed startled when he caught her staring, he touched his dark gray hat to her and bowed slightly from the waist. *Good.* He was a gentleman without being rakish. She waited to see if anyone joined him. He appeared to be alone, which was even better. A single man. There were too many women at Paragon Springs already. With a little luck, she'd be taking him back with her.

"Sir," she said, moving toward him, "you seem a bit confused. Perhaps I can give you directions. Are you looking for a hotel? The livery, perhaps?" *Idiot,* she reprimanded herself about her approach. The air was thick with the strong odor of the livery, which was in plain sight a few yards away. There were two plainly marked hotels in view.

He eyed her with caution, as though afraid she might bite.

"I beg your pardon?"

Get to the flat-footed facts, Meg. "The truth is, if you don't have a specific destination in mind, sir, I'd like to discuss a job offer with you."

A spark of interest showed in his eyes, along with relief, but he was still wary. "Have you mistaken me for someone else?" He glanced around with a puzzled frown, then back at her. "We haven't met somewhere before, have we?"

No wonder he was suspicious. How many times did a man step off a train to be met by a strange lady ready to snatch him up for a job? "We haven't met." She smiled and explained, "I don't have the privilege, as a man might, to look for help in the many saloons in this town. I decided the train depot was my best chance to find a newcomer seeking work in these parts."

He nodded slowly, doffing his hat. "Perhaps you have found the right person; I'm very much in need of work. My name is Owen Symington. Friends and family back home in Sandusky, Ohio, call me Smart Symington."

Her brow quirked at the unusual name and he explained, "The name 'Smart' got started way back in school when I

216

helped slower students to master their studies, for a price, of course." His grin was wide, his expression open and friendly.

Intelligent. A head for business. Lord, but could she pick them! She held out her hand, "Nice to meet you, Mr. Symington. I am Meg Brennon. Perhaps we can talk over a glass of cider at Hattie's Restaurant?"

They loaded his belongings—a greatcoat folded neatly and strapped atop his small leather trunk along with a shiny new Spencer rifle—in the wagon. They would pick up her goods later.

"I need a hard worker with a good head for business," she told him when they were settled at an oilcloth-covered table at the cafe. He had ordered a plate of fried potatoes and steak, and, after she deferred from joining him in a meal, he ate slowly and listened as she sipped her cider and told him about Paragon Springs.

"We've been pretty much in the middle of nowhere until recently. The area was opened to settlement a few years ago. But lack of interest in dry country, some bad turns of weather, along with the persuasive methods used by cowmen to change the minds of the few who wanted to locate and establish farms, has kept the area thinly populated. That's changing." She described the Paragon Springs family and their growing community, and her plans for the future of the community.

"We have a main, well-traveled cattle trail running south to north just three miles west of us. Cowboys and new settlers to the country come to us for meals, sometimes for overnight stays; they often buy supplies from us. Without really intending to originally, we've developed into a road ranch."

She described the rock quarry, leaving out that the plan to mine The Rocks came to her as she secretly buried a man close by. "Besides the quarry business, we've begun a freight line. We will make ourselves a major supply point for new settlers, as well as travelers passing through. There are presently too few of us at Paragon Springs to carry on these business ventures adequately."

Owen Smart Symington interjected, "If you're seeking an investor in your enterprises, I have to tell you I don't have a nickel in the way of capital."

She gave him a wry smile. "I won't say additional money or funding wouldn't have been welcome. But right now, as much as anything, we need extra help, a strong hand. A bonus would be good business sense in the help we take on. Given those, the money will come, *amply* for all of us, if my guess is right."

He nodded, a bright gleam in his soft brown eyes. "I'm very interested in what you propose, Miss Brennon. It is Miss?"

She nodded yes. The lie was effortless after so long. "But please call me Meg."

"Since I'm starting all over out here, I think I would prefer to be called Owen, my real name, for a change, if you don't mind. I got tired of being called Smart," he grinned, "even as a compliment."

"Fine, Owen it is. I'm interested to know how you made your living in Sandusky, Owen. And how you happened to come to Dodge."

"As I'm sure you might guess, I came looking for new opportunity." He grinned. "But I didn't expect to have my chance the moment I stepped off the train. Now that I've heard you out, I bless fate for bringing me here. I had rather another idea, that I'd made a huge mistake, when I first saw Dodge City from the train window. What an ugly, desolate place! Before that, one of those 'ladies of the evening' that got off at the same time I did, the pretty blonde one, stole my gold

Waltham pocket watch, I'm convinced. There was some crowding on the train as we found our seats after a stop in Kansas City. I had the watch before she squeezed by me, afterward it was gone."

Their conversation had sidetracked, but Meg smiled and asked, "Did you call her to account and ask that she return it?"

"In the most gentlemanly way possible. Of course she denied taking the watch, and posed great feminine indignation." He grinned. "Men, almost as often as women, can be at a disadvantage in the other's world, you know. Had she been a man, I could have pounded the truth from her with my fists—gotten my watch back. Being female was her protection. I could do nothing but smile and accept her word and my loss."

"It was nice of you to handle the situation that way; some men wouldn't have." She was thinking of Teddy Malloy who hadn't let her sex stop him from using his fists on her. By the same token, she supposed she *could* go into the Long Branch and order whiskey, but she didn't care to. "Now, what did you do in Sandusky, Owen?"

He laid his knife and fork across the top of his plate, pushed the plate aside and used his napkin. "I worked for my uncles in the family department store. Between them they had enough sons—my cousins—to fill the higher-paid jobs as buyers, managers, partners. There was no chance to advance, and I simply couldn't see being a lowly clerk all my life."

"Are you married?"

"That's the plagued trouble of it! I couldn't support anyone but myself on the miserly salary I received, and someday I hope to have a wife, a family."

She hadn't intended to have his personal story, but over his pie he told her, "I've never been rich enough to appeal to the kind of quality lady I'd like to marry. In fact, I've given up in that quarter. I decided to settle for being a country merchant in the newly developing West as they say, and, if necessary, once established, mail order myself a bride, just an ordinary, nice lady."

"You might not have to send off for a bride." At his shocked, but pleased expression, she said quickly, "Oh, no, I don't mean—me. I was just thinking you might meet someone out here, one of the new people to the country."

Actually, she'd been thinking of Aurelia when she made the remark. The stranger, who seemed a good friend almost, after the hour and a half they'd spent together, looked just about perfect for Aurelia. But better to let those matters take their own course, if such was to be, or not.

Activity had died away on their return to the depot. A lone scruffy brown dog sniffed at rubbish tossed away on the tracks. Meg and Symington loaded up her goods for the journey to Paragon Springs. "I see you have a rifle," she said, nodding at the Spencer carbine strapped to his bundle in the wagon behind her.

He climbed up, sat down beside her, adjusted his hat in the blowing wind. "I bought it just before leaving home, for protection once I reached the 'wild west.' " His earnest face filled with color. "But I confess I've never shot it. I hardly know the first thing about weapons."

So she'd lost out on one point. "You may have to learn fast," she told him soberly as they struck off on the wagon trace toward home. She decided to save confession of Jack's hired assaults against her and others for later.

She clucked her tongue to move the team faster, but the horses picked up their pace only a little. As they rumbled along, she was glad to see how engrossed her passenger was in their surroundings. Until he said, "My God, I've never seen such godforsaken country! There's nothing out here!"

"Look again, Mr. Symington," she said as spiritedly as she could, although her heart drooped in disappointment. "Surely you see something." *Potential.*

"All right," he said, waving his arms at the brown distances stretching in waves to the horizon in front of them, "I've seen a few cows. A mud hovel or two with chickens scratching in the yard. But other than that, miles and miles of—nothing."

Miles and miles of *hope,* of *promise,* she thought. "You'll change your mind, Mr. Symington, once you've been here awhile. I guarantee it." She hoped she was right; she wanted him with them badly. "And at dark we'll be pulling in to one of those *hovels* to spend the night, before continuing on to Paragon Springs in the morning." Ma Jewett loved company. She had extra beds, and a pot of coffee always on. Of course they would have to pay for their stay by having their ears talked off. She clicked her tongue at the team—smiled to herself.

The rifle fire was sudden, from a draw off to their left, lifting Owen Symington's hat. Stunned at first, Meg jerked her head toward the origin of the sound, but she saw nothing. A second bullet twanged against her wagon wheel's iron rim, followed by a quick third shot that thunked a chunk from the wood where her booted foot rested.

Her skin became bathed in cold sweat. "Get your Spencer, Owen," she ordered tightly, "I can't shoot that far with my pistol." She steadied her grip and popped her whip over the team's back, shouting at the top of her lungs, "Haaay, get on there! Git up, Butterfield, and you, Crow." The sudden lurch of the wagon as the team swung into a trot nearly unseated Owen, who was reaching behind the seat. But he came up with the rifle and a handful of ammunition. He loaded the weapon slowly and carefully as the wagon swung side to side, mumbling to himself as though remembering lessons.

Meg leaned forward, her whip cracking like a rifle shot. She ached with panic, her thoughts dismal. The team swung into a gallop, but Owen fumbled on. When she was about to decide it would never happen, he got off a shot behind them. His face had lost color, but he managed a shaky smile her way. "Doubt I hit anything but a dirt ridge."

"Good enough. Can you see them?" she shouted over the rumble, rattle, and thumping of her careening wagon and the team's thudding hooves.

"Not a blessed thing! Shall I fire again?"

A bullet whined past her ear, like the sound of a hornet but a lot more deadly.

"Yes!" *For God's sake, yes!* "We have to let them know we're not spineless, that we'll fight back with every means." The horses couldn't move any faster. "Fire the damn rifle, Owen! So they know we're not scared."

He followed her orders, then turned back to yell at her. "But I *am* afraid, aren't you?"

"Yeah, but if we show it, we're finished." She had bit her lip until she tasted blood; her insides felt both hot and cold.

When she was positive the ambushers' plan was to frighten them out of their wits but not come after them, she drew the team to a slower, less punishing, trot.

"What was that all about?" Owen asked. "Were they intending to rob us? Would they have killed us if we hadn't fired back?"

She shook her head. "If they wanted to kill us, they would have." She sighed, deciding she had to tell him the truth even if it meant his insistence that he be driven back to Dodge to catch the eastbound train. "There's a couple of outlaws, hired by a local rancher, who have taken to shooting at anything that moves and calling it an 'accident.' "

At his gasp of disbelief, she explained. "They take pot-shots at whoever looks like a would-be homesteader—'nester' or 'squatter' as the cowmen refer to farmers—to scare them witless, so they'll run for their lives. If they don't leave—" She left the comment hanging in the air.

Owen looked bothered and ran a finger around under his tight, white collar. He said, "You didn't mention trouble when you hired me on. You spoke only of the potential, my chances for success out here." He didn't sound particularly unhappy with her, he was just stating facts.

"I told the truth: the land is free, opportunity wide open as the sky." She looked at him. "I assumed a smart man like you would surely know that anything worth having is not easily come by. You have to fight for it, work your fingers to the bone for it. Be willing to bet your very life on winning in the end. If you feel I've deceived you, say so. I'll drive you back to Dodge, right off."

"No," he shook his head, "I don't want to go back."

She sighed in relief, smiled to herself and felt better.

He looked embarrassed, and he grinned nervously. "I kind of expected it to be this way, anyhow. Risky. Dangerous. It's not so different where I came from. Three times back in Sandusky, when it was up to me to deliver the store's deposit to the bank, I was beaten up and robbed."

"*Good!* No, I don't mean that, exactly." She turned again to face him on the wagon seat. "What I mean is, it's good you know trouble and are willing to keep going in spite of it, not give in. That's the way of it out here." As an afterthought she added, "I'm sorry you were robbed and beaten back in Ohio."

They talked the rest of the way, about dozens of things. By the time she drove into the yard at Paragon Springs, she was convinced Owen Symington was a gem, indeed. And she could hardly wait to introduce him to Aurelia.

Aurelia led the group spilling into the yard to meet them. She walked slowly. Her lifted face wore a curious smile as she focused totally on Owen Symington. Owen was staring back.

Well there you are! Meg thought, her pleasure followed by a twinge of envy.

Chapter Twenty

Meg had meant to skip supper, turn in early, and sleep away her exhaustion. But she couldn't have slept, anyhow, with gunfire popping off up toward The Rocks. Ad was teaching the greenhorn newcomer, Owen, how to shoot. Ostensibly to bring down game but for protection, too, against human marauders—in particular, Jack's hired ruffians.

Increasingly, she feared that Jack's determination to keep the country for cattle and drive out settlers would lead to a killing. Maybe his, maybe someone else's. Along with that, she felt the burden of Finch's death more than ever.

She had joined the other women, and the children, at Aurelia's and sat giving Lucy Ann's toddler a bouncing ride on her foot while Aurelia, Lucy Ann, and Emmaline cooked and Selinda set the table. "I should be helping," she said, leaning down to smile tiredly at Rachel. Was it just being raised by Admire that made the child look so much like him? When she kissed the dusky little nose, the child's beautiful, raisin-colored eyes lit up, she giggled, and asked to "go fasser, Aunt Meggie."

"You are helping." Lucy Ann smiled over her shoulder. "Rachel is getting over the ague. For the first time this week, she isn't fussing. She loves you, Meg. Rachel, sweetie, don't wear your auntie out, hear?"

Emmaline threw in, from where she stirred gravy at the stove, "You ought to be having babies of your own, Meg."

Meg laughed, at the same time struck by a twinge of longing. She drew Rachel up into her arms, stroked her hair. "Rachel, you are a love, and you do make me want my own." She looked at the women. "But when would I have the time? And besides, having a baby requires a husband."

"So what's stopping you?" Lucy Ann said, nodding toward the sound of shooting outside. "Mr. Symington seems like a fine catch to me."

Aurelia's back was to them as she worked at the stove. Meg saw the fork she'd been turning antelope steaks with poise in the air, as Aurelia became motionless.

"Owen is an admirable man," Meg answered. "He'll make someone a fine husband, but he's not for me." Aurelia's shoulders relaxed. She turned the meat, lifted a lid to check a pot of steaming carrots, opened the oven door to check the biscuits.

Lucy Ann was likely not aware that since Owen came a few weeks ago, he had spent evenings in the kitchen with Aurelia, later playing checkers with her. Their late evening walks had become a regular occurrence. Meg guessed, from Aurelia's new glow, that she'd been kissed a few times, too.

"Tell us about 'your type,' Meg." Aurelia turned from the stove. She smoothed her apron—smiled.

She was saved from answering when Lad strode through the door. "More company," he said. "Mr. Potter has just come. He wants to talk to you, Aunt Meg, outside. He wanted to know if you are going to Dodge soon, and I told him yeah."

She nodded, put Rachel down to play, got her shawl from the hook by the door, and pulled it around her shoulders. She sighed. "I'm in for a haggle, I'm sure. Joe Potter likes our freighting service, but would rather not pay for it."

She went out to meet Potter, a blocky, ruddy-faced farmer with a graying red beard and stern eyes. "The wife's folks are sending her one of those newfangled sewing machines, a couple lamps and things. I told her you'd pick the crated stuff up for her in Dodge as long as you're goin' anyways." He nodded toward her freight wagons loaded with stone and ready to go.

"Certainly. But of course I have to charge the usual freighting fee, by the weight of your goods." She smiled at his expression of resistance.

"You're goin' to Dodge anyways, and comin' back home, ain't you?"

She nodded, "Yes, I am."

He went on, scratching his neck. "Then it don't seem neighborly you'd charge fer this, since it don't cost you nothin' extry to haul."

"I'm in business, Mr. Potter, it isn't that I'm not willing to be neighborly. I'm in *business*," she repeated. "Freighting isn't the safest job. We've been fired at. Surely you've heard about the trouble? This is lawless country."

He spat on the ground. "I've heard. I've heard some vigilante talk aimin' to take care of it, too."

"Well, that hasn't happened yet. There are other concerns, besides being harassed. Financially, there is horse feed to buy, the wagons and gear to keep up. My time is involved, as is my partner's, whoever is riding shotgun with me."

She lifted her hands and turned to go back inside. "But if you don't want my service, if you'd rather go to Dodge and do your own hauling, that's fine with me." She looked at him.

"Well, I can't do that!" he burst out with a fierce frown, his red beard jutting. He came after her. "I got my fall plowing to finish, I can't go traipsin' to town."

She shrugged and looked to where Owen and Ad were coming from The Rocks, talking with confidence, pointing at the rifle in Owen's hand. The shooting lesson must have gone well.

Potter, after another minute dickering with her, decided to hire her to do his hauling for him, as she knew he would, rather than take the time to go himself and let his plowing wait.

"Thank you, Mr. Potter. We'll be extra careful with your wife's things. We'll be back from Dodge by the end of the week. You can pick up your goods here or, if you want us to deliver to your claim, it will cost another dollar."

"I'll come for it," he growled. He talked a moment with the men who had just walked up, shook hands with Owen as they were introduced. Meg invited Potter to stay for supper. He accepted. He would want something free out of the deal, or else. Considering the fine meal Aurelia and the other women were preparing, he was getting a very good deal.

So was she. She had plans for every nickel she could earn.

Lightning zigzagged across the western Kansas sky, thunder cracked and boomed. Clouds split over Dodge City and rain gushed down.

Meg and Owen hurried to unload their shipment of stone at the building site of Tog Elsberry's new office. She wondered how Admire and Lad were doing, with their load taken to Larned. The bare ground under their feet quickly turned into a quagmire, making moving around more difficult.

They finished unloading and Meg leaned back against the side of the wagon to rest, wiping her arm across her brow. Her clothes were soaked through, but she felt exultant as she usually did filling a profitable work order. "We'll look for Tog at the stockyards—find out if that's all he needs." In a way she felt she was getting back some of the money for her cows she had accepted so little for, after the bad grasshopper troubles. Tog was prospering; he had paid top price for her stone.

She and Owen were driving toward the train depot to pick up the Potter order when she saw the backs of a familiar-looking pair—one in a frock coat, the other in a shaggy buffalo-hide coat that hung to the ground—disappear into the noisiest saloon on that part of the street.

Pond scum, Ad had called them. She had learned their real names: the tall man was Elam Frey, the other was called Little Hammett. She wondered if they had spotted her and Owen in town, and were fortifying themselves with whiskey before following Jack's orders to hound them.

"We have to hurry," she told Owen in a flat voice. "I wish we had time to let the team rest longer, but I think we'd better head for home as soon as we load up."

He frowned at her. "Is there trouble?"

She explained about the men she'd seen, elaborated on who they were, what they could be up to. "I could be wrong and they might not know we're anywhere about. I don't want to take any chances."

The road back had turned slick as glass from the cold, driving rain. Driving the team, she could hardly see. Owen sat beside her with his rifle under canvas on his lap. The wind howled like demons around them.

She looked over her shoulder every now and then to make sure the larger canvas was still tied down over their load. She had guaranteed Mr. Potter she'd bring his shipment to him in perfect shape. She meant to keep that promise.

She cracked her whip over the team's back, sorry to work the animals so hard, but anxious to get out of reach of Frey and Hammett, should they be following.

The day had turned dark as night, the heavy rain concealing everything beyond her team's heads from view. As she strained to see, she concluded that they were headed in the right direction, but she wasn't sure they followed the road anymore. If a wheel went over the edge of an unseen ravine, they could tip over. "Can you see the road?" she shouted at Owen, "We have to stay on it, or as close as possible." The plains only *looked* flat; in reality they were corrugated with gullies.

He shouted back as he hung over the side of the wagon, peering ahead, "You're all right, so far." He added in a shout over the din of wind and rain, "Maybe you oughtn't to drive so fast."

"Got to," she answered. They rocketed about, off the road, then she got them back on track. They made slow, steady, but near-blind progress. Owen yelled instructions over the sound of the storm each time they started to veer off course. There had been no time to dry out and her bones had turned to icicles.

"Confound it, I can't see a blessed thing!" Owen shouted suddenly. "We had better slow down, stop and get our bearings."

His warning came too late. With a sudden jolt, a sickening drop, the right back wheel dropped over the edge of a draw. They began to slide backward, the horses taking clawing backward steps with them. She shouted, cracked the whip over the team's back to keep them pulling the wagon onto solid ground. The wagon tipped, then was rolling over onto its side in slow motion. She felt herself slide into emptiness, clawed for something to hold onto, then she landed hard in the mud of the draw. She heard Owen's drawn-out yell just before he struck muddy ground a few feet away.

"Goddammit!" he shouted into the howling wind and

rain. "If you don't mind my saying so, Miss Brennon!"

"I don't mind," she panted, lying flat on her back, rain drenching her face, "but we've got to get this wagon righted and out of this draw." She sat up in the mud, panting, wanting to catch her breath before she tried to stand. She wriggled her fingers, moved her arms and legs. Nothing broken. The team still looked to be hitched to the tilted wagon, but they stood precariously on the upside of the bank, the hitch lines twisted and ready to break. If it happened, the horses would likely run.

Meg struggled to her feet, slipped and slid her way to the tipped wagon, Owen close behind. Overhead, feeble sunlight began to bleed through the dark of the storm. The wind died down; the torrent of rain slowed. Rain clouds blew across the sky, leaving a faint path of blue. "Hardly enough blue to make a Dutchman's britches," Grandma Spicy would say. The storm was over, at least temporarily.

The team waited, straining forward in the harness. Meg hurried to their heads, stroking and calming them. Below her, Owen shoved his bulk under the downside of the wagon and heaved upward. The wagon began to tilt onto four wheels, then slipped back. With a loud groan, Owen shoved again. After three tries, he got the wagon settled on all four wheels, but still at an angle at the bottom of the draw.

"I'll get in and drive the team," she called, "if you'll shove the wagon from the back, keep it steadied and on course."

"Go ahead!"

"But if the wagon starts sliding back, you get out of the way, Owen. I don't want you run over and killed."

He grumbled, "Just drive the horses, Miss Brennon. If I stay in this muck any longer, I'm going to put down roots and grow like a tree."

In spite of their dire situation, she chuckled. The laughter died in her throat when she happened to turn her head in the other direction. Through the gloom, two rough figures rode along the bottom of the draw toward them from the south. Hammett and Frey must have been close behind all along, the storm making too much noise for them to be heard following. Shivers streamed up and down her spine.

"Owen, where's your rifle?" she called quietly. "We have company." She reached under the wagon seat, fingering to find her holstered pistol. It wasn't there, it must have fallen out when the wagon tipped over.

She heard Owen's sharp intake of breath when he spotted the pair coming at a steady pace. She saw him looking frantically about for the rifle. "Damned if I can find it!" he called back in a whisper.

Without weapons, they were at the jackals' mercy. She got down from the wagon on the side opposite the men's approach. She peeked around the edge of the wagon seat to watch them, their coats and mounts dripping from the rain. She tried to convince herself that it was the hard spill in the mud, and the cold, that caused her teeth to rattle like gourds. She clamped her jaws tight.

It happened so swiftly, she couldn't believe her eyes, couldn't move. Frey and Hammett lifted their pistols and began to fire into her canvas-covered load, so close to where she stood she could have been killed by a ricocheting bullet. That done, they sent their mounts lunging up the bank and, without hesitation, shot each of her horses between the eyes. The ground shook when the horses dropped dead where they had stood, still in harness.

Her scalp tightened painfully, a soundless cry clogging her throat.

Owen said, "Goddamn you two! Why'd you have to do that?" In a whipping stride he headed toward them.

She came to and rushed to catch his arm. "Don't, Owen." She held him in a white-knuckle grip, afraid for their lives.

The riders laughed and swung their horses around. The taller, pasty-faced Frey said over his black-cloaked shoulder, "That's only a taste of what you'll get, lady, if you don't take yourself and your friends and hightail it out of this country!" The squattier one, Little Hammett, sent a last bullet into Butterfield, already dead, to emphasize the warning.

Meg flinched. She almost passed out. She held to Owen to steady herself as Hammett turned to laugh at her.

"My God," Owen said, as the men rode away, "if stealing a man's horse is a hanging offense out here, what is it when two good horses are shot dead like that? Folks can't survive without their animals."

She held her tears until the gun-devils were gone, and then she ran through the mud to fall to her knees by Butterfield's head. She stroked his golden neck, over and over. Finally, she let Owen pull her away and hold her close. "H-he was my h-horse, my dear good friend and helper for y-years. Why did they have to kill him, kill an innocent horse? And poor old Crow—"

"To hurt you, dear, just as they have. And to leave you with a huge loss, which they've also done."

By the time he released her, her shivering had stopped and she had turned numb. *What, who* was next? Frey and Hammett had to be punished for what they'd done, or human slaughter could be next. She needed the law's help. But in order to use the law, she had to be free of worry from them on her own account.

She dried her face on her sleeve and, mind whirling, went to examine the load while Owen unhitched the fallen horses.

The Potters' sewing machine was ruined. She and Owen went through the rest of the load. They sorted out undamaged dishes, other things not bullet-riddled. They divided them, tied them into two canvas bundles, and hefted them onto their backs for the long walk home to Paragon Springs. As she walked in the coolness of late afternoon, she welcomed the time to think. She knew with heavy finality that she must find a way to *end* the insanity. She had ridden the fence too long.

She was tired of the constant threat of Teddy Malloy finding her. She had to face him and get a divorce if possible.

She had felt free there in the West, but had never really *been free*. She had been a fool to try and live with the deceit, guilt, and worry as she had these past few years. Particularly lately, needing the law, but afraid to go to them. In spite of the burden on her back, she took long strides, limping only a little, sure of her decision.

She had every reason to be proud of what she'd accomplished in western Kansas, making a new home, a new life. But that didn't mean she hadn't made some mistakes.

She recognized how truly ashamed she had been all along of what happened in St. Louis. It was not only fear that drove her to silence, but humiliation at how her marriage turned out. But the shame was not hers, it was Teddy's. Had he not beaten her whenever he was displeased, their love might have grown, they might be married yet. His true colors that eventually showed had sent her away, not any flaw in her.

With a divorce, she would be free to meet someone else, a heady possibility she hadn't before allowed herself to consider at any length.

The small potbellied stove in Bassett's Dodge City office glowed with heat. Meg turned down his offer of a cup of fragrant coffee, took the chair he offered, and clenched her clammy hands in her lap.

Without getting into all the details of her marriage, she told him about the death of Frank Finch. How he had tried to take her with him by force, and had beaten her with his gun. How she had shot him to save her own life. That he was buried on her place. She wasn't sure whose jurisdiction the case might be in, possibly the state marshal's.

Sheriff Bassett listened carefully, then had her repeat the story. "Sounds the same as when the boy told me about the killing, only he said he did it."

"What boy? What are you talking about?" She sat forward stiffly in her chair, her heart pounding in her ears. She had told Lad what to say. Surely Sheriff Bassett wasn't talking about Lad. But of course he had to be. She felt fierce denial rising. Lad was not to be the one—!

Bassett pulled open a desk drawer, carefully shuffled some papers, drew one out. "Here is his confession. Signed his name Leonard Voss. Sometimes he's called Lad Voss, he said."

She was dumfounded. "When did this take place? No one came to question me. I don't understand. If you knew, why didn't you come discuss the killing with me? You should have! Lad didn't do it, I did!"

"I don't think you did." He smiled, but his manner was dead solemn. "I believe he told the truth. He came in here one time, maybe more than a year ago. He wanted to clear his conscience. But he wasn't going to tell me anything unless I promised it wouldn't get back to you. He said he'd sworn to you he'd never tell anybody the truth of how it happened." He hesitated, went on, "Seemed to me a clear case of the boy defending your life. But I wrote and told Frank Finch's wife I would investigate further if she wanted me to, and if she wanted me to press charges—"

"His wife?"

"The boy, Lad, slipped items out of Frank Finch's pockets. He said you were close to being unconscious from the pistol-whipping at the time. There was an address for Finch's wife on a letter. I sent Mrs. Finch her husband's pocket watch, a few other things, asked her what she wanted done about the killing. Odd," he mused, mouth puckered as he looked toward the ceiling.

"What do you mean? What—did she say?"

He looked at her. "Well, Mrs. Finch seemed *glad* to hear she'd been made a widow. Seems she already had another man in mind to fill poor Mr. Finch's shoes. She said there was no need to investigate, or prosecute anybody. She accepted the facts as I gave them, a justified killing. She asked that her husband's remains be left where they were, as she said, 'in peace.' "

Meg sat there, her mind whirling to grasp these new facts. "Sheriff, I don't know what to say. This is all such a surprise to me." She took a deep breath. "But I suppose I agree with Mrs. Finch that there is nothing more to be done. Providing as far as the law is concerned, the matter is settled?"

"It is settled, Miss, or—I should say, Mrs. Malloy." He took the chair behind his desk. "Was there anything else?"

Hearing the name she hated unsettled her anew, but she managed to tell him about the vicious killing of her poor horses, the outrages against the other settlers. She told him what she knew about Frey and Hammett and the man who hired them, Jack Ambler.

Bassett sat back in his chair and listened, his smooth jaw set grimly. He nodded. "I've heard some upset talk about the doings of Frey and Hammett, but until now nothing concrete and provable. I've gotten no formal complaint. This time I got plenty of cause to bring them in." He shook his head, his eyes blazing. "You understand right now is the first I've heard what they did to your horses? That outright needless slaughter is enough to put them away for a long time, if the jury doesn't vote to hang them, and they might."

She nodded, feeling a relief she hadn't felt in ages. Any further violence was in the law's hands. Bassett would have fine help in his new deputies, Bat Masterson and Wyatt Earp, who would be more than a match for the jackals.

She had lied to herself that there was no law to go to when Finch was killed. She had been terribly afraid, but all the same she should have gone to Bassett then and asked for help. She wished that she had faced Teddy Malloy, too, and insisted on a legal separation, a divorce, long before now.

Running from troubles only postponed the inevitable. Sooner or later, buried problems would fly up to strike a body down, like a stepped-on stick in the woods. She realized suddenly that her thoughts had taken her away from what Bassett was saying. "Beg pardon?"

"It's not to put innocence on Jack Ambler," he repeated, "I know him too well for that. But about your horses, it wouldn't be like Jack to have ordered those animals killed that way. That's just too low-down. I believe that that time Frey and Hammett acted out of their own ignorant, evil hearts."

She absorbed his words, knowing that he was likely right. Jack, ornery and trouble-causing though he could be, would have some scruples when it came to shooting innocent horses. Even so, she wanted an end to his harassment of herself and others, whatever the form. The open range days were gone. He had to see that, before there was loss of human lives.

Bassett seemed to read her mind. "I think what Frey and Hammett done will put an end to all this, as far as Jack is concerned. Jack's already lost what he wanted out of this, he just ain't seen yet that farm folk are in these parts to stay."

"I'll take him to court if I have to, if there's further trouble."

Bassett nodded. "We'll both see him there if there's any more trouble."

Meg sighed, feeling again that a tremendous load had been lifted from her shoulders. She would return to St. Louis and, at long last, face up to Teddy Malloy, be truly free to go ahead with her life. She stood up and smiled, shook the lawman's hand. "Good-bye, Sheriff, and thank you very much."

As she strode down the street to the livery to retrieve her wagon and head home, she whistled the sweet melody of the lark. She would get her divorce, she would, and then she would come home to the only place where she belonged, where she would ever belong.

She had plans for Paragon Springs, big plans! And if she met her own true love, her soulmate, at long last—and she thought that a very likely possibility to happen now that she would be free and her heart ready—what a wonderful gift that would be.